YASMINE

NEW YORK TIMES BESTSELLING AUTHOR

GALENORN

THE SILVER STAG

A WILD HUNT NOVEL

NOVEL

BOOK 1

A Nightqueen Enterprises LLC Publication

Published by Yasmine Galenorn
PO Box 2037, Kirkland WA 98083-2037
THE SILVER STAG
A Wild Hunt Novel
Copyright © 2018 by Yasmine Galenorn
First Electronic Printing: 2018 Nightqueen Enterprises LLC
First Print Edition: 2018 Nightqueen Enterprises
Cover Art & Design: Ravven
Art Copyright: Yasmine Galenorn
Editor: Elizabeth Flynn

A Nightqueen Enterprises LLC Publication
Published in the United States of America

Acknowledgments

Welcome to the world of the Wild Hunt. This is one of those series that has been haunting me for a while, and now, it's time to put pen to paper (fingers to keyboard) and let the stories out.

Thanks to my usual crew: Samwise, my husband, Andria and Jennifer   without their help, I'd be swamped. To the women who have helped me find my way in indie, you're all great, and to the Wild Hunt, which runs deep in my magick, as well as in my fiction.

Also, my love to my furbles, who keep me happy. And most reverent devotion to Mielikki, Tapio, Ukko, Rauni, and Brighid, my spiritual guardians and guides.

If you wish to reach me, you can find me through my website at Galenorn.com and be sure to sign up for my newsletter to keep updated on all my latest releases!

Brightest Blessings,
~The Painted Panther~
~Yasmine Galenorn~

Welcome to Silver Stag

Once on the other side, going was more difficult. My footing was precarious, the rocks covered in slippery moss. I was holding on to the side of the embankment as I jumped from stone to stone, trying to keep from falling into the stream. The slope was getting steeper, and the rocks fewer and farther between. I would either have to follow from the cliff above, or jump down into the water and wade upstream. I glanced back at Vik, who was watching me carefully.

Turning back to the water, I tuned in, listened to it as it cascaded along.

It whispered to me, asking me if I would follow it up-stream a ways. There was a sadness to it, a melancholy feeling that made me want to cry.

Finally, I eased my way down into the water and, knee-deep, pushed against the current, slogging over the slippery rocks in the streambed. I had only gone a few feet when I noticed something ahead, lodged against the side of the embankment. Whatever it was, it sparkled in a sudden spate of sunlight that burst through the forest, slicing through the clouds.

Taking a good look around to make certain noth-ing was waiting to pounce on me, I followed the water over to the sparkling item. I found myself staring at a necklace, the chain of which had been broken. I slowly reached for the pendant, and as my hand met the water to scoop up the necklace, a shriek ran through me as sure as if I had heard it aloud. I let out a shout and stumbled back, surprised by the sudden pain that ac-companied the cry.

The Silver Stag: Book 1 of the Wild Hunt Series

Chapter 1

I CREPT THROUGH the backyard, keeping a close watch on the thick copse of trees to the side of the property. The coyotes were thick around here, and plenty of cougars and bears frequented the area as well. I skirted my way around the hen house. I could hear chickens rattling around inside, uneasy when they should have been asleep.

The urban farmers were my clients, and they had complained about some creature raiding their henhouse and asked me to look into it. They were shifters of some sort—I hadn't asked what kind, because that would be rude. But they seemed more reticent than most of the shifters I was used to dealing with, and I suspected they were too afraid to take on the intruder themselves. I had been keeping watch most of the night, and was about to call it done when a figure slipped into the yard, creeping toward the hen house.

I stayed close to the side of the shed, skirting around to where I could peek more clearly. A large man-sized creature was skulking near the door. I froze, resting my hand on the dagger that was strapped to my thigh. Easing back so the intruder wouldn't see me, I leaned my head against the wall. Well, it wasn't a coyote or fox, that was for sure.

A gust of cool wind blew past me and I shivered, even through my leather jacket. Early April in the Seattle area was cool and wet. At five A.M., we still had nearly an hour to go before sunrise, and the clouds were so thick I doubted they would burn off before noon, if then.

The creature fumbled with the lock. Whatever it was, it showed no signs that it sensed my presence. I could move softly when I wanted and now I crept to the right of the shed, then paused. The ladder was leaning against the side of the building. It would be simple to climb up onto the roof and peek over the edge. I could gain an advantage from up above, I thought, maybe get the drop on him. Keeping my step light, I shimmied up the rungs, grateful that I had worn gloves as the aluminum of the ladder chilled me right through the material.

The roof of the shed was slanted with an incline toward the front. I squinted at the shingles, wondering whether they would hold me. There was no way to find out except to start climbing. Praying that I wouldn't fall through, I slowly eased myself up the shingles toward the front of the rise. At the top, I cautiously leaned over the edge.

Great. Just dandy.

I found myself staring down at the head of a goblin. He reeked even from up here, and it was a wonder that I hadn't smelled him before. I must be coming down with a cold, I thought.

Goblins were nasty, dangerous creatures. Wiry and tough, they stank to high heaven when you were close enough, and they were ravenous. They ate people. Dogs. Cats. Cows. Anything they could fit in their mouths was fair game. They preferred human flesh, though they'd settle for whatever they could catch. As long as it was raw and live on the hoof, they were happy. Seattle, along with the surrounding suburb communities, had laws in place prohibiting them from entering city limits, but that didn't stop them, even though hunting season was wide open on them. Truth was, the cops wouldn't respond to calls about them, and chances were good the creatures would luck out and get away with whatever scheme they had going. So most of them thought it was worth the risk. This one's luck, however, had just run out.

Luckily, he hadn't heard me yet. At least, I didn't *think* it had.

I eased my way to the very edge, staring down at him. He was intent on breaking the padlock. I quietly unfastened the snap holding my dagger peace-bound, to give myself easy access. I had learned the hard way *not* to jump off a building holding my blade. I still had the scar from that mistake right above my left knee.

I perched on the edge, waiting for the right moment. Then, taking a deep breath, I launched myself off of the roof, landing square atop the goblin, taking him down beneath me.

The creature let out a nasty hiss and a string of obscenities, although I couldn't understand him. But it was obvious he was cursing.

"Would you speak to your *mother* like that?" I had knocked him down, and now I straddled him, trying to pin him between my knees. He might be tough and wiry, but I worked out six days a week, and I was Fae—which meant I had some extra strength going for me. I managed to hold him down and, in the dim light of the approaching dawn, I got a good look at him. Tufts of fur covered his head, patchy and rough like steel wool, and his face was a mass of wrinkles—common with goblins. His eyes were small but wide-set on his face, and he had yellow, sharp teeth.

"You're an ugly sucker, aren't you? Even for a goblin."

He struggled, managing to free one hand. As he lashed out, his claws dangerously nearing my face, I ducked back to dodge the attack.

Enough. I drew my dagger. I couldn't keep him down much longer and I was getting tired.

As I raised my blade, he thrashed again, and this time he succeeded in slashing my arm. Luckily, my leather jacket took the brunt, and he ripped a hole in the material but not in my skin.

"That's going to cost me good money, you freak."

I raised my blade and his gaze met mine. For a moment he looked afraid, but then he snarled and I brought the blade down, throwing my weight behind it. The tip of the dagger pierced his windpipe, sliding through to stick inside the ground below him. The goblin let out one last hiss, thrashed, and then lay still.

"I didn't charge enough for this gig," I muttered to myself. Truth was, I hadn't expected a goblin, so I had given the couple a low bid. I had thought I'd be facing a wild dog or a fox. So much for assumptions.

Making certain he was dead, I took a picture before he started to bubble, then rolled over to spread out on the grass next to him, resting. The chill morning dew sceped through my jeans as I caught my breath, staring up into the sky. The faint hints of dawn were spreading across the eastern horizon, thin ribbons of red piercing the clouds, but they only heralded an incoming storm.

At that moment, my cell phone rang. I pulled it out of my pocket as I rolled to a sitting position. Next to me, the goblin was beginning to bubble. I reached over to yank my dagger out of the creature's neck before my blade got any messier than it already was, and wiped it quickly on the grass to remove most of the gunk. I scooted further away as nature began to take its course on the goblin as I answered my phone.

"Hello? Do you *realize* what time it is?"

I hadn't glanced at the Caller ID, so I wasn't sure who it was, but I didn't care. If this were any normal morning, I'd still be in bed, asleep. Most of my work was done at night and I usually slept till noon. I just happened to have a job that kept me up till dawn.

"Yes, I *do* realize what time it is. Did I wake you?"

Damn it. Ray Fontaine.

Ray owned a bakery called A Touch of Honey, and he made the best bread in Seattle. He also happened to be my ex-boyfriend. Or rather, we had dated a few times. I had liked him enough that I broke it off before anything happened between us. Given my track record, he was a lucky man.

"No, I'm finishing up a job. What do you need?"

I shivered, suddenly cold. I slipped my finger through the ring attached to the back of my phone so I wouldn't drop it, and scrambled to my feet. The goblin was dissolving, melting into a pile of bubbling sludge. Within half an hour he would soak into the ground as if he had never existed. At least I wouldn't have to clean up the mess. I started for the kitchen door to ask the O'Malleys for payment, then paused. Their lights were off, which meant they weren't awake yet.

Ray cleared his throat. "My shop was broken into. I thought maybe you could come take a look?"

I blinked. "Why haven't you called the cops?"

"I did, but they took one look and said it wasn't a human matter. They said it looked like some sort of Crypto attack. Ember, you're the closest thing I know to a SubCult PI."

The "SubCult" was a blanket term referring to the combined Fae courts, Shifter Alliance, and Vampire Nation. Most humans referred to all of us as *Cryptos* if they didn't know what our heritage was, but it was better than the slang used among the holdouts who still wanted an all-human world.

I let out a sigh. I had just finished one job, and

I really didn't feel like working another, but I felt like I owed Ray. I really didn't want to see him, but it was the least I could do, given how hard he had taken it when I dumped him.

"Lovely. All right, I'll be down there in a while. I need to get my pay, then stop off for coffee and a bite to eat first."

"Don't bother about breakfast. I've got fresh croissants, gouda, and coffee here."

Finally, something to cadge a laugh out of me. "You always did know how to win me over." And with that, I pocketed my cell phone, and knocked on the kitchen door.

Ten minutes later, I had pounded long and hard enough that Mrs. O'Malley answered the door, squinting. She was in her bathrobe and seemed surprised to see me.

"Oh, are you still here?"

I blinked. "Of course I'm still here. I caught your chicken thief. Goblin." I held up my cell phone to show her the picture I had snapped. "No doubt about it. One dead goblin."

She stared at the picture, then started to shut the door on me. "Thanks. We appreciate it."

I stuck my foot in the door, wedging it open before she shut it all the way.

"Hold on! You owe me for the rest of the job." They had paid me half up front, with the promise of the rest of payment upon proof of job completion.

A sly smile stole over her face. "You can't prove that you caught him on our land. That could be a picture of any goblin, anywhere. We won't pay."

"What the fuck?" I stared at her, trying to comprehend what she was saying. "You're actually trying to stiff me? Lady, take a good look. That's your shed in the corner of the picture, and one fucking dead goblin. I came all the way over from Seattle to help you. I saved your scrawny-assed chickens. I undercharged you. I sat in your backyard all night guarding your stupid birds. You are going to *pay* me for my work." I glowered, leaning in.

She wrinkled her nose, trying to stare me down. "We never promised."

"Like hell you didn't." I paused, irritated. I worked on a verbal contract for most small jobs and I stuck to my promises. Most of my customers stuck to theirs. This was an unwelcome surprise. "All right," I said, turning back to the yard. "You want to do this the hard way? I notice you have a sprinkler system out there."

I focused, searching through the moisture in the air until I touched on the lines running below the ground. Forcing as much energy as I could into my thoughts, I coaxed the water to pour through the system, faster and harder until there was a sudden *pop*. A geyser of water broke through the soil, gushing into the yard.

"What did you do?" Mrs. O'Malley jumped, pushing past me into the yard. She flailed, glaring at me. "Make it stop."

"I guess your sprinkler pipe burst. Gee, I wonder what would happen if I found a water elemental to check out the pipes under your house? What if they all froze and then broke?" I probably wouldn't go that far, but *she* didn't have to know that.

The bluff worked.

"All right, all right! I'll pay you." She started back inside. "I have to get my purse."

I pushed inside, close behind her, not about to give her the chance to slam the door on me. "Fine. Cash only, please."

WOODINVILLE WAS PART of the Greater Seattle metropolitan area. Northeast of Kirkland and south of Navane—the city of the Light Fae—for a long time it had flourished as a techie wonderland, but as the tech companies migrated to north Seattle proper, the Eastside eventually became a forested haven, a metropolis of suburbs. Oh, there was still plenty of crime—for one thing, it was easier to hide given the growth of the forests around and in the cities—but for the lower-income areas, it felt spacious and beautiful.

A Touch of Honey was located on the Redmond-Woodinville Road NE, on the border between Redmond and Woodinville. As I eased into an empty parking spot a few spots down from the bakery, I leaned back in my seat. I was so tired that I could barely keep my eyes open, but I had promised Ray, and I kept my promises.

I slipped out of the driver's seat of my eight-year-old Subaru Outback and headed into the bakery, where Ray was busy behind the counter. He looked up as I entered and waved.

"You look like hell," he said. "You're covered

with dried mud." He paused, then grimaced. "Is that blood?"

I glanced down at my shirt where the goblin had bled on me. One more for the rag bag.

"I took down a goblin this morning. That's enough work for one day."

"Nasty business, those little freaks." Ray was all too acquainted with goblins. He had a long scar on his leg from where one had tried to take a bite out of him when he interrupted me on a job and my target had turned on him. It was at that point that I had decided our relationship had run its course. Before he got himself killed, I broke it off. I couldn't face another heartbreak. I had already lost two loves and I felt like I was under a curse.

"There's been an upsurge in their numbers lately. They always think they'll beat the odds, and the cops are paying less and less attention to them." Tired of thinking about goblins, I changed the subject. "You said you have croissants and gouda? And caffeine?"

"Rolls are hot out of the oven. The cheese is fresh and creamy. And the coffee's hot and strong."

The bakery was overflowing with a warm, yeasty scent that sent my salivary glands into overdrive. My stomach rumbled, demanding food. As Ray fixed a tray, I headed over to the coffee pot and poured myself a cup of coffee. I preferred espresso, but caffeine was caffeine and I sorely needed my fix. And Ray bought quality coffee—Caribbean Dark Roast from the islands. Adding cream and three sugars, I sat down at one of the tables.

The bakery was fair size, with four tables, each

seating three people. The counter display case was filled with cookies and breads, and I suddenly felt weak-kneed. I needed food and I needed it now. As if he had read my mind, Ray returned with a tray filled with warm croissants and a small wheel of cheese. The flesh was a creamy yellow, and my guess was that he had bought it off one of the local farmers who sold homemade cheese at the farmers market.

I glanced around. The bakery seemed unusually empty.

"I don't see any of your regulars in here," I said, slicing a thick wedge of cheese off the wheel. I placed it on the plate, and then broke open one of the croissants, inhaling deeply as the warm rush of yeast filled my lungs.

"The regular city crew that normally comes in every morning is apparently filling potholes on the other side of town. I don't see them until afternoon now. Otherwise, yeah, it's been a quiet morning. Then again, the rush usually doesn't start until around seven-thirty or eight."

Sure enough, even as he spoke, the bells jingled as the door opened and two women entered the shop. I gauged them as both human. Ray excused himself to wait on them, and I busied myself with my croissants and cheese.

I mulled over my schedule, pulling out my day planner to check what was on the agenda for the day. I was scheduled to make a run over to Wesley's Blades to have him sharpen my dagger. I needed to go grocery shopping unless I wanted to eat cardboard for dinner.

Ray returned to the table, pulling out the chair next to me. Flipping it around, he straddled it and leaned his elbows on the back. He was a tall man, with soft black hair that waved down to his neck. He was also as human as they came. He handed me a hundred and fifty dollars.

"Will this cover the bill for looking over my storeroom?"

I pocketed fifty and handed him back the rest. "You get the friends and family discount." I suddenly felt awkward. Ray and I hadn't talked much since we broke up, at least no more than polite formalities. I shifted in my seat.

He seemed to feel it too. "So, are you seeing anybody?"

At least that was an easy answer. I shook my head.

"No. I think I'm better off on my own." I met his gaze, searching for any signs that he was still angry. "I wish I could tell you why I broke up with you, but Ray, it wasn't you. At least, not in the way you think."

He gave me a rueful smile. "After you dumped me, I was really angry. I never wanted to see you again. Then Angel told me about Robert, and about Leland. Anyway, I understand. Thank you, for looking after me." He lingered over the words, then shrugged. "I'm still game, if you are. I'll take my chances."

I gave him a long look. "Ray, don't do this."

"But we were—"

"Look, it's done. Over. Angel told you about Robert and Leland because she's my best friend and she knew it hurt me to push you away. Please, don't make it harder than it already has been."

He let out what sounded like a cross between a sigh and a huff. "Okay. But don't be mad at Angel for telling me."

"I'm not. I'm glad she told you about them. I don't want you to hate me." With a sigh, I pushed back my chair. The last thing I wanted to do was get into a discussion of my tangled mess of a love life and I wasn't about to open the door to Ray again. "Okay, let me look at your storeroom."

Ray frowned, looking like he was going to argue, but then he shrugged and led me into the back. After he unlocked the door, I saw that the entire room had been trashed. Flour bags were ripped to pieces, honey jars had been tipped over and smashed and two of the bigger buckets of honey had been slashed. Nothing had been spared.

"Holy crap. Who did you piss off?"

"I have no idea. All I know is that no animal did this. The cops told me it was probably a raccoon. But what raccoon can do this much damage in a short amount of time? And the windows weren't open. How did it get in?" He scuffed his shoe on the floor. "I thought maybe you could pick up on whatever came through here."

I nodded, taking care not to enter the room, at least not yet. The cops were wrong. This hadn't been the work of an animal. Nor did the damage feel human in origin. For one thing, Ray was right. The window was intact, so either the vandal had a key or could spell the door open.

I knelt, touching my hands to the floor just inside the door. Sometimes I could feel when strong emotions had passed through an area. They imprinted in space, or in the walls of buildings, or rooted into the very ground itself. Here, the residual feeling of anger hung heavy in the air, anger and...*revenge*.

"Whatever or whoever did this, I think they have a grudge against you. I can't pick up more than that, but yeah, it wasn't human or animal. I suggest you hire someone to ward your place. There's a very talented witch who has a shop called Magical Endeavors. Her name is Lena. I suggest you talk to her, and while you're at it, figure out who you've pissed off lately. My guess—somebody hired one of the sub-Fae to come in and tear up the joint."

The sub-Fae were the dregs of Fae society, usually nasty tempered and often hiring themselves out as mercenaries to anybody at the right price. Like goblins, they weren't welcome in the city, but all you had to do was hang out at one of the Sub-Cult dives around town and you would run into at least one of them.

"Thanks, Ember. I appreciate it. You wouldn't be interested in taking on the case and helping me out by hiring Lena...and so on?" He was standing too close for comfort.

I backed away a step. "Sorry," I lied. "My schedule is booked up." I yawned, pushing past him to return to the front of the shop. "I'd better get going. I have errands to run before I go home and crash." I glanced over at the counter. "Wrap me up a loaf of French bread and a dozen white chocolate raspberry cookies, if you would."

Ray crossed to behind the counter and fixed my order. As he handed it to me, our fingers touched. A familiar spark raced through me, but I ignored it. I didn't dare go down that road again, not if I wanted him to be safe. Besides, I didn't do clingy well, and Ray had shown definite signs of wanting more from me than I could give.

"How much do I owe you?"

"On the house. And it always will be."

And with that, I headed back to my car as the morning rush began to trickle in. Overall, Ray was a good guy, and he was alive. I wanted him to stay alive.

MY CONDO WAS over in Seattle, in Spring Beach. At one time, the neighborhood had been suburban—the home of the rich. But now, it was row upon row of high rises and commercial buildings. Shiny chrome-and-glass blended in with older brick, making a hodgepodge of urban dwellings. Parks dotted the neighborhood, replacing the vast swaths of foliage that had surrounded once-massive estates. My building—the Miriam G Building—overlooked Puget Sound, and the rich colors of cloud and sky and ocean greeted me every morning when I got up.

I lived on the fifteenth floor, in unit 1515. Every now and then I worried about what might happen should we see another large earthquake like we had some years back, but the buildings in the area had been retrofitted—the ones that hadn't crashed to the ground—and the newer ones were built to a strict code.

As I parked in the parking garage, it occurred to me that I might want to think about selling the place and buying a house on the outskirts of the city at some point. The condo was small, around eight hundred square feet, and while I had two bedrooms, my guest room also housed my arsenal of weapons.

I glanced around the dark garage. Even during the day it was spooky. The building had been built about thirty years ago, and the developer had gone bankrupt. The bank had repossessed the apartments and sold the Miriam G to another buyer, who had decided to sell them as condos. Eventually, when I was looking for a place, a unit came up for sale and I bought it. I'd been living here since I was twenty-five. It wasn't fancy, but the view was worth the money, although the area I lived in wasn't exactly a safe haven.

I slipped out of the car and quickly made my way to the elevator. Luckily, there was nobody else waiting—I didn't trust all of my neighbors—and within a few moments I was at my apartment door.

MR. RUMBLEBUTT WAS waiting for me. He was a Norwegian forest cat, sixteen pounds with fur that made him look like a giant tribble on legs.

He was sitting on the back of the sofa, staring at the front door. When I entered, he let out a disgruntled purp, jumped down, and headed toward the kitchen.

"All right, I know breakfast is overdue." As I opened the can and put his chunky chicken on the floor, I started to yawn, so tired I could barely think. I crossed over to the floor to ceiling windows that overlooked the Puget Sound and pulled open the curtains. A wash of daylight broke through the gloom and I leaned against the armchair that looked directly out onto the balcony. The thought of falling asleep staring at the water sounded good to me, but I knew my back wouldn't thank me when I woke up. So I trudged into the bathroom, stripped and, leaving my clothes on the floor, stepped into a hot shower.

I was too tired to wash my hair, so after I finished up, I dragged a brush through it and padded to my bed. I debated on opening the curtain so I could look out on the water as I slept but decided the light would probably keep me awake. So I slid under the covers, closed my eyes, and within minutes was dead to the world.

MY PHONE WOKE me up. I cracked one eye, rolling over to stare at the clock. It was 2:30 P.M. and I had managed about six hours of sleep. Yawning, I scooted back against the headboard as I grabbed my phone off the nightstand. The Caller

ID read Angel, and I quickly punched the talk button.

"Hey, what's up?" I yawned again.

Angel was my best friend, and I was surprised to see the call was from her. She seldom called during the day. Texted? Definitely. But phone calls from her job? So not approved by her boss. After work, she would go home to take care of her little half-brother. She had taken in DJ when their mother died, and she was doing her best to make sure he didn't end up on the streets.

"I'm worried about DJ. I'm afraid something's happened to him." She sounded frantic. Angel hardly ever let her nerves get the better of her. If she was worried, something was wrong.

"What's going on?" I asked, pushing back the covers. Angel and I had each other's backs, we'd been best friends for years, and if one of us was in trouble, the other one was always willing to come to the rescue.

"Last night he stayed over with a friend. He was supposed to come home this morning, but when I called home from work half an hour ago, he didn't answer. I called Sarah—the mother of the boy he was staying with. She said he left at seven-thirty this morning. He should have been home by nine, shortly after I left for work. So I came home and I don't see any sign that he's been here. This isn't like DJ. *You* know him. He's a good kid, and he always lets me know where he is. I checked my texts, I checked voice messages. Not a word from him."

"He didn't have school today?"

"No, today's a teacher's day. That's why I let him

stay over last night with Jason."

I could hear the tears in her throat. DJ was ten years old, and as she said, he was a good kid. He had been a change-of-life child, and Mama Jackson had conceived him when she was forty-eight. Mama J. had died a year ago, the victim of a car crash. Her death had left a hole not only in Angel and DJ's life, but in mine. Mama J. had filled the void when my parents were killed.

When Mama J. died, Angel took DJ in and the arrangement had worked out fairly well, although it hadn't been easy for her. For one thing, DJ was Wulfine—a wolf shifter. Angel was human, and she had no clue how to help him transition through the changes as he grew up.

"I'm on my way over. Meanwhile, call all his friends if you haven't done so already. Maybe he stopped off somewhere and got busy playing and just forgot."

Even as I suggested it, I knew it wasn't true. DJ wasn't the type to space out on his responsibilities. Even when Mama J. was alive, DJ had been a somber child, focused on helping his family. Angel often told me that he seemed to feel old before his time, although neither of us could figure out what had brought that on. It just seemed to be his nature.

"Thank you." Angel paused, her voice hushed. "Ember, I have a horrible feeling that he's in real trouble. You know that most of my premonitions are spot-on. I'm afraid."

"I'll be there in fifteen minutes." There was nothing else I could say. As she hung up, I was al-

16652

ready sliding into a pair of leather pants. I fastened my bra and then pulled on a black ribbed tank top. I jammed my arms in the sleeves of my leather jacket, and then slipped on my ankle boots, zipping them up the side. I dragged a brush through my hair and then pulled it back into a ponytail. After kissing Mr. Rumblebutt on the head and filling his dry food dish, I grabbed a chocolate chip breakfast bar and headed back to my car.

Chapter 2

ANGEL LIVED ON the Eastside, in the UnderLake District. Once a thriving suburb, it had fallen into decay, with weathered houses lining roads riddled with potholes. It wasn't Angel's first choice, but when she took over DJ's care, her limited salary had to stretch and so she had moved to an inexpensive area that still had decent schools. Mama J. had left a lot of debts and the sale of her restaurant barely covered them. Angel had traded apartment living for renting a small house, with room for DJ to play out back.

Both bridges spanning Lake Washington were toll bridges, so I opted to drive around the north side of the lake. It wasn't that I couldn't afford the tolls, but at this time of day they were slammed. Actually, gridlock was a common problem here except during the dark of the night. I'd actually get to Angel's house quicker by taking a roundabout way.

Heading east on 145th Street, I then swung a left on Highway 522 and followed it around the northern tip of Lake Washington. When I reached Kenmore, another small suburb, I turned right on 68th Avenue, which took me directly into the UnderLake District.

UnderLake had once been a thriving suburban area, but now there was an abandoned feeling permeating the air, like a party at three A.M., when most of the guests had packed up and gone home, with only a scattered few remaining, trying to finish the scattered remains of a buffet. The houses were weathered here, with paint peeling off their sides, and the roads were riddled with potholes and cracks. The entire neighborhood felt ignored. The schools were decent, if underfunded, but there was a growing darkness to the UnderLake District and it cast a pall over the entire suburb.

Up north, near Bothell, the Shifter Alliance had taken over, as they had down south in the Renton, Kent, and Federal Way areas. When you went further east to Woodinville, Snohomish, and Monroe, the Fae had moved in, creating two large districts, Navane and TirNaNog.

Navane was run by Névé, the local Queen of the Light Fae, and TirNaNog was run by Saílle, Queen of the Dark. I avoided both like the plague, considering my background. My heritage guaranteed me a swift kick to the ass when I tried to interact with the Fae. I was a half-breed, unwelcome at either court. Half Dark Fae, half Light Fae, my blood ensured that neither side wanted to claim me.

As I eased my car through the streets, it struck

me that the only humans still living in this area were either poor, or they had been here a long time and didn't want to move. The fact that spring was a little late this year and the trees were still bare of leaves—although the buds had started blossoming—made the area seem even more desolate. The sidewalks were uneven, and grass grew through the cracks along the way. A number of the houses looked abandoned. For-sale signs were plastered on a number of the sagging fences.

I eased into the driveway of one of the few houses that looked neat and tidy. While the rental would require a lot of work to bring it back to its former glory, Angel had done a remarkable job on tidying up both the cottage and the yard. She given it a new coat of paint, and the crisp white walls stood out in a sea of weathered gray. The yard was neatly trimmed, and daffodils and crocus flourished at the base of the tree trunks that surrounded the cottage. Her landlord hadn't objected to her working on the place, and even gone so far as to supply the paint.

I hurried up to the porch, hoping that in the time it'd taken me to get there, DJ had come home. But when Angel answered the doorbell, my hopes were dashed. Her expression said it all.

"He's not home yet?" I didn't bother with small talk. She wouldn't be up for it, and I wasn't much good at it.

She shook her head. "I've called every place where he could possibly be, and nobody has seen him today. Sarah and her son Jason walked the route from their house to here, but there was no sign of him. I'm really worried."

She was trembling. Angel could have been a model, she was so tall and lithe, with rich black skin and a halo of black hair that curled down her back. She was human, although her half-brother was a wolf shifter. His father had vanished before he was even out of the womb. Angel was psychic, and her precognitive flashes were usually right on the money. And that had me worried for DJ.

"How far is it from here to their house? What's the route?" Given that DJ was almost always good to his word, I doubted that he had stopped off anywhere along the way home.

"Sarah lives over on 151st Street. Sometimes DJ takes a shortcut to get home through UnderLake Park, but he knows I don't like it when he does. He usually avoids it, but now and then when he's in a hurry, he'll cut through there. Sarah doesn't know which way he decided to go. She was busy in the kitchen when he left."

I could hear the fear in her voice. The Under-Lake District was bad. But UnderLake Park? It was a whole different level of dangerous. Heavily wooded, it had once been the home of an order of monks that had long since left, leaving the monastery still there, crumbling and haunted. Over the years the park had been renamed, but no amount of changing the name could alter the fact that there had been a lot of violence and disappearances there. Anybody who lived in the Seattle area had heard of it.

"Why don't I go check it out? You stay here in case he comes home."

"Thank you." A grateful smile spread across her face. "I called the police, but you know how they are. Until it's dark, they won't even consider looking for him. If he were two years old, they might get their asses in gear, but they think every black kid able to talk is mixed up with a gang."

The police were overburdened, underfunded, and overwhelmed. They were also—for the most part—corrupt. Oh, they responded to homicides, vicious attacks, and burglaries, the latter mainly at wealthy estates. Over the years, you'd think things would have changed for the better in terms of racial tension. But the world only seemed to get worse and that tension had extended into the Crypto community. The cops were bought and paid for by rich humans, the vampires, and the Fae.

"Do you know what he was wearing?" If he was trapped or hurt in a hard-to-reach area, it would help to know if he was wearing bright clothing.

"If I remember right, he was wearing a red hoodie and a pair of blue jeans. I don't remember what color T-shirt. I wish I had told him to take his bike, but it's still on the porch so he must have walked over there yesterday."

"Why would he take the shortcut?"

"If he's tired, or he thinks he's late, he'll sometimes cut through there. If he had taken his bike he probably would have taken the long way." She bit her lip. "I'm afraid."

I took Angel's hand and gave it a long squeeze. "We're going to find him. We don't know that he took the shortcut, but I'll check it out. Meanwhile, you make yourself some tea and try to calm down.

Don't borrow trouble."

She nodded, biting her lip. "It's just that... Since Mama died, DJ and I are all that's left. You know? My father's dead, and DJ's father vanished the minute he found out Mama was pregnant. Any aunts or uncles we have are back east, and we don't have much to do with them. Or rather, *they* don't have much to do with *us*. Mama's sister, Maria, was pissed as hell when she found out that DJ was Wulfine."

"About that—how much control does he have over his shifting? If something scared him, could he have changed shape? Does he have trouble transforming back? Should I be looking for a young wolf as well?"

Angel considered the question, then gave me a short shrug. "He's still getting the techniques down for shifting. He can shift at will, though he's shaky about it. The full moon still makes him shift. I take him out to the country a couple times a month so he can practice and run around in his wolf form without any worries. It always takes him a while to transform back. So I can't give you an answer. I suppose it could be possible."

I stood up, glancing around the tidy living room. The cottage was small, with two bedrooms, a living room–dining room, a bathroom, and a kitchen, but every surface sparkled, and what little clutter there was belonged to DJ. Angel had done her best to turn it into a home, and to make a safe place for DJ to grow up in.

"I'll find him. I'll do everything I can." I gave her a hug.

She dashed away a tear. "Bring him home, please," she whispered. "Bring my brother home."

AS I HEADED back to my car, I pulled out my phone.

"Search UnderLake Park history."

I figured it might be a good idea to get a better idea of just exactly what I was dealing with. Even though I knew the park was dangerous, I didn't know all the specifics.

"Which city should I search?" the search engine asked.

"The UnderLake District, near Kirkland, Washington."

Seconds later, a string of search links popped up on my screen. I noticed one of them was a news article and tapped on it first. I slid into the driver's seat, glancing over the site. It was a local pseudo-news site, more touristy than anything but not clickbait.

The UnderLake Park, which borders Under-Lake, Washington, and Kirkland, Washington, sprawls across five hundred acres. Part of the land was originally donated to the city by a monastery when it closed its doors. An additional fifty acres adjacent to the park was donated to the city by Trina Castle.

Ms. Castle inherited the Castle Hall estate when her mother and father were brutally murdered in their home. Police found blood everywhere, but no bodies. John and Vera Castle were never found, but DNA samples verified that the blood belonged to them, and the medical examiner stated that with the amount of blood found at the scene, there was virtually no chance either one could still be alive. No motive was ever discovered, although many theories were proposed, and the bodies have never surfaced.

Castle Hall sat empty for several years until Trina Castle donated the estate to the city, claiming she couldn't bear to live there. The old mansion still stands on the grounds, half a mile from the crumbling monastery, abandoned and in a state of disrepair. City officials have repeatedly discussed razing it, but nothing has ever been done. There are claims that the mansion is haunted, and amateur ghost hunters have visited the estate numerous times. The Castle Hall estate was established in 1920, passed down through the Castle family until the disappearance of John and Vera Castle in 1998.

Over the years since then, five unsolved murders—all gruesome—have happened within proximity to the Castle Hall estate, and numerous reports of missing persons have been logged within UnderLake Park as a whole. Speculation abounds about the possibility of a serial killer but has been repeatedly denied by the police.

I blinked. I knew the park was dangerous, but had no clue of its bloody history. I pulled up my maps app and traced the route that led through the shortcut. Angel watched from the front porch as I eased out of her driveway and headed toward the trailhead.

The entrance to the park was wide and broad, marked by long cedar logs to which the UnderLake Park signs were attached. I turned onto the paved drive and immediately felt the shift in energy. The park was a tangle of old growth, mostly fir and cedar, their trunks massive with moss dripping from their branches. The branches formed a canopy over the road, entwining over the narrow road. Two cars could go abreast, barely, and there were no shoulders on which to turn off if you had car trouble. Over the years, the forest had thickened and a riot of vegetation flourished, spreading out to surround the tree trunks and cover the ground.

Stands of birch, with its startling white bark, dotted the park, breaking up the constant clamor of forest green and the dark trunks of the trees. Light could—and did—peek through the foliage, but only in patches, and as I crept along, looking for the trailhead that led to the shortcut, I found myself quickly descending into a brooding watchfulness. I opened my window even though it was chilly and humid, and listened to the call of the birds.

To my left, a murder of crows had set up a racket, and to my right came the shriek of a redtailed hawk, which was setting off the crows. The hawk was hunting, that much I could tell, and as I listened, a gust of wind came rushing through. For a moment, I could swear I heard voices on it—talking, as though a group of people was passing by. I squinted, but could see nothing. I wasn't good at catching a glimpse of the Unseen, although I could sense when they were around. Angel was better at that than me.

As the energy settled around me, I felt like I had entered claimed territory. I was an intruder here, and there were eyes all through the forest. I breathed a sigh of relief when I finally arrived at the Wonder Trail, the shortcut DJ usually took, and guided my car into one of three parking spots. Turning off the ignition, I leaned back in the seat, listening.

Below the layer of the crows and hawk, below the voices I had heard, there surged a current of energy. I followed it, sourcing it back to the trees and the soil and the animals that made up the forest around me. City park or not, this was a Wild Place, and even though I was Fae and used to them, that fact made me nervous. Wild Places could be dark and brooding areas, and they were dangerous for the unwary—human or otherwise. They were tied into the very heart of the planet, the deep forces that made up the bones of the world and there were spirits and creatures in them that were far more deadly than anything walking on two legs.

I focused on lowering my vision to below the level of the trees, diving deep into the core of what made up UnderLake Park.

The sentience that ran below the surface of the park was thick, like a shadow creeping through the night. It coiled around the roots of the trees, trickling through the soil like rivulets of water, seeping into the rocks and vegetation. It crept up the tall trunks to filter between the branches and around the limbs of the trees. It seeped into the water and the debris that littered the forest floor.

Foggy and dangerous, it had an edge that could slice through flesh like a razor blade. The spirit was angry, with a voracious appetite that felt like it would never be satiated and it churned with all the fervor of an ocean wave, threatening to sweep me under as it rolled by.

"Holy fuck," I muttered, pulling myself out of the trance. I hadn't expected to key in so easily. Most places that had experienced great violence had some sort of sentience, but this was like a monster, frothing below the surface as it waited for the next victim. And I could only hope that the chosen target hadn't been DJ. If he was in here, I had to find him and fast, because there were numerous dangers that lurked within the woodland.

Grateful for my tracking skills, I retrieved my backpack from the backseat, then jumped out of the car and locked it. I kept a pack with all my tools ready to go. Rope, a first-aid kit, a spare knife, water bottles, food, a thermal blanket, and a flashlight took care of most of my needs.

While most of my jobs were simple *track and catch*, occasionally I found myself on a search and rescue mission, and I wanted to be prepared. I slipped the pack over my shoulders and headed down the trail, into the forest.

Some forests were dark and brooding, obviously dangerous places for creatures of any sort. Others were welcoming, while still others gave the illusion of tranquility, when in truth, they sought to lure in victims. As I headed to the entrance of the trail, I listened to the trees murmur around me and quickly realized that, though they were dangerous and didn't trust humankind nor any of its ilk, neither would they play favorites. They would harbor both good and evil, favoring neither.

Pausing at the entrance, I inhaled a deep lungful of air, paying attention to the scents.

My sense of smell was heightened, thanks to my Fae heritage, and as I let myself sift through the layers, I searched for anything that would tell me whether DJ had come this way.

Beneath the fragrant smells of water dripping from the cedar and fir branches, I could smell moss and the mildew, the tang of decaying leaves that had fallen from the trees last autumn, the smell of mushrooms and fungi that were so prevalent in the woods here.

I patiently sifted through them, discarding the ones that were obvious. Below that I could smell the faint stench of skunk. One must have passed this way within the past twenty-four hours. And a faint musk hung in the air, suggesting that a deer or an elk had crossed through the park. Lowering my sense of smell even further, I stretched out my awareness as far as I could. There, on the edge of my perception, I could smell chocolate and nuts, and fear.

I began to head along the trail, staying on the center of the path. Overhead, the canopy of trees wove their branches across the path, forming a lattice-work roof.

Deciding it best to trace the chocolate, I focused my attention on the scent. That was the only clue I had. DJ loved chocolate, I knew that much.

About five minutes in, the scent abruptly veered left, into the undergrowth. I had been watching the ground carefully, looking for any sign of footprints or anything to tell me that he had come this way. Even though it had rained, the soil of the path was compacted, with few mud puddles. Pausing, I stared into the foliage. Finally, deciding that following the scent would be my best chance, I turned to the left and forged my way into the tangle.

Within a few minutes, I found myself at the top of a ravine. The grade was steep and I paused to yank a broken branch off of a nurse log to use as a walking stick. Grateful for the nonskid tread on my boots, I began to make my way down the slope, half-sliding, half-stumbling down the hill.

At least it wasn't raining, although clouds had socked in and we were due for a good spring drenching. A rustle to my left caught my attention, but it was only a small animal, out hunting. A breeze coasted past and I closed my eyes, inhaling deeply as I tried to read whatever I could from the flowing breeze. Once again, the smell of chocolate came over me, coming from down below, and I picked up my pace as best as I could.

The ravine was steep and slick, but the trees were thick enough that I was able to weave my way, using their trunks to steady myself. It was slow going as I slogged through the undergrowth, and I tested each step to make certain I wouldn't turn an ankle, but as I built my rhythm, the going began to get easier.

"Thank gods I wore long sleeves," I muttered out loud. I passed through a tall stand of stinging nettles. The barbs on the plant caused severe welts, even for the non-allergic.

A moment later, I realized a low mist was beginning to rise. I froze, sensing a faint sentience to the fog. Wrapping my hand around the hilt of my dagger, I breathed softly as I waited. There was danger everywhere within this park, and I wondered whether whatever had killed John and Vera Castle was still around. Maybe not a serial killer in the usual sense of the word, but a deeply entrenched danger? After a moment, the mist rolled lightly across the ground, ignoring me, and I continued.

I came across a small puddle of water at the base of a tree, and squatted beside it. Placing my palm on the surface of the water, I reached deep with all of my senses, searching for the essence behind the element. All elements were sentient to a degree, and if there were any elementals around, I should be able to pick up on them. At least *water* elementals.

I could feel the connection of the water in the puddle to the water running through the roots of the trees, to the water dripping off of the needles and branches of the trees, to the moisture in the air. And then...behind that, a presence.

Is anyone there? Will you speak to me? I sent out the emotion, a questioning energy. Elementals didn't respond to words, but to feelings and images.

A flicker of awareness signaled that I had caught

the attention of the water elemental. I hesitantly reached out, extending my respect, and the elemental reached back, lingering around the edges of my aura. It was hesitant and wary, but seemed open to communication.

I formed an image of DJ in my mind, surrounding him with a sense of worry. I pushed a sense of urgency into every ounce of my inquiry, focusing on the danger that I thought he was in.

A moment later the elemental responded. The image of the streambed formed in my mind, deep inside the ravine, and I saw what looked like a concrete culvert. I sensed a warning in the message, but couldn't see what I was supposed to watch out for. The elemental broke off contact, and I whispered a *Thank you.*

I leaned back against the tree, considering my next move. If I could trust the elemental, then DJ would be somewhere near a stream. Maybe he was caught in a culvert and couldn't get out? And if there *was* a stream, it was probably at the bottom of the ravine.

The question was, which way should I go once I found it? I thought about calling out for DJ, but something stopped me. This woodland would be the perfect place for the goblins to hide in, and while I could take care of myself, DJ couldn't.

Unable to shake off the feeling that there was something dangerous nearby, I began to descend through the ravine again, trying to make as little noise as I could.

Finally, I reached the bottom, and sure enough, found a small stream, about ten feet wide. On the other side, the ravine climbed back up.

I looked to the left and then to the right. Both directions vanished into the forest, curving out of sight. Frowning, I reached into the layers of scent again, searching for the scent of chocolate. A few moments later it bloomed again, coming from my right. At least the going would be easier, now that I was on level ground.

I made my way parallel to the stream, following the smell of candy. The water wasn't extremely deep, but it ran swift, with foaming whitecaps as it burbled along.

I navigated around tree stumps, slogging around the soft banks of mud as I eyed the ground for any sign of footprints. I had gone about twenty yards when I caught a flash of something bright off a bush off to my right. Hurrying over, I saw that it was a red bandana. When I picked it up, I saw a smear of chocolate on it. There was a candy bar wrapper at the base of the bush as well.

I pulled out my phone and called Angel. Reception down in the ravine was full of static, but I managed to get through.

"What's DJ's favorite candy bar, and do you know if he had a red bandana with him?"

When she spoke, I could hear the fear in her voice. "Yes, he did. And it's Choco-Nutmallow."

I stared at the wrapper in my hand. *Choco-Nutmallow*, all right. DJ had come this way. "Don't panic. I haven't found anything to show that he's hurt, but I'm on track. I'll call you later when I have anything else to report."

I pocketed the bandana and the candy wrapper,

and started out again. The bush wasn't far off from the stream, so I decided to keep going along the streambed.

Not far ahead, I spotted a disturbance in a pile of leaves. It looked like somebody had been rolling in them, or scuffling in them.

I knelt to examine the ground. Here and there I could see a footprint—the tread of a boot heel, I thought. And it looked like some of the surrounding plants had been trampled. Unless I missed my guess, some sort of altercation had taken place here. I inched ahead, looking for any sign I could find that DJ had been part of the tussle.

The moss wasn't conducive to prints like mud or dirt were, but I spotted a few places where boots had made some sort of an indentation. But it couldn't be DJ—not for that deep of an impression. He was too small. Either someone heavier had been through here, or several people had been walking in formation.

A noise alerted me and I turned around, wondering if I had been spotted. But all I could see was a faint silver glow up the slope in a thicket of the ravine. I gazed at it for a moment, and then I saw antlers.

It must be a stag, I thought. *Caught in a beam of light, maybe*. At that moment, the stag vanished behind a tree.

As I started up again, following the streambed, the undergrowth grew thicker as the stream narrowed. Up ahead I could hear something—water splashing. I could also hear voices. I froze, straining to hear what was being said. But even though I had good hearing, the water and the wind muffled everything into a blur of sound. I crouched down and began to creep forward, doing my best to avoid making any noise. There seemed to be a clearing up ahead, and I sure as hell didn't want to accidentally out myself before I knew what I was dealing with. Or who I was dealing with.

I inched my way forward, gritting my teeth as I snapped a branch below my hand. But the voices continued, so I figured that I hadn't been overheard. In fact, it sounded like I was going to interrupt what seemed to be a heated argument. When I was almost to the edge of the undergrowth, I stopped and slowly parted one of the bushes so that I could just peek through.

I was at the head of the streambed, and sure enough—there was a culvert at the end. In fact, that was where the water feeding the stream originated. The culvert rammed into the side of the hill, about four feet above the ground. Directly in front of it, I could see DJ. He was sitting on the ground, his hands tied behind his back, and he was gagged with what looked to be a white cloth.

Standing near him, arguing full force, were two men. They were Fae, I could tell that right off, both dressed in jeans and leather jackets. I could see daggers strapped to their belts. One was about five-eight, with long dark hair hanging down his back in multiple braids. The other was a little taller, and his hair was blond and shaggy. Both looked beefy enough to make tangling with them problematic. I focused on what they were arguing about.

"I don't like killing kids," the blond one said. "Can't we just take him back to Névé?"

"She told us to get rid of anybody who overheard us. I'm not questioning a royal decree." The dark-haired man laid his hand on his dagger. "It doesn't matter what his age is, he overheard our plans and that makes him dangerous."

Blondie shrugged. "We don't know if he heard us or not." He opened a small wallet and pulled out a note, reading it. "Kid doesn't live too far from here. His name's Derrick Juan Jackson."

Crap. They knew where he lived now.

"You really want to thwart the Queen's orders? I knew you were addled, but not that stupid. We have to do something because if he's missing for too long, they'll come out looking. We can stuff him deep in the culvert and they won't find him for days. But if we stand around arguing any longer, we might get caught."

"Don't blame *me*," the blond one said. "You're the one who wanted to come out here and look for *thalacious*."

I grimaced. Thalacious was a poisonous plant that was often used on daggers and arrows by more unsavory types. Given they were talking about taking DJ back to Névé told me they were from the Light Court.

"I didn't think we were going to be overheard out here in the middle of the woods. Besides which, we were instructed to gather the herb by Quariala. I'm not disappointing Névé's right-hand witch, thank you. I prefer to keep my dick intact. Besides, the kid's a wolf shifter. One less shifter in the world isn't going to do any harm." Brownie snorted.

"Then you're the one who's going to have to take care of him. I won't do it." Blondie took a step back and crossed his arms. "I doubt if Sasha would agree with you."

"Sasha's not here right now. I told him to see if anybody else is snooping around. He's doing *his* job." The dark-haired man glanced over at DJ and a sly smile stole across his face. "He'd make a lovely little play toy, but alas, we don't have time to draw this out." He began to reach for his dagger.

DJ struggled, his eyes wide. He knew what was about to happen.

I had to do something and do it quick, or DJ's days were over. I unsnapped the binding on my dagger and drew it. Coming out of my crouch, I lunged out of the undergrowth and launched myself into a tackle. Before he could react, I landed on the dark-haired man and took him down.

He was strong, and even though I caught him by surprise, he reacted immediately. He wrapped his legs around mine as I straddled him, reaching around to grab me by the ponytail. As he caught hold of my hair, he yanked hard, jerking my head back to expose my throat.

I had to keep him from drawing his dagger. While I couldn't get a good aim, considering he had hold of my ponytail and it was hard for me to see, I remembered his dagger had been on his right side. I brought my blade down swift and hard, hoping to hit his arm.

He let out a sharp cry, and let go of my hair. I

had landed dead center on his bicep. But my dagger was embedded in his flesh, so I clenched my fists together and brought them down as hard as I could on his nose.

Dazed and in obvious pain, instinctively he reached for his face and I grabbed the hilt of my dagger, yanking it out of his arm. At the same time I looked up to see where the blond man was, not wanting to be caught unawares. To my surprise, I saw the stag I had seen come down out of the forest and attack the other Fae, thrashing at him with his hooves.

Blondie staggered back from a blow to the head, and I returned my attention to my opponent. I had broken his nose and probably crushed one of his eye sockets, but he was starting to shake off the shock. I had no choice. If I didn't take him out, he'd take me out.

I dragged my dagger across his throat. Blood spouted up, a geyser of red, and he began frothing from the mouth as I rolled off of him, staggering back. I turned to see the stag trampling Blondie.

I met the gaze of the massive deer, and he backed away, inclining his head toward the prone man. I raced over and drove my dagger into the Fae's heart before he could get up off the ground.

Panting, I dropped to the ground. I had killed goblins over the years, and other sub-Fae, but I had never really taken on anyone quite so human. I felt—shell-shocked. Everything seemed so surreal. Dazed, I glanced around and saw DJ, struggling with his bindings. I scrambled over to him and slashed the ropes holding his hands tied behind his back. I quickly untied his gag.

"Are you okay?" First things first. Always make sure the victim is all right.

He nodded, shaking as he threw himself into my arms. "I think so. They were going to kill me." He looked around. "Where's the other one?"

I shook my head. "I don't know, but we have to get out of here before he comes back." I was covered with blood, but I pulled him into my arms and held him as he leaned against my shoulder, trembling. "That's why I'm here, DJ. I came to find you."

By now, it was growing darker in the ravine. Sunset wouldn't be for an hour or so, but down here, at the bottom, it was already nearly dark. We had to find our way out, now, before Sasha returned. It would take me a while to work my way back up the hillside, especially carrying a cold and scared boy, and then we had to get back to my car. And that was assuming there was no one else out here to stand in our way.

At that moment, the stag stepped forward. In the growing darkness the silver glow surrounding him flared. He looked like a massive red stag, the kind commonly found in Europe, but his fur was white, tinged with silver, and he had an otherworldly feel to him.

"Thank you," I said, sensing that he could probably understand me.

The stag nodded, and knelt on his front legs. He seemed to be waiting for me to do something.

"I think he wants us to ride on his back," DJ said, glancing over at the deer.

"You think so?" I looked at the stag again. "Is he right? Do you want us to get on your back?"

Again, a nod.

I grabbed DJ's hand and we headed over to the massive animal. He had to stand at least five feet tall at the shoulder. All I knew was that this was no regular deer. There was something magical about the stag and right now, considering he had helped us, I was willing to trust him.

I swung DJ up on his back, then scrambled on, holding DJ back against me. There were no reins, but as the stag began to stand, I motioned for DJ to lean forward and I leaned over him, doing my best to hold onto the deer's sides.

The next moment we were off, racing through the forest, heading up the slope of the ravine. We were flying along, so fast that I was terrified we were going to fall off, but somehow we managed to keep our balance as the stag nimbly wove in and out through the trees. Everything was a blur, the trees and undergrowth blending together into a trail of motion behind us.

I began to feel queasy, not so much from the movement but because everything around us seemed hazy, and only DJ, the stag, and I felt real. And then, as quickly as we had taken off, we came to a halt at the edge of the road. I realized we were near my car. The stag knelt again, and DJ and I slid off. I wanted to know so many things, but before I could open my mouth to say thanks, the stag turned and vanished back into the forest.

"Come on, get in the car." Dazed, feeling almost numb, I hustled DJ into my car and quickly started the ignition. I wanted out of here before anybody found those bodies, because there was no way in the world I could prove myself against the Light Fae Court if they decided to push matters. Yes, I had been defending myself and DJ, but Névé always got her way.

As we headed out of the park, my thoughts were a million miles away, still at the bottom of the ravine with the two dead Fae, the one still alive, and the silver stag.

Chapter 3

ALL THE WAY back to Angel's, I kept looking in the rearview mirror, trying to tell if we were being followed. I hadn't asked DJ anything yet because I wanted to wait until we were safe behind closed doors. He looked like he was in shock, his hands stuffed in his pockets as he leaned forward, trying to hunch out of sight. As we rounded the curve and pulled into Angel's driveway, I was relieved to see that no one had seemed to have followed us.

"Come on, kiddo," I said, taking a deep breath. "Let's get inside and figure out just what the hell happened."

Angel must have been watching out of the window, because she came running out the door as she saw us get out of the car. DJ dashed toward her, and as she wrapped her arms around him, he burst into tears. She let him inside and I followed, making certain to lock the door behind us, letting out a little cry as she glanced at me.

I looked down at myself. In the light of the living room, I realized that I was covered with blood. It was sticky on my skin and clothes, beginning to dry, and I suddenly felt sick to my stomach.

"Are you all right?" Angel knelt beside her brother, yanking his hoodie off so she could check him over. "Are you hurt?"

"Don't worry. This isn't DJ's blood. He's all right as far as I could tell." I quickly moved over to the window and glanced outside, looking for any sign of anybody passing by.

"What the hell happened? Where did all that blood come from? Are *you* okay?" Angel's voice was trembling, and I realized that her shock was giving way to a flood of suppressed panic now running free.

"I don't know. Or rather, I'm not sure what happened. As far as the blood goes, not mine either. I'll tell you in a minute, but do you have anything I could change into? I need to get out of these clothes or I'm going to throw up." The metallic tang of the blood was starting to make me queasy. Even though I was used to taking down sub-Fae, this was a whole 'nother matter. I had killed two men in cold blood, and even though I had done so to protect both DJ and myself, it hit me hard and I couldn't stop shaking.

"Of course. Go take a shower and then go through my closet. I have a couple of loose gowns that should fit you. I'm going to wash DJ in the kitchen, and check him over for any injuries." As she hustled him into the kitchen, he was slowly wiping his eyes on his sleeve.

I stumbled into the bathroom, not wanting to take too long. I stripped off my clothes and climbed in the shower, scrubbing all over with a vanilla bath wash. I washed my hair and the blood poured down off my body in a stream of red water. Finally, the water was clear and I finally felt clean.

After I toweled off, I glanced through Angel's closet. She was five-ten, and thin. I was five-six and one hundred and fifty pounds of muscle and boobs. I found a loose tank dress that would fit me, but I knew her bras wouldn't begin to work for me, so I went without. My own was so saturated with rain and mud and blood that I couldn't bear to put it back on.

I gathered my clothes in a pile and dropped them in her bathtub. I would put them in a plastic bag before I went home.

As I returned to the living room, DJ was sitting on the sofa, eating a sandwich. I hurried over to the window and glanced outside again. Still nobody driving by, which I took as a good sign. I motioned for Angel to join me and we sat next to DJ.

"I'll tell you all about it, but first I want to talk to DJ." I turned to him. "DJ, we need to know what happened. Tell us everything you can. Don't worry—we won't be angry. Tell us everything you remember." I grabbed a notebook that was sitting on the coffee table and opened it to an empty page. "Angel, I need a pen."

She handed me a gel pen, and I prepared to take notes.

DJ swallowed a bite of his sandwich and set it back on the plate. He took a deep breath.

"I was headed home from Jason's, and Mrs. Harris was out in her yard."

"Who's Mrs. Harris?" I asked.

"She's one of Jason's neighbors. She's an old lady but she's really nice. She asked if I could help her out for a moment and she would pay me for the help. I know how hard you work," he said to Angel. "I thought if I could help out..."

"Oh honey, I wish you wouldn't worry so much." Angel winced. "You don't ever worry about money, all right? I'll always take care of you. What did she want you to do?"

"She had some weeding that needed done, and she wanted me to help her plant some flowers. She said she'd pay me twenty dollars if I'd help her out for a few hours. So I decided it would be okay. I was going to call you, but then we got busy and I forgot. I worked there until about two o'clock, and then I realized that I had forgotten to feed Barney last night." Barney was a tortoise that hung out in their backyard. "I didn't want him to be hungry, and I knew that Angel would be worried if she called and I wasn't home. So I decided to take the shortcut."

Angel started to say something but I motioned for her to be quiet.

"Go on."

"I was part of the way through—almost to where your car was—when I heard something in the woods. In the ravine. It sounded like somebody calling for help. I thought somebody was in trouble, so I ran over and started down the slope." He was staring down at his hands in his lap. "I know you always tell me not to go through the park if I can help it, but I thought somebody was in trouble."

"I know," Angel said. "And you always want to help people when you can." She glanced over at me.

I nodded. DJ was one of the most helpful children I had ever met, and he had a keen sense of responsibility.

"It's okay," she said. "I'm not mad. Please go on."

DJ bit his lip, then continued. "I heard them call out again and it was louder this time. It sounded like somebody was hurt. I followed the voices until I saw three men down below in the undergrowth. That's when I realized nobody was calling for help. They were yelling and screaming at each other, and at first I thought one of them—the blond man—was hurt. I slowed down because I didn't want to interrupt if they were okay. And that's when they quit yelling so loud and started to talk."

"What did they say? Was it the same men who had you tied up when I found you?"

He nodded. "Yeah, it was them, and a friend of theirs. I'm not sure what they were saying, but I heard them making plans about bows and arrows and poison."

I let out a long sigh. The Light Fae were probably looking to ambush their icy cousins. Par for the course, given the two factions hated each other. "Lovely. What happened then?"

"I got really scared and I tried to sneak back up the hill but I stepped on a branch and it broke. They heard me and started chasing me. I knew I could run faster if I wasn't running uphill, so I took off to the side and then ran down toward the stream. I got tangled up in the bush, and lost my handkerchief. By the time I got free they almost had me. I tried to get away, but they knocked me down. They tied me up and started arguing about what to do with me. And then they dragged me over to where you found me and talked about stuffing me in the culvert after they killed me. The dark-haired man told the other one—he had dark hair too—to go see if anybody else was sneaking around."

Angel let out a cry. Her hand fluttered to her mouth. "This is worse than I thought."

I had to agree. "Did you see any others there? Besides the three of them? Anyone at all?"

DJ shrugged, scrunching up his face as he tried to remember. "I don't know. All I know is that the blond one didn't want to kill me and the one with dark hair did."

"Is there anything else that you can remember? Anything else that you heard?"

DJ was fretting now, looking frantic. "I don't know. I don't know!"

I had the feeling we had gotten everything we could out of him, at least for now. He might re-member more later, but right now he just needed to finish his sandwich and get some rest.

"Eat your sandwich and then take a hot bath." I turned to Angel. "My clothes are in your bathtub.

Do you have a plastic bag that I can put them in?"

"They're in the kitchen, on the microwave," she said.

While DJ finished his sandwich, I hurried to wring out my clothes and scoop them into the garbage bag, tying it shut. Then I washed up the tub and drew a hot bath, pouring in a few bubbles. As I returned to the living room, carrying my bag of bloody clothes, I nodded over my shoulder.

"The bathtub's ready."

"Thanks," Angel said. She patted DJ's shoulder. "Why don't you go take a bath, kiddo?"

He had finished his sandwich, and I saw a cupcake wrapper sitting next to it. "I see you had dessert," I said, forcing a smile to my face.

"Do you want one?" he asked.

I nodded. "I'd love one. Thank you." I couldn't help but wonder what he thought of me now, considering he had watched me kill the two men. But he brought me back a cupcake, a smile cracking the solemnity of his face.

"Thank you," he said quietly, handing me the treat.

I took the cupcake and peeled away the paper. The fragrant smell of chocolate wafted up to set my stomach to growling. "What did I do?"

"You saved my life. I know they were going to kill me. I'm just sorry you had to hurt them instead, but thank you."

And then, he threw his arms around my neck. I juggled both DJ and the cupcake as he gave me a quick hug before running off into the bathroom. Watching him go, I bit into the cupcake and closed my eyes as the frosting melted in my mouth.

Angel was sitting cross-legged on the sofa. She waited until we heard the click of the bathroom door before letting out a long sigh and turning to me. "What the hell do we do? There was somebody else there, he said? Do you know if they found out who DJ was?"

"I can answer part of that. I didn't see the third man, but there was one there, DJ said. They found DJ's wallet and...damn it, I didn't think to pick it up when we left. Let me tell you what happened. DJ didn't mention the stag, but I'm not surprised because he was so shaken."

I told her everything, including how the silver stag had come to our rescue. "I have no idea what that creature was, but I can tell you this, he wasn't from this world. Or if he was, he's some species I've never encountered before. I'm thinking I should go back and see if the bodies are still there. If they are, I'd better dispose of them somehow."

"You *can't* go. If this Sasha is still there, he'll be waiting for you." She shivered. "I'm afraid to stay here. The third man will find DJ's wallet... Maybe he has already. He'll know where we live." Angel nervously paced over to the door, peeking out the front window. "I don't want to stay here tonight."

"Should I call the police?" I already knew the answer to that one, but it felt like something that I should say.

She shook her head. Angel might be human, but she understood all too well the nuances in politics concerning interspecies relations. "They aren't going to help us. For one thing, we know that there are Cryptos on the police force. If any are secret agents for Névé, then you'd be toast and so would DJ and me. I don't think we can chance talking to any of the authorities."

"Yeah, and I can't plead our case before Névé, because she wouldn't allow me to come before the throne. I'm half-breed, caught between Light and Dark, anathema to both." To say I was carrying a bitter streak against both sides of the Fae world was putting it mildly. I kept out of their machinations, preferring the company of other Cryptos and humans.

Angel frowned. "Even if we did call the cops, they would just find some way to blame DJ. He's a young black boy and that pretty much seals his fate with the authorities."

I nodded, all too aware that racism still ran deep against anybody who wasn't white and rich in the country.

"Come back to my place for the night. We can figure out what to do tomorrow. I suppose by then, it might be safe for me to return to the ravine to see if the bodies are there. Maybe I can call a friend to help me." But when I thought about it, I really didn't have many friends. Angel was my bestie, of course, and I had a few other buddies, but when it came down to it, I really didn't hang out with people very much. Angel was my go-to girl, and that was about it.

"I'm going to call in sick to work tomorrow. I don't know what else to do."

"After DJ finishes his bath, get him dressed. Pack a bag for a couple days. I'm pretty sure that if this Sasha saw me, he wouldn't know who I was. They have your address, but there's no way they'll know to come over to my apartment. We can figure things out when our heads are clear and we're not so tired."

While Angel packed for herself and DJ, I raided her refrigerator for anything perishable. We could take the food with us so it wouldn't go to waste. Once DJ was dressed, Angel and I carried the bags out to my car.

"You should leave your car here. I just feel you'll be safer if you ride with me."

"As long as you drive me back for it tomorrow. Then I suppose we can tell if anybody has been in the house. I wish I was a witch—I could cast a spell to booby-trap the place."

"Well, I can work some magic, but nothing along those lines. I suggest that you lock every window, and when we lock the doors, leave a piece of paper between the door and the door jamb so that if the door opens, the paper will fall. Put it down low enough and make it small enough and an intruder probably won't notice it." It was the only thing I could think of at the moment.

It was dark out by the time we packed the bags into my car and took off for my condo. For the first mile or two, I kept a close eye behind us, looking for any sign that we were being followed. But the only cars on the road seemed to be intent on their own destinations, and by the time we were over the bridge to Seattle, I was breathing easier.

We reached my building without any problems, and as we headed up the elevator, I was doing my best to figure out who to call to ask for help. In a metro area of over three million people, I was suddenly feeling very alone.

I TUCKED DJ into my bed, and he fell asleep immediately with Mr. Rumblebutt watching over him on the foot of the bed. As I looked out of the window, over Puget Sound, I was suddenly grateful that I lived on the fifteenth floor. Nobody could come sneaking in, unless they were a vampire. And vampires were the last thing we were worried about.

When I returned to the front room, Angel was in my kitchenette, making grilled cheese sandwiches for us. The cupcake had only whetted my appetite, and while she sliced cheese and buttered the bread, I found a bag of potato chips in the cupboard. I also dug out a bottle of brandy and poured us a couple of drinks. Handing one to Angel, I held up my snifter.

"Here's to a long life and good health," I said, sipping the fiery liqueur. "The gods know, I needed this."

"You and me both. Once again, I can't thank you enough for saving DJ. I almost lost him, Ember. I don't know what I would have done without you. You saved his life." She paused, then staring down at the toasting sandwiches, said, "What the hell are we going to do? We can't go to the cops."

I shrugged, not sure of the answer myself. "First,

we have to be very careful mentioning this to anybody. You know how capricious the Fae courts are."

"Thalacious? Really? I can't believe they were gathering that. I thought it was illegal. Couldn't we use that against them?" She flipped the sandwiches as I poured the potato chips into a large bowl.

"I doubt it. The poison may be illegal but it's in use by both the Light and Dark courts. Nobody's going to do anything about it."

I paused, thinking about my childhood. "My father was going to teach me how to distill it, you know. He thought one day I might need to know. But the Fae courts got to my parents before he could teach me that." I paused.

"I'm sorry, Ember. I know it still hurts." Angel flipped the sandwiches.

I shrugged. "Nothing I can do about it. How my mother and father ever managed to get together, let alone spawn me, I have no clue. But their love got them both killed."

My mother and father fled both TirNaNog and Navane because of their forbidden love. They had tried to live among the rest of the Cryptos and humans. Unfortunately, my mother was fairly high placed in the Light Court, and her family didn't take well to her defection. When I was fifteen, I had come home after school one day to find her and my father brutally murdered on the kitchen floor. If I had been home, they would have killed me as well.

I had recognized the daggers still in their hearts as Fae made.

When I had called in Mama J.—Angel's mother—for help, she had read the cards and told me Light had done the deed. But if they hadn't, the Dark would have come along sooner or later to finish the job. Mama J. was a witch woman, a tarot reader of incredible ability as well as the best damned cook in Seattle. Angel had inherited her psychic abilities from her mother. Unfortunately, Mama J. had ended up on the wrong side of a drunk driver.

"I think we should just try to fly under the radar."

"But we can't do that. One escaped, and he'll find DJ's wallet and track us down. Also, can't the Fae call in one of the Morte Seers? If they can, you're in danger just as much as we are." Angel handed me a plate with two sandwiches on it. She had fixed one for herself. She knew that I had a bigger appetite than she did. We carried our plates over to the kitchen table.

"That's why I want to get rid of the bodies, if they're still there. If they don't have the bodies, they can't call on the spirits for help. It only works when the Morte Seer has a body to work with." I paused, realizing that wouldn't fix the problem. "I don't know. Let's eat and clear our heads and then think about it."

As I bit into my sandwich, I realized I really wasn't looking forward to going back to those woods. I had just added two more spirits to an already haunted park, and I wasn't inclined to pay another visit to it. But I couldn't just leave them there to be found. I wasn't worried about the cops.

Unless the Fae were nobility, they wouldn't pay much attention. Just two more dead Cryptos. But a Morte Seer could ask questions of the dead, and even get visuals from them.

I polished off one sandwich and started on the other.

Angel retrieved the brandy bottle and refilled our glasses. We had been best friends since we were eight years old—twenty-two years ago we had met in grade school. Most of the Fae studied in their own courts, but I couldn't because of my heritage, so my parents sent me to the local school, where I met Angel the first day.

She had shoved me in a mud puddle, and I dragged her down with me. After a scuffle, we were both sent to the principal's office, soaking wet and covered in mud. Our mutual fear and dislike of authority spontaneously created a bond by the end of the day and after that we were fast friends. When my parents were murdered, Mama J. took over as a second mom to me. I sold just about everything that my parents owned, tucking what money there was left in the bank for when I would be on my own. I lived with Angel and her mother for three years, until I turned eighteen. Over the years I had done what I could to thank them and repay the debt.

DJ had come along when Angel was twenty. Mama J. had fallen in with a Wolf shifter, who had stuck around until he found out she was pregnant, and then he lit out. DJ had inherited his father's blood, and Mama J. and Angel did their best to help him grow up in human society. They had befriended a couple lone-wolf shifters, asking for help in teaching DJ his heritage. But just like the Fae turning their back on me, the Wolf shifter society seldom allowed *whelps*—what they called crossbreeds—into their fold. They weren't as cruel as the Fae, but neither did they look fondly on anyone who wasn't of pure blood.

I knew that Angel still stayed in touch with the wolf shifters who had helped her and Mama J. "Do you think Ben and Lyle could help us? Do you think we could trust them?"

"You know how the shifters feel about the Fae, at least in general. I don't think it's a good idea. They may be lone wolves, but the truth is, shifters don't get along with many people except humans. Who knows what they might do?" She glanced at the door to my bedroom. "I'm doing my best to bring up DJ without those biases, but it's difficult. Some of them seem inbred, to be honest."

"Then I'm not sure who to contact. Or if we should even try."

"You may not be in danger, but I still have the problem of how to protect my little brother. I can't go home again until I have some answers." Angel gave me the look she always did when I had totally missed the point.

I let out a sigh. "Right. I'm sorry, I didn't think." I was running through a list of people I knew in my head, trying to zero in on somebody who might be useful to us, when the doorbell rang.

Angel and I both froze. I slowly rose out of my chair and motioned for her to join DJ in my bedroom. When she had closed the door behind her, I readied my blade and quietly approached the front door, peeking out through the peephole.

A man stood there. He was tall—at least significantly taller than I was—and with wheat-colored hair that fell below the shoulder blades and the scruff of a beard. He didn't look Fae, and yet he didn't look human either. I hesitated, my hand on the doorknob, when he rang the bell again. Slowly opening the door a crack, I peeked out, ready to slam it shut at the first sign of trouble.

"Yes?"

"Ember Kearney?" His gaze met mine, and it felt like he drilled a hole right through me.

"Who wants to know?" I wasn't used to visitors, and that he was here so quickly after what had happened this afternoon made me wary.

"My name is Herne. You don't know who I am, but I know who you are, and I know you're in trouble. And I know you need my help. That's why I'm here."

He was wearing biker's leathers, and carrying a helmet in his hand. I tried to read his energy, and the strength of it blasted me back. Rubbing my head from the sudden pounding, I wasn't sure what to do. He *could* be Fae, although I didn't think he was. And how did he know my name and that we were in trouble?

"You'll have to do better than that. I need to know who you are and why you're here."

"I know you're protecting friends right now, and that's a good thing. But you won't be able to protect them much longer without my help. I took care of the bodies in the woods, but I couldn't find the third man."

I hesitated. He obviously knew what had happened, but if I let him in, was he a greater danger? There was no other way out, given I lived on the fifteenth floor. And I'd be the only one standing between him and DJ and Angel. While I was good with my dagger, I wasn't sure that I could take him on. He looked muscled, and it looked like he had a wicked blade strapped to his belt.

"You can either let me in, or I can leave and let them find you."

I pressed my head to the door, struggling with the decision.

"You have my help, if you choose it. I give you my word, I'm not here to hurt you."

"Your word? And what would you swear on?"

Herne held out his hand, then drew his blade. Immediately, I reached for my dagger but he shook his head and slashed his blade across his palm. Blood sprang forth, and he held it out toward me.

"Under the name of Cernunnos and Morgana, I swear to you on my blood that I will not harm you. For they're the ones who sent me."

At that, I knew he was telling the truth. He swore on the name of the goddess my mother had been pledged to, and it would be an easy thing for me to call down her vengeance if he broke his oath. Magic was rife in his voice, and he had just infused it into his oath and his blood.

I stepped back, opening the door so he could enter. At that moment, Mr. Rumblebutt ran out into the foyer beside me. He looked up at Herne, then turned around and sauntered off.

He came in, glancing around. "You need to get your friend out here. We all have to talk."

Angel eased the door open to my bedroom and slipped out. "I was listening." Her gaze was fastened on his face, and I glanced over at her, looking for confirmation. She was psychic enough to tell if he was lying.

"What do you think?" I asked.

"He's telling us the truth. There's more, but I don't get the sense that he's here to harm us." She joined us at the table and we all sat down.

I turned to him. He was a striking man, with brilliant blue eyes, and he felt familiar, though I knew I had never met him before. "All right, we're listening."

As he settled into his chair and leaned forward, his elbows on the table, I retrieved a paper towel and handed it to him for his hand. But he opened his fist just in time for me to see the wound close and vanish. He wiped off the blood that was still clinging to his fingers, but the cut itself was gone.

"Are you a vampire?" The only people I knew who healed up so quickly were vampires.

He let out a snort. "Hardly. I'm as alive as you are. You saw the blood. If I was a vampire, I would have bled far more slowly. I told you, my name is Herne. My father is Cernunnos, the Horned One, the Lord of the Forest. He and Morgana sent me. I've come to offer you and your friend jobs and safety, of a sort. My father has agreed that you should join the Wild Hunt. Welcome aboard."

Chapter 4

WHEN NEITHER ANGEL nor I moved, Herne reached across the table for the brandy bottle. He waited a moment, then opened the bottle and was about to upend it into his mouth.

"I'll get you a glass," I said then, shaking myself out of my stupor. I hurried into the kitchen and brought back another snifter, handing it to him.

"My thanks," he said, pouring himself a stiff belt. He slammed it back and then poured another. "Not bad, not bad." He glanced up at us, the smile still tilting the corners of his mouth. "Nothing to say? I'm not surprised. That's all right, news like this takes a while to assimilate."

I held out my hand. "Hand me that bottle."

He passed it to me and I poured drinks for Angel and me. This time, we didn't sip the booze, just slugged it back, the way he had. I poured another round, and the liquid fire rolling down my throat seemed to drain some of the disbelief out of my system.

"So, let's start from the beginning. You were out there in the woods?" I paused, then made a connection. "Did *you* send the stag to me?"

"Guess again," he said, as he poured himself another. He held up the glass, staring at the brandy. As I gazed into his eyes, I caught a silver tinge that looked familiar.

"You *are* the stag," I whispered.

He just arched his eyebrows and winked, then drained the snifter again. "As I said when I was standing outside of your door, I took care of the bodies for you. They'll never be found. But that doesn't solve the problem of the fact that there was a third participant."

"We were worried about Morte Seers. You didn't happen to pick up DJ's wallet and ID while you were there, did you?"

"Morte Seers are a deadly possibility. And no, I didn't notice it. I was too busy trying to keep you both from being killed." He turned to Angel. "Your brother is in danger. And you, too."

"What am I going to do?" Her eyes were wide, and I could feel the fear rising. Angel was brave enough for herself, but if something threatened her brother, it triggered her fears.

Herne stared at the table for a moment before answering. "Your best bet is to send him away."

Angel let out a faint cry. "I'm the only family he has."

"That's why you need to keep him safe. I know a family who will keep him safe and sound and cared for. You do *not* want to underestimate the treachery of the Fae—either side. They would kill him for spite, as quickly as they'd stomp on a bug." He glanced at me. "No offense intended."

I wasn't sure what to think. He was right about them, and yet he was including me by default. "No offense taken. At least, I don't think so. You said that Angel and I should join the Wild Hunt? What the hell is that?"

"I'll explain in a moment. But in order to do so, first, I must explain the nature of the Fae."

"I know their nature. I was born with it and stay as far away from my kin as possible."

Herne ignored me. "From the beginning of time, the Dark and Light courts have fought. It is the nature of the balance. As the world grew smaller—and the populations of all beings increased—their battles went underground, and a squad of bounty hunters were formed to keep that war from spilling out into full-scale conflicts that would affect everyone else. We're stationed around the world. My agency is called the Wild Hunt."

"So, you're peacekeepers?"

"In a way," he said. "Cernunnos and Morgana spearhead the efforts. Basically, we clean up the mess that the Fae make, and when situations arise that could endanger the rest of the world, we put a stop to them."

"How does this relate to DJ and Angel? Or me?" I was trying to follow the flow of information.

"It wouldn't, normally. But given the way things played out, they'll spin it so that DJ will be considered the main instigator—regardless of the way it happened."

He yawned, stretching. His muscles rippled beneath the form-fitting muscle shirt. I found myself musing as I watched him. He was extraordinarily handsome, in so many ways that I found attractive. He was fascinating. Probably *too* fascinating for my own good.

He's the son of a god, after all, I thought. *Of course I'm going to find him attractive.*

"I have no clue what you're talking about," Angel said, startling me out of my reverie. "All I know is that my brother's in danger and you're telling me I have to send him away? And then I have to help you stop the Fae from murdering each other? I think you're barking up the wrong tree, dude. I'm *human*."

Herne gave her a dry look. "If I have to, I will take you back to my father and let him explain things. But I guarantee, he's a lot more *intimidating* than me. Or I can just let you go on your merry way, until they find you and kill you and your brother."

"Fucking hell, you're just full of good news, aren't you?" Angel let out an exasperated sigh. "Why should we trust you? And what good would it do for us to work for you?"

"You should trust me because without my help, your brother and Ember would be dead by now." His words stopped us both cold. Arrogant he might be, but he was also correct on that score.

I took a long breath and counted to three before releasing it slowly. "We need a moment to clear our heads. You're dropping a lot of information on us right now."

"I realize that," Herne said. "It's a lot to take in." He glanced at the kitchen. "How about some tea to go with the booze?"

Angel nodded, mutely rising to fix a pot of tea. I kept a variety of flavors around, along with a teapot, just for her. I crossed into the living room, trying to collect my thoughts. I had no clue what was happening. Everything from this afternoon on felt like chaos had descended. It had been this way when I came home to find my parents murdered, too. Sudden confusion and the feeling as though my world had turned on end.

A few moments later, we gathered at the table again. Angel brought a pot of peppermint tea over, along with three mugs.

I was trying to sort out things. "So we're all in danger, especially Angel and DJ? Will the Light Fae ever stop looking for them?"

Herne leaned his elbows on the table. "The truth is, all three of you are in jeopardy from both sides, for differing reasons. The moment you get mixed up in the machinations of Fae politics, you're fair game. But we can help."

"And the answer to that is to join your agency?" It didn't make sense to me. "I mean, thank you—I suppose I should say that because thanks to you, DJ and I are alive."

"You would never have managed both those assassins." Herne's voice was grave. "They're highly trained."

"Be that as it may, the fact remains that Angel and I know very little about what you're referring to. Why should Angel have to give up her brother to strangers? And what good will joining the Wild Hunt do?"

"I can protect Angel—and you—to a degree by taking you into the agency. But as long as DJ is visible, the Fae will have the chance to blackmail Angel. They aren't above using children as pawns."

My headache was steadily growing. I realized that I was both exhausted from my encounters out in the woods as well as from the fact that I had only had about six hours of sleep after a busy night of goblin bashing. "I need some aspirin."

Angel refilled my mug. "Peppermint's good for a headache." She turned to Herne. "Please, explain so we understand."

"All right. I'll start from the beginning." Herne leaned forward. "The Fae have been at war since the beginning of time. I don't know if you know that or not, given your heritage."

"Mostly, yes. If you want me to be a liaison, it won't work. Neither side wants anything to do with me."

"No worries on that. The Light and Dark courts hate each other. It's a wonder they didn't kill your parents earlier." He paused as I winced. "I'm sorry, that was insensitive of me. You'll find that I tend to be direct. At times, blunt to the point of offensive. It's because of who I am and what I am here to do. I mean no harm."

I nodded, accepting his apology. "Go on."

"As I said, the Fae have been at war with each other since the beginning of time. They were in danger of devastating the world, so my father and

Morgana stepped in. She is the goddess of the Fae, both Light and Dark. Before you say anything, I know there are other goddesses who exist within that realm, but Morgana connects with the Fae more than any of the others."

"My mother worked with her. She was pledged in her service," I said quietly.

"Yes, and that is a plus for you. The Fae truly believe they will always be at war, and it's lodged in the bones of their very nature. Very few exist who are like you, Ember. You contain both bloodlines, and you're a rare specimen among your people. You are a threat—an example that the blood of either line will not poison the other side."

"I never thought of it that way. If I can exist, then peace might actually be achieved. I'm not trying to kill myself out of self-loathing, that's for sure."

"Right. Morgana favors neither side and helps keep a balance of power between the two. She also happens to be my mother."

I blinked. So he *was* part Fae—divine Fae, at that.

"When I grew to an age where I could be on my own, Cernunnos sent me into this world to keep watch. There are others like me around the planet, but this area is my territory. We keep a close watch over the battles, and step in when necessary. We enforce the necessary balance. One of my duties is to ensure that as little collateral damage happens as possible. Especially to those not of Fae blood, like your brother, Angel."

All this was a great deal to take in. I found myself desperately wanting fresh air, and held up my hand for him to pause as I opened the door leading up to my balcony.

Fresh air swept in on the night breeze as the sounds of the city filtered in, ambulances and sirens wailing, traffic grinding its way through the night. I stepped out on the balcony, leaning against the metal railing. I had never given much thought to my heritage or the people who made up my bloodlines. They had no love lost for me and I had no love lost for them. But now it occurred to me that I should at least know the history of my ancestors, whether or not I ever was welcome there. There was so much about my parents that I would never know.

Overwhelmed, I suddenly felt dizzy. I grabbed hold of the railing, inhaling deeply, then let out a slow breath and returned to the table, making sure to close to the door so the cat wouldn't get out there.

"So basically, the Fae are always at war, and you keep things from getting out of hand?"

He nodded. "That sums it up. Yes. I, and others like me. During the down times, the Wild Hunt Agency hires itself out for SubCult investigations."

"And the Fae don't try to kill you?"

He shook his head. "They are forbidden. Anybody who works for me, or anyone of my kind, is under what you might call divine immunity, which is why it would benefit the two of you to come work for me."

"You can't be killed?" Angel asked, her voice hopeful.

"Oh, we *can*—at least those who work for me can, given they aren't of divine birth. But both sides—Light and Dark—agreed to abide by the rules Cernunnos and Morgana set forth. If we find out they're breaking those rules, they are subject to dangerous punishment. That doesn't mean some haven't tried, and if they hire someone from the sub-Fae or one of the other Crypto races, those outlier agents are not bound to the agreement."

I was beginning to get a picture of how this worked, although it was still confusing. Angel crossed to my cupboard and pulled out a box of cookies. She brought them back and tore open the package. It was covered with dust, and was probably stale, but in a pinch, anything would do.

"I don't know about you, but I need chocolate and I need it now," she said. "It's past the expiration date, but I'm willing to take a chance, if you are."

Herne laughed. "Mind if I join you?" He accepted a cookie. "It will fall into place eventually. But to cut to the chase: since you and Angel have ended up embroiled in this mess, I'm bringing you into my agency. You'll have diplomatic immunity. Nothing else I can do stands as good a chance of keeping you both alive. Given they know DJ's name and address, do you really want to take the chance? Are you willing to risk your brother's life? Or your own lives? Ask yourself that before you answer me."

Angel slowly raised her hand. "May I ask a question?"

"Of course. I will answer as thoroughly as I can."

"Why are the Fae courts allowed in the United Coalition, if they are at war with each other?"

The United Coalition was the governmental structure in place that was composed of the Shifter Alliance, the Vampire Nation, the Human League, and the Fae courts. Most of the nations had adopted something similar—at least those that espoused democracy of any sort—once the human world realized it was not the primary inhabitant on the planet.

"Because it's recognized that the Fae are like this. The other groups know, but they also know we do our best to keep the balance. If they tried to kick the Fae out, then Light and Dark would launch all-out open war on each other, and the rest of the world be damned. This way, it's a delicate balance that's kept and no one group can try to push out the others."

He paused, then added, "I would have come to see Ember even if today hadn't happened."

I blinked. "Why?"

"As I said, you're a rare specimen—half Light Fae, half Dark Fae. There are qualities about yourself that you haven't yet realized because of your breeding. Both sides know this, and for that reason, if you had been at home the day your parents were killed, they would have killed you as well. When Morgana found out about your parents' deaths, she visited Névé and Saílle and forbade them to touch you as you were growing up. Over time, we believe they forgot about you. And you've never done anything to bring yourself to their attention until now."

"And now, if this Sasha is able to identify me, it will mean that I'm on their radar again. Just what kind of *qualities* are you talking about?"

He shook his head. "That, I cannot tell you. I don't know and my mother has not seen fit to tell me. But if you join my agency, you'll have some semblance of safety." He paused, then added, "Did you know that your father was pledged to Cernunnos? You have a birthmark on your lower back—the right side—don't you?"

I stirred, uncomfortable. "How did you know about that?"

"It's the head and antlers of the stag, isn't it?"

I nodded, not sure of what to say. He was correct. I had a jet-black birthmark at the base of my lower right side, right above my butt cheek. It was the head and antlers of a stag, all right. My mother never told me why I was born with it, only that I would learn when I was older. But they were killed before I did.

Herne cleared his throat. "You were born with the mark of the silver stag. It marks you as one of my father's chosen hunters. *Your* father served Cernunnos, just as your mother served Morgana. So you see, you were already on my father's radar."

I caught my breath. I worked with Morgana with my water magic, because my mother had been pledged to her. But I had no clue my father had dedicated himself to Cernunnos. The Lord of the Forest was a primal hunter, and more often than not, it was humans who gravitated to him.

"You're for real, aren't you?" For months now, I had felt like something was about to happen. I hadn't known what, but the anticipation, almost an anxiety, had been nagging at the back of my mind.

He nodded, looking solemn. "You will always have a choice, but if you choose to walk away from this, you're fair game for both Fae courts. And there are rumors they've begun a purge of all those who are of mixed Fae blood. Not half-human, half-Fae, although they don't care for them either, but of Light and Dark blend. There aren't a lot of you out there. By joining the Wild Hunt, you'll be protected as much as we can protect you."

Stunned, I slumped back in my chair. "Why not leave us be?"

Herne cupped his brandy snifter in his hands. "I don't know. Something has escalated, but we don't know what. Maybe it's as simple as what we were talking about—that you and those like you represent a threat. A potential for co-existence."

I hated being funneled into anything. I hated authority in general, but it was obvious that I didn't have much of a choice. I was a walking target. And with Angel and DJ now involved, I wasn't about to hedge my bets with their lives on the line.

The truth was, I had been drifting through the days, not quite certain how I wanted to spend my life. Hiring myself out as a freelance hunter was what I knew best, but it hadn't been a conscious choice. I hadn't woken up one day and decided, *Gee, I want to go hunt goblins.* I hated feeling like I didn't have a purpose. On that level alone, Herne's invitation appealed to me.

"And me? What about me and DJ?" Angel looked like she was about to cry.

"I can guarantee both of you safety—as much as anybody can guarantee anything—if you come work for me as well. But we should send DJ away. This is dangerous work, Angel, and it's better if your loved ones aren't in the immediate vicinity. Especially someone as young and vulnerable as your brother."

"Where would you send him?"

"We can place him with a foster family where he can learn more about his Wulfine heritage. I can arrange for you to visit him several times a year. No one need know that he doesn't belong to that family." Herne cleared his throat. He poured another round of brandy. It was almost empty. "As I said, I know this is a great deal to take in, but I need your decisions tonight. We need to declare you as part of the agency tonight just in case they're searching for you. The two of you are at a crossroads, and the rest of your life depends on what you choose to do. I'll excuse myself and visit the restroom while you talk it over."

ANGEL AND I sat there staring at each other after he walked away. As the bathroom door closed behind him, I slumped back, shaking my head.

"What the hell?" I looked over at Angel. "I had no clue. I had no fucking clue."

She looked on the verge of tears. "I wish DJ had never stayed overnight at Sarah's last night. But if wishes were pennies, I'd be rich. What's done is done, and now we have to make a decision."

"I think we can trust him. I don't know why, but there's something about him that tells me he's straight up."

She nodded, her shoulders sagging. "Oh, we can trust him. I can sense when people are lying—and even though he's a god, he's telling us the truth."

Pausing, she trailed her finger along the rim of her teacup. "I have to say yes, Ember. I don't want to give DJ up, but I can't put him in danger." Then the tears began to trickle down her cheeks. "I hate myself for saying this, but I'm almost relieved. I don't make much money. I'm doing my best to give him the life he deserves, but I don't think I can help him grow into an adult and learn how to handle his wolf. I have no clue what it means to be a shifter, and most of his own kind won't give him a second glance. If Herne can find a family to willingly and lovingly take him in, and show him what it means to be Wulfine, then I can't stand in his way."

I knew how hard it was for Angel to say that— how hard it was for her to willingly give up her brother. I reached out and took her hand and squeezed hard, holding on tight.

"Do you remember when we first met, after I told you who my parents were? I expected you to sneer and make fun of me. A couple of the other Fae children were taunting me and calling me names. You beat the crap out of them and told them that if they ever did that again there'd be more where that came from. I've never forgotten how brave you were."

She squeezed my hand back. "I couldn't let them pick on my bestie. I had your back, and I've always known you had mine."

"I still have your back. We'll join the Wild Hunt. We'll make sure DJ's okay, and that we're okay. I guess this is what they call fate."

She sniffed back her tears and gave me a wide smile. "Destiny's a bitch, isn't she?"

"She sure is, Angel. She sure is."

BY THE TIME Herne returned, we had wiped our eyes. One thing that Angel and I had in common: when we made up our minds, done was done. We weren't wishy-washy people. I refilled our glasses and pushed Herne's snifter over to him.

"Shall we drink to our new alliance? You'd better pay well, and give good benefits." I raised my glass and Angel raised hers.

Herne stared at us for a moment, then his lips curved into a sensuous smile. I found myself noticing him far too much for my own good. His eyes were twinkling.

"You don't know how relieved I am to hear that. To the Wild Hunt's newest employees. And for your information, I doubt either one of you has ever made as much money as you're about to. You're not going to be rich, but you'll be able to pay your rent and bills without worry. As far as benefits go, health and life insurance are included." He leaned forward, crossing his arms on the table. "Angel, I suggest you move over to this side of the lake. My agency is down in the Old Town section of Seattle. The Pioneer Square area."

I grimaced. Old Town was a seedy place. At one point it had been the center of business, but business moved north, and the downtown sector of Seattle had become a seedy wasteland. Now, there were a lot of clubs and taverns down there, and a number of brothels. Once prostitution was legalized, it had become a major moneymaker for most city governments. Taxed high and regulated strictly, it had put the pimps out of business and kept the kids from walking the streets. Punishment for anyone breaking the rules was strict and swift.

"Don't turn up your nose. Rent is cheap, and down there nobody asks questions." He pulled out his wallet and tossed us each a card. "There's the address. As soon as I leave here, I'll contact Névé and Saílle, and put your names on the roster of people they cannot touch. Or that they shouldn't touch. As I said I can't guarantee anything one hundred percent, but at least you'll be on the registers."

"What about DJ?" Angel's voice was quivering, but she was trying to keep it together.

"I've already been in contact with the family where he'll stay, just in case. They live down south a ways, in the Chehalis area. A lot of shifters live there, and the family he'll stay with are very open-minded as to parentage. They'll say he's a cousin from back east, and if anybody questions them, we will forge papers to prove that his parentage was approved by the Alpha."

"What if somebody checks? I mean, a busybody could look into it and find out that he really wasn't from back there."

I had the feeling Angel was grasping at straws, trying to figure out some way she could keep DJ with her even though she knew it was in his best interests to let him go.

"We have an arrangement with the Alpha of the New Hampshire division of the Shifter Alliance. He owes Cernunnos a great debt, one that he's not likely to work off in this lifetime. As a result, we utilize his services in this manner when need be. He also happens to be one of us—one of Cernunnos's bounty hunters."

Angel let out a long sigh. "I guess that's it, then. When does he have to leave?"

"The father of the family is waiting for my call. He's just down the street. We believe in being prepared. He'll take DJ with him. I'm not going to tell you the family's last name or anything about them. I'll make arrangements for you to see him at least four times a year for a week or so. The holidays, if you like. But the less you know about his foster family, the safer he will be. He'll have a new name and a new life."

"You're asking a lot on trust," I said.

"At some point, you have to take a leap of faith. One thing I have learned over the years I have been alive is that nothing is ever guaranteed. Oh, the sun will rise and set, the world will turn, and birth and death come to us all. Other than that, there is absolutely no surety." Herne leaned forward again, propping his chin on his hands. "You have to do what your heart tells you is right."

"I thought the gods were immortal." Angel seemed to be almost holding her breath, her gaze so intent upon our visitor that I thought she might burn a hole through his head.

"My father is. My mother became a goddess. She herself was born of a god and a mortal. She can die, if wounded gravely and not attended to. As can I, though it takes a lot to bring us to death's doorstep."

"I trust you," Angel said. "My heart tells me to go on faith. I will entrust you with my brother's life. I'm going to hold you to it. I know you can't control everything that happens to him, but if the people you give him to hurt him in any way, god or not I'm coming after you."

"And I will be at her side." I reached over and took her hand again. "Angel and I have a bond that goes beyond friendship. We are oath sisters."

Herne gave us a solemn nod. "I would expect nothing less, given what I've heard about you. *Both* of you." He turned to Angel. "Your brother will be loved and cared for. And I will make sure that you see him several times a year, without interference, and you can judge for yourself then. Shall I call for his new foster father to come by?"

Angel bit her lip, pressing one hand against her stomach. She nodded, very slowly. "Yeah. Call him. I'm going to go spend a little time with DJ till he gets here. I don't know how I'm going to tell him about this."

"Tell him that he's going to a safe haven. A sanctuary house. That's the truth of the matter and he will hear the truth in your voice. Tell him that what he witnessed this afternoon may not be over, and that he will put you out of danger by going into sanctuary. That will speak to such a brave young man."

Angel vanished into my bedroom, softly closing the door behind her.

I held my breath for a moment, then let it out slowly. "What's a sanctuary house?"

Herne held up his hand as he pulled out his cell phone and punched in a number. "It's set," he said to whomever answered. "The Miriam G building—fifteenth floor. I'll meet you by the elevator in ten minutes. Bring the sanctuary flag."

As he hung up, I felt like the world was shifting beneath my feet. Angel had to be feeling the same way.

"A sanctuary house—or building—is a place where no one—be they from the Shifter Alliance, the Vampire Nation, the Fae courts, or the Human League—can interfere. Anyone who claims sanctuary in one of those places will be safe until a decision is made by the Grand Council. And I suggest you not ask questions about the Council at this moment. There are some things better off left in the dark, if you know what I mean."

I felt like I was getting a schooling on a world I had grown up in, but never truly knew. Everything seemed different, and all of my *normals* were flying out the window.

"Do most people know about all of this?"

Herne shook his head. "Not really. There's a vast

network running below the surface of the governments in this world, whether they be human, shifter, Fae, or vampire. And that doesn't even account for the rest of the Cryptos, most of whom have some sort of representative on the Grand Council."

I hugged myself, suddenly cold. "So most of the world goes through the motions without any understanding of what's taking place?"

"Most of the world goes through the motions of life in general, blissfully unaware of anything beyond their lives. And if you gave them a choice, ten to one they'd pick ignorance over knowledge. Knowledge carries great responsibility. Ignorance offers most people an out."

I nodded, thinking he was right. "I know a lot of people who don't want to take responsibility for their lives. It's easier to blame somebody else when something goes wrong than accept their part in whatever happened."

Herne stood up. "I should wait by the elevator." He paused, glancing back at me. "It really is for the best, sending DJ away. Angel's brother would be in grave danger. I can't have him working for the agency at his age, and while families of my employees are supposed to be immune to retribution, it doesn't always play out."

I wanted to ask him if he could send Angel with DJ, but I knew his answer would be no. I wasn't sure why, but I instinctively knew there was some reason that she couldn't go with him. And maybe Herne was right. DJ would grow up with other wolf shifters. He would learn what it meant to be part of that society.

As Herne waited outside my front door, near the elevator, Angel escorted DJ out into the living room. Both of them looked like they had been crying. She sat down and pulled him toward her, brushing the myriad of tiny braids back from his face.

"Remember, you promised to be strong for me."

There was so much pain in her voice that I wanted to dive in, say *No—both of you run away as far as you can get.* But that wouldn't solve the problem.

DJ nodded, straightening. A frightened light filled his eyes, but he was doing his best to be brave.

"I promise. You promise that I'll see you before school starts again?"

"I promise with all my heart. You spend the summer with these nice people, and I'll see you before you go back to school in the fall. Herne promised. And you know I can tell when somebody's lying. He was telling me the truth."

DJ let out a hiccup and wiped his nose on his sleeve. "I don't have my toys or my schoolbooks."

"We'll make sure you get them. Now give me a hug—as long and hard of a hug as you've ever given me. It will have to last until I see you again, so it better be a good one." Angel held out her arms and DJ flung himself into them.

I looked away, wanting to give them privacy. I was crying, wondering how everything had become so convoluted in the space of one day. If only I could go back to the morning, knowing what I knew now, and call Angel to go pick up DJ before he left Sarah's house. But there was no going back. What was done was done, and we had to move forward.

The next moment, Herne entered the apartment again, a burly man standing behind him. I glanced up into the man's eyes and saw that, as rough as he looked on the outside, his eyes held nothing but gentleness. He walked over to Angel and DJ, and knelt beside them.

"Hey DJ, you can call me Cooper. I know this is hard for you and your sister. I'll make the transition as easy as possible for you. I have two girls and a boy. We could sure use another young man around the place. My wife bakes the best chocolate chip cookies ever, and she loves children. We're all wolf shifters, and we're going to teach you how to handle your inner wolf. You'll go to school with my kids, and we'll get you all squared away." His voice was modulated, soft and soothing.

DJ looked frightened still, but his voice was a little less shaky as he asked, "Can Angel come visit me before school starts in the fall?"

"We'll make sure that she does, and we'll be sure that you get to spend Thanksgiving and the holidays with her. It may have to be down near where we live, but we'll figure out a way. I promise you that. I give you my word."

"You'd better hurry. You may have the sanctuary flag flying from the antenna, but that doesn't mean that you won't be followed. I have a cloaking spell that you can use, but you have to use it before midnight. It's time-sensitive."

Cooper stood up, and held out his hand to DJ. "Don't worry about clothes or anything. We have everything you need." He turned to Angel. "I give you my word, he'll be safe and happy. I know you're going on a lot of trust right now, but we'll uphold our end of the bargain."

DJ tucked his hand into Cooper's, and then glanced back at Angel. "I love you."

"Be brave and make me proud. I don't want to hear that you've given them any trouble when I get there to visit you." Angel stood up, squaring her shoulders. "You hear me? Mama J. will be watching over you. You know she's always there."

As Cooper led DJ out of the apartment, Herne glanced back at us.

"I'll make sure they get off safely. I want to get the cloaking spell into their car." He shut the apartment door behind him.

As I turned back to Angel she collapsed on the sofa, crying so hard I was afraid she might break a rib. I hurried over and wrapped my arms around her, pulling her head onto my shoulder. I had a horrible feeling that this was just the first in a long line of drastic changes we were both facing. But at least we'd be facing them together.

Chapter 5

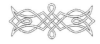

ANGEL AND I had moved over to the sofa by the time Herne returned. I was doing my best to help Angel keep from losing it. He gave us a weary smile, then dropped into the chair next to the window, staring out at the night.

"How much more is there that we don't know?" I asked. I wasn't sure exactly what I meant, but the world seemed overwhelmingly complex all of a sudden, and I felt out of place in my own skin.

"Where should I start? For now, you should rest for the night. I've notified Névé and Saílle that you're on our roster. Both were suspicious as to why I called them so late, but I figure better now than waiting till tomorrow. You should be safe tonight." He paused, then added, "DJ got off safe. He'll be fine, and I will make arrangements for you to see him sometime during the summer. Tonight, get some sleep and then meet me down at the office tomorrow around noon. We'll get you situated away into whatever respective jobs I feel you're best suited for."

"I don't like my job, but I should give notice—" Angel started to say, but Herne cut her off.

"No. Call in tomorrow morning and say unavoidable circumstances have forced you to resign. Don't worry about picking up your things, I'll have someone go do it for you. It's not like you need references to work for me and, as of now, this is your job for the foreseeable future." He pushed himself to his feet, stretching and yawning. "Sleep. Rest. Cry if you need to. Tomorrow's a new day, and a whole new world."

With that, he headed for the door.

"What about my house? My car is still there."

"Give me your keys. I'll have your car down at the office tomorrow. I'll send someone home with you to gather your things. But you really should move over to Seattle. Even though you're on the clock with me, I just feel safer if you were here, in the city."

Angel tossed him her car key, and he pocketed it. Then, giving us a wave, he headed out the door, shutting it firmly behind him.

I ran over and locked the door behind him. Turning, I wasn't sure what to say. I expected to see Angel in tears again but she was staring out the window over Puget Sound. She was breathing softly, and when I walked over to stand beside her, she smiled.

"He's going to be okay. The worry about him that I've had all day? About him being dead or close to it? It's vanished. I didn't tell you after you found him and brought him home, but I was still afraid and I didn't exactly know why. But now, I feel like he dodged a bullet. My brother's going to be safe. And right now, that's all that matters."

"Then you have a good feeling about this Cooper?" I had come to trust Angel's instincts.

"That's not his name. He didn't give us his real name. But it was so that my brother would be safe. I think DJ will finally have the father figure that he needs. Mama J. tried but she couldn't be both mother and father to him, especially since she wasn't a wolf shifter. And I could barely be even a substitute mother. But he's going to have a family now, and they'll take care of him."

I knew Angel well enough to know that she wouldn't say it if she didn't feel it to her very core. Exhausted, and suddenly feeling like if I didn't get into bed I'd drop in my tracks, I turned to her.

"We should get some sleep. Are you all right on the sofa? You can sleep in the bed with me if you want—it's big enough for two."

"I think I'd like to sleep on the sofa tonight. I like looking out at the city from this angle. I like seeing the water. Is it all right if I crash here until I find a place?"

I nodded. "Of course. But you know, I've been thinking of looking for a house. Maybe we should find one together. We make good roommates, you have to admit that. We've done it before."

"That's a good idea. We can talk about it in the morning."

I rustled her up some blankets and a sheet and

a pillow, and then I took a long hot shower before dropping into bed. I was afraid that I'd toss and turn half the night, replaying what had happened throughout the day. But everything seemed to glide off of me, falling away as I crept into bed. I closed my eyes and wrapped my arm around Mr. Rumblebutt, his purr began to lull me to sleep, and the next thing I knew, the sun was peeking through the window and it was morning.

COME MORNING, EVERYTHING seemed a little brighter. As I was dressing, I glanced in the mirror at my birthmark. The stag's head and antlers suddenly made sense. How far had my father's connections with Cernunnos gone?

I brushed my hair back, binding it into a high ponytail. I looked more like my father than my mother. He had had raven black hair just like mine, and green eyes like mine as well. My mother had been a redhead, with bright blue eyes and a voice that could charm the morning birds.

After I shimmied into a pair of jeans, I slipped on a corset top, inhaling deeply as I fastened the busks. I found that corsets supported my boobs better, and they also—if not cinched too tightly— supported my back, especially when I was out on the job, although acrylic boning was a must for being able to move quickly. I wasn't a tomboy, although I certainly couldn't be described as prim and proper. I liked makeup and I liked pretty clothes, but I liked my look with an edge.

After I finished dressing, I slipped on a pair of ankle boots with two-inch heels. They were chunky, and had good tread so that I could run in them. I threaded a studded leather belt through the loops in my jeans, and then, after a quick splash of powder, eye liner, and lip gloss, I headed out to the kitchen.

Angel was already up, whistling as she prepared pancakes. I was surprised she seemed so cheerful, but Mama J. had taught her to trust her instincts. If she thought DJ was safe, then he was safe.

"How long have you been up?"

"About an hour. I took a shower, and I'm grateful I packed a bag for a few days. I'll need to get the rest of my clothes soon. I thought I'd make bacon and pancakes for breakfast. There weren't enough eggs so I hope you don't mind going without on those. I've already fed Mr. R. and he's off playing in the living room."

Mr. Rumblebutt loved Angel because she always brought him catnip toys.

"Mind? Hell, I'm just grateful you're cooking. My specialties are pizza and toast. But you know that." I grinned at her. We had gone to community college together, rooming together, and she had done most of the cooking for those two years. I had pitched in with housecleaning. I'd rather scrub the toilet any day than figure out how to prepare dinner. Most nights, I ate sandwiches and opened cans of soup. Or I'd stop for takeout on the way home.

"Ready to start our new jobs?" She flipped three

pancakes onto the plate, added five rashers of bacon, and handed it to me. I carried my plate and the maple syrup over to the table. She followed with the butter and her own plate.

"Coffee? *Coffee coffee coffee*?" Angel didn't share my obsession with caffeine—at least not with coffee. She had her own raging addiction going in the form of black tea, however.

"I don't know how to work your espresso machine. So you're going to have to fix that yourself." Her eyes were twinkling as she spoke.

"You're going to have to learn how to use it if you expect to live with me. Just like I know how to make your tea. You like two tea bags in the cup, so strong that you could stand a spoon up in it. I don't know how you can gag that stuff down." I wrinkled my nose at her, grinning. "I'm glad you're feeling okay this morning. I was so worried about you last night."

"I told you, he's going to be fine. He's safe where he's at. Meanwhile, I have to admit that I'm kind of excited. I hated that job, and you've got to admit, this is going to be a whole new way of life. No more drifting. And at least I know DJ will be looked after and that they can afford to take care of him. There were months where I ate ramen for dinner so that he could have a halfway decent supper and breakfast."

"I wish you would have told me."

We had very few secrets from each other, but there were matters we were both embarrassed about. Or maybe, too proud. Money was one of them, on Angel's part.

"There's not much you could have done. You weren't that much better off."

I shrugged. "I could have figured out something to help." I dug into my pancakes. "Where the hell did you find pancake mix? I didn't have any in the cupboard."

"Flour and eggs, baking powder and milk. A pinch of salt. I know my way around the kitchen, girl."

I frowned. "I don't remember buying flour and baking powder."

"My house. You brought them with us last night."

"Oh! That's right. I just grabbed whatever I found. I wasn't paying close attention." The pancakes were soft and fluffy, and the syrup tasted slightly different but good.

"I *know* I didn't have syrup. Your place?"

She shook her head. "I was out of syrup, too. But there was brown sugar and cream, so I made a form of caramel. So you want to be roomies again?"

I nodded. "I'm game if you are. We can look for a house after we go visit Herne. Or rather, after we go to work. I must admit, it will be a relief not having to freelance anymore. It gets scary when the clients run thin. Or when they cheat you."

She gave me a solemn nod. "While my job was more secure, I got really tired of being cussed at when things went wrong, and watching the guys get promoted right and left. Not to mention having the scuzzball boss hit on me. But if I had filed a sexual harassment suit, he would have found a way to turn it around on me. And I couldn't afford to be out of work, given taking care of DJ."

I bit down on a piece of bacon. Several times, I had wanted to pay a visit to Angel's boss and set him straight on how to treat her, but she begged me not to. And I knew she couldn't afford to get on his bad side.

"I'll put the condo up for sale. I should be able to find a little house on the outskirts of the city for not much more than I paid for this. Mortgage shouldn't be too steep, and you can rent a room from me. That work for you?"

She nodded. "All right. I'll give thirty days' notice on the house, it's not on a lease so at least I've got that going for me. The only thing I ask is that you don't buy anything near a frat-boy hangout or party house. The one thing going for the neighborhood I lived in was that it was quiet."

"And dangerous. We can ask Herne for some recommendations." I paused, glancing sideways at her. "Am I the only one who thinks he's pretty hot?"

Angel let out a laugh. "You better watch yourself. Getting involved with a god could be dicey."

"Do you know how long it's been since I've had sex? After what happened with the last couple guys..." I fell silent, my giddy mood suddenly vanishing. "Thank you, by the way. For explaining to Ray. I just couldn't tell him."

"I thought you might be mad, but I felt he deserved to know. He deserved to know that you weren't being a bitch. You did what you could to save his life."

"Well, thank you anyway. I still can't talk about it very easily. I don't know what happened, and I don't know if I ever will. The first time I thought it was a fluke, but after Leland I knew it was just being in proximity to me and my work."

I closed my eyes, trying to keep away the images that kept running through my mind. First there was Robert, who tried to help me on a job putting a stop to a batch of will-o'-the-wisps, but they lured him away when I wasn't watching and drained him of his life force. I blamed myself, and it had taken me months to regain my equilibrium, and a couple years before I felt strong enough to date again.

And then I met Leland, and I had fallen in love with him. He was a cougar shifter from Mount Rainier. We dated for several months before I would even let him kiss me, and then slowly, I let the relationship move forward. He was a gentleman, waiting for me to give the okay. Finally, I took him into my bed, made long slow love to him, and in the middle of our tryst, he had a fatal heart attack. The doctor said it was too much rich food—and Leland did love his expensive pastries and carb-rich pasta dishes—but that kind of put a damper on things for me.

Then Ray showed up. He almost made me almost change my mind, but the closer we got, the more flashbacks to Robert and Leland I had. And then, Ray was attacked by the goblin I was going after. He hadn't died, but the scar was a nasty one, and I decided that I liked him too much to chance him getting killed because of me.

"So you're thinking, maybe because Herne's a

god, that he won't fall under whatever curse you think you carry that killed Leland and Robert, and almost killed Ray?" Angel smiled. "Just make sure that you *really* like him first, okay? I know you're hard up, and trust me, I understand. But don't jump your employer's bones just because you're horny. That could be bad in so many ways, and I'm not just talking about finding him dead on the bed."

"I suppose you're right." I gave her a wry grin. "It's been so long since I worked for anybody else that I've forgotten the nuances of social interaction on the job. I guess it would be like sleeping with one of my clients. Not such a good idea."

I hated to admit it, but she was right. I also didn't like owning up to the fact that I found Herne absolutely gorgeous. I had a thing for the biker boys, especially the bad ones. Pushing lascivious thoughts away, I finished my breakfast and stood up.

"I suppose we better go find out what our new lives are going be like." I paused, then added, "I'm glad you're okay. Last night was harsh."

Even though Angel insisted she was all right, there had to be a place deep inside where she was devastated. She took her responsibility for DJ so seriously that I couldn't imagine that every-thing was quite as hunky-dory as she said. But I wouldn't push matters. Angel would deal with this in a way that was easiest for her. If that meant pushing away her own feelings of loss, that was probably what she needed to do. At least, for now.

We carried our dishes to the sink. Then, grabbing our jackets and purses, we said good-bye to Mr. Rumblebutt and headed for the elevator. It was time to go to work.

ON THE SURFACE, Seattle was a beautiful city. Over the years it had grown into its nickname—the Emerald City. Set on Puget Sound, it was a major port for the country and an international hub, airport-wise.

A mix of old buildings amidst gleaming new ones, the city was as diverse as a box of crayons. It was a high-tech magnet, and yet there was a startling level of poverty in the city. Rents were steep, and for every penthouse owned by some computer guru, there were two-bedroom apartments filled with families of eight or nine people, trying to make ends meet.

There was a sector of homeless transients, as well. Tent cities cropped up here and there, some by the freeways, some under the numerous overpasses that connected suburb to suburb. For a long time, people had protested their existence. But when the recession continued, the arguments faded and the transitory neighborhoods became just one more fact of life. The rich moved to the suburbs on the northern outskirts, or over to the Eastside, and the core of Seattle—its heart—was left to the lower classes.

I took Greenwood Avenue, southbound, until it turned into Phinney. Then I followed Phinney until we hit Thirty-fourth, where I turned left. From there it was an easy hop onto Fremont Avenue and over the bridge to the Queen Anne area. Another fifteen minutes of stop-and-go traffic saw us down to First Avenue, where I pulled into a parking garage across from the address Herne had given us.

The streets in downtown Seattle were wide, riddled with potholes, and notorious for their awkward placement. But the city felt like home, and the multitude of beautiful old brick buildings and tree-lined streets were in direct juxtaposition to how gritty the city could feel on bleak days in midwinter. As I eased into the parking garage, I grimaced when I saw the rates, but the skies opened and a hard spring rain began to pound down and I was grateful we weren't parking on the street three or four blocks away.

"Well, at least we're only across the street from the Wild Hunt. We won't have far to walk in this mess." I eased into a parking stall, and pulled out my credit card. "Let me pay for the afternoon and then let's get going."

Now that we were actually here, some of my excitement had worn off. I was more nervous than anything else. I kept telling myself that if it was really bad, we could nullify our agreement and take our chances.

Angel and I dashed through the rain, weaving through the pedestrian traffic that filled the sidewalks. A lot of the small boutiques that used to line the streets were gone, and now a profusion of neighborhood markets and delis took their place, along with the brothels that had become so popular. They catered to the fetish personality, each one offering a specialized service. I averted my eyes from one with the name of "Spank-o-Rama" as we passed by. I had my own kinks, but that wasn't one of them.

The Wild Hunt Agency was in a five-story brick walk-up. There was an elevator, but an OUT OF SERVICE sign was plastered across it.

"Wouldn't you know it? He's four flights up."

"Of course." Angel grinned. "Quit complaining and start climbing stairs. It's good for you."

The Wild Hunt Agency took the entire fourth floor.

As we got off the elevator, we found ourselves in the lobby of a spacious waiting room. There was a desk in the center, facing the elevator, and a seating area to the right, with a leather sofa and several upholstered chairs. A water cooler sat in the corner, along with a couple large plants in vivid blue porcelain urns.

There were two doors on the wall behind the desk, a window that overlooked the city streets to the left, and against the right wall, a hallway led further back into the agency. The brick walls were clean, and the lighting was bright, giving an airy feel to the reception room. It was a pleasant surprise, considering how old and grimy the building had looked outside.

We crossed to the desk, but there was no one behind it. Instead, a bell sat on the edge, with a sign propped next to it that read, PLEASE RING FOR SERVICE.

I glanced around. There was no one in sight, so I reached out and tapped the bell. A loud chime reverberated through the room, louder than I expected.

"I'm surprised there isn't somebody waiting for us." I craned my neck, trying to see around the corner down the hallway, but we were too far from it. I decided it wouldn't be polite to go snooping just yet.

Just then, the door directly behind the desk opened, and Herne entered the waiting room. He shut the door behind him, and when he saw us he broke out into a smile.

He certainly didn't look as messy as he had the night before. His hair was smoothed back into a ponytail, and though he still had the closely cropped beard, it looked like he had trimmed it. He was wearing a pair of blue jeans and a suit jacket with leather patches on the elbows. Beneath the jacket, he wore an olive green sweater with a V-neck, and he had a bronze necklace around his throat, but from this distance I couldn't tell what the pendant was. He looked just as good as I remembered him looking last night.

He was carrying a file folder, and when he saw us he closed it. "Welcome to the Wild Hunt. I'm glad you actually showed up." His eyes were twinkling as he said it, but there was a serious note to his voice.

"Has anybody actually *not* shown up who said they would?" Somehow, it had never occurred to me to stand up a god.

"Actually, yes. Several people. They were in similar situations as you, and unfortunately, they decided to bail on me." He sat on the corner of the desk, dropping the file folder by the laptop.

"What happened to them?" Angel asked.

"They vanished. Unfortunately, people who make enemies of the Fae often do." He shrugged, then stood and straightened his jacket. "So are you ready to get to work?"

I nodded. "I guess we're as ready as we'll ever be. But you haven't told us what we're going to be doing."

"Well, as you can tell there's nobody manning the reception desk. Our last receptionist left the agency to have a baby and she's decided to stay home. Angel, I thought you would be best suited at being our new receptionist. Your ability to read people will be a great help."

"How did you know that I'm able to read people?" Angel gave him a suspicious look.

He snickered. "Being the son of a god has its perks. I knew right away that you have precognitive abilities. I'm able to sense such things. But when I was doing research on Ember, you came up as her best friend."

She let out an exasperated sigh. "So of course, you researched my background?"

"Of course. And given what happened with your brother, I'm glad that I did. Otherwise, we wouldn't have been able to move so quickly on getting him into a sanctuary house. By the way, over the next few weeks, I need both of you to acquaint yourselves with all the sanctuary stops around the city. And that includes the Eastside as well. You'll have to have that information at the tip of your fingers should the client need it—and that goes beyond the scope of our dealings with the Fae. But we can go into that a little later."

I was beginning to realize that we weren't just going to be poking our nose into the skirmishes between Light and Dark. It sounded like the Wild Hunt dealt with a number of life and death situations.

"So, Angel, this will be your station. Ember, I've decided to put you out on the front with us. You'll be assisting us with cases. Your background as a freelance bounty hunter will fit right in for that. You already know how to research and track. You'll have to learn our procedures, of course, but that's just a matter of memorization. For now, come meet the rest of the team."

He motioned for us to follow him.

I wasn't sure why, but I hadn't expected there to be a "team"—which seemed ridiculous, when I thought about it. He couldn't work alone, not and run an agency like this. But for some reason I hadn't gone so far as to wonder who else we'd be working with.

He led us around the corner, into the hallway that I had been curious about. It ran back about fifty feet to an end wall, with three doors on the right side, and one door at the end on the left, near the end. He led us to the first door on the right. The frosted glass pane in the upper half of the door was stenciled with the words BREAK ROOM on it. He turned the knob, and led us in.

THE BREAK ROOM was about a third of the size of the waiting room, with a long table in the center, a small range and refrigerator on one side next to a counter, and on the other side, another counter with a small sink, several drawers and cupboards beneath it, and a microwave. A sofa sat against the end wall, with a pillow, and a couple blankets neatly folded over the back. The lights were fluorescent, and there was a glare to the room that made mc feel alert. *Definitely* a working room, not a hangout space.

Three people sat at the table, two men and another woman. One of the men was burly, and looked like somebody you might meet in a dark alley. He was bald, with a Snidely Whiplash mustache. Dressed all in black—black jeans, black turtleneck—he looked muscled and fit.

The other man was thin and tall, with wire-rimmed glasses and long brown hair that reached his ass, pulled back in a neat braid. His eyes were deep brown and right off the bat I pinned him as Native American. He was wearing a striped polo shirt and blue jeans.

The woman must have been in her mid-sixties, with a narrow nose and a hawkish face. She was busty, with a narrow waist and curved hips, and she was wearing a neat, brick red, linen pantsuit. Her long silver hair was pulled back away from her face by two thin braids on either side, and I had the immediate sense that she was Crypto. What kind, I couldn't tell, but one look at her eyes was enough to tell me I didn't want to mess with her.

All three of them looked up as we entered the room. Herne sat at the head of the table. He placed the file folder he was carrying in front of him, but left it closed.

"Meet Ember and Angel, our two new employees. As I told you this morning, Angel will be taking over the receptionist desk, while Ember will be joining us on the investigations team. I've told you about both of them, but they don't know who you are yet. So, introductions."

He motioned to the woman. "This is Talia, our head researcher. She does all the legwork. She prepares the dossiers, finds out all the background information on people and places. Basically, anything I need information about that isn't of a technical nature, I turn to her."

Talia looked us over carefully. "Hello, girls. Welcome to the agency."

On the outside, she seemed friendly enough. But there was a reserve beneath the pleasant demeanor. It would take time to get to know her, and if we pressed, I sensed she'd slam down a wall so fast it would smack us in the face.

The burly man went next. "I'm Viktor. I'm head of security, and you need my okay before you check out any weapons from our armory. I'm also here as backup and muscle."

"Don't let Viktor fool you. He may be the muscle of the agency, but he's also one hell of an investigator and he's got an IQ of 180. Brains and brawn in one package."

"I just wish my family felt that way," Viktor said. He glanced over at us. "You'll find out soon enough, so I might as well tell you. I'm half-ogre. My family disowned me because I took after my human mother. If I'd been a girl, they wouldn't have cared, but men in my race are expected to be brutish. And by *brutish*, I mean big. Really big." He grinned as he said it, shrugging. "You do what you can, and hope it all falls together in the end."

I blinked. I'd heard of ogres but had never met one. "You look plenty big to me," I said before I realized that I was actually saying the words aloud. I blushed, but that broke the ice and everybody laughed.

Viktor slapped the table. "From your mouth to my father's ears, I wish. But it is what it is, and at least I have a good job, thanks to Herne."

"I wouldn't have anybody else on my team," Herne said. He motioned to the other man, who looked younger than any of us. "And this is Yutani. He's our computer programmer and all-around tech guru. He's also one of our investigators."

Yutani saluted us with two fingers. He was leaning back in his chair, staring at us with an unreadable expression. But he didn't seem angry, or unfriendly, just observant.

"Welcome to the company. Before you ask, and because you probably should know, I'm a coyote shifter. Great Coyote dogs my heels, so fair warning in advance. Sometimes his energy splashes over onto the other people I run with."

I rubbed my forehead, trying to suppress a groan. The last thing we needed was Coyote's energy running rampant in our lives. It felt like we already had enough chaos as it was.

"That's the same look my last girlfriend gave me when she found out who I'm bound to." But he laughed, and motioned to the chair next to him. "Brave enough to sit near me?"

Angel snorted. "Dude, don't ever dare Ember. Trust me on that one."

I grinned at him as I took the chair next to Talia. "I've got enough chaos in my life, thank you."

Angel sat next to Yutani. Viktor pushed back his chair and headed over to the coffee pot, which was sitting next to the small sink.

"Care for some coffee?"

I raised my hand. "I never say no to caffeine. A splash of milk and a spoon of sugar, please."

"I'm a tea girl myself," Angel said. "Black tea, two teabags in one cup, as strong as I can make it."

"I think we can rustle up some tea." Viktor put a teakettle on the burner, then opened one of the cupboards and pulled out a box of teabags. When he returned with our drinks, Herne cleared his throat.

"I expect everybody here to help Angel and Ember as much as possible. Before we get to our new case, which is a doozy, I'm going to reiterate the rules for the girls." He glanced over at me with a frown. "I don't mean any disrespect by calling you 'girls.' You're both women, but you're both young compared to most of us. But if it bothers you, just let me know."

I shrugged. "I've been called far worse. So long as you don't ask me to get you coffee."

Angel shook her head. "Trust me, where I was working before, I had far less respect. And as receptionist, I suppose coffee is one of my jobs?"

"Whoever gets here in the morning puts on the first pot. But yeah, I may ask you to grab a cup for me now and then." Herne cleared his throat and opened one of the file folders in front of him. "The rules of the agency are simple. You are both required to sign an NDA. Trust me, if you break them, I will find out. Punishment is up to my father, and you do *not* want to get on the bad side of Cernunnos. You will discuss the cases and events in this office with *no one* except those in this room. Understood?"

"Understood," I said. "I had confidentiality agreements with my clients. For me, the ability to keep quiet meant that I had returning clientele."

Angel just nodded. "Understood."

"All right, next: we begin work at eight A.M., generally. You're expected to be on time. Some cases will take us into the nighttime hours, and we adjust as necessary. You're both on salary. Angel, you're *required* to be here from eight A.M. until six P.M., Tuesday through Saturday. You get an hour lunch break, and of course, two coffee breaks. One in the morning, one in the afternoon. As long as you man your desk and get the work done, I don't care if you sit there playing video games afterward, though only on a private laptop. Absolutely no visiting sites with the work computers where you might download a virus. When in doubt, ask Yutani."

She jotted down notes. Angel was a perpetual note-taker.

"Ember, you work the schedule that the rest of

us work. Investigators work as needed. If we're on
a case, you may be working around the clock. Angel, at times you may be called in as well. You both
get sick leave, and after six months you both get
two weeks' vacation a year. After two years, you get
three weeks' vacation per year. Keep your noses
clean—we do our best to fly under the radar of the
cops. They know we exist, but there's not much
they can do about us, except to make life difficult.
We work outside of their jurisdiction, but only
when we're on a case. If you're speeding and they
catch you, you get a ticket."

He let out a long sigh, scrunching up the side
of his lip as if he were trying to decide how to say
something.

"What?" I asked.

Herne gave us a long look. "All right, here's what
you don't know. What I haven't told you so far.
None of this is discussed in public, because if it
were, whoever was doing the talking would be in
one hell of a lot of trouble."

"Why do I have a feeling we don't want to know
what you're about to tell us?" I asked, trying to in-
ject a little levity into the conversation. But Herne
wasn't smiling, and neither were Yutani, Talia, or
Viktor.

"This is no laughing matter," Herne said, and
I felt duly chastised. "Are you the least bit curious why the cops wouldn't even follow up on your
parents' murder?"

I shrugged, "I figured it was because the cops
were underfunded and understaffed."

"That's true enough, but no. It's because your

parents were Fae. Light, Dark, doesn't matter.
The fact that they were Fae meant that there was
never any real investigation, no matter what they
told you. You see, Névé and Saílle both keep the
authorities' pockets well lubricated so that they'll
look the other way. Like the vampires own Wall
Street, the Fae own the cops. And the governor,
for that matter. Anything to do with Fae politics
is paid lip service, only. Neither Fae Queen wants
interference, and they pay well to keep the authorities out of things."

"Bribes? That doesn't surprise me, but what
about the United Coalition? Don't they take exception to what you just said? Both the vampires and
the Fae?" That was what the alliance was called
between the Shifter Alliance, the Vampire Nation,
the Human League and the Fae courts.

"Nothing's in writing, the money is laundered
so well that it's squeaky clean, and if there were
any allegations made, it would lead to all-out
war between the factions. The Fae courts and the
vampires are so powerful that the other members
of the UC choose to look the other way. If either
side were to make inroads to control *everything*,
I'm pretty sure it would be a different matter. But
neither the vamps nor the Fae are looking to rule
the world. As long as they keep out of most personal affairs, the money is too good to ignore, and
it crosses too many hands."

"Essentially then, with the Fae, we have two
warring factions who are allowed to play out their
internal spats, as long as collateral damage isn't
too high and the payout is worth it." I had always

been jaded, but now I felt even more so. "It's just lovely, knowing I belong to both sides and yet, to neither."

Herne shrugged. "And you represent an unacceptable union of opposites to both Light and Dark." He leaned back in his chair. "Which leads us to the next rule. Under no circumstances are you to accept money from anybody other than the Wild Hunt. Not even a free lunch unless it's a good friend. No gifts, unless it's from a good friend, and I'm talking a person you see regularly. No bonuses unless I pay them. *Nothing*. The cops know we exist. The Fae know we exist. So does the United Coalition. They all know why we're here, and they stay out of our work, as long as we don't take sides. We keep the balance. We've taken on Light and we've taken on Dark. Cernunnos and Morgana have the last word and both sides grudgingly accept that. We're balance keepers, more than anything else."

"Then we're not here to *stop* this war?" Angel asked.

"Nothing on earth can do that. It's a continual battle that the gods have long come to accept. We keep it from breaking out into the human world, into the shifter world, and into the Vampire Nation. We keep the members of the United Coalition from taking sides. That means that at times, we take on blood vengeance debts. The Fae know and accept this—both Névé and Saílle."

"Then we're not really the good guys," I murmured.

Talia spoke up. "You'll come to learn that there

aren't really any truly *good guys* in this matter. As Herne said, we're balance keepers."

The room fell silent for a moment. I glanced over at Angel, who was staring at me. I knew what she was thinking because I was thinking the same thing. The world was a rough place, and it had just gotten a whole lot rougher.

Chapter 6

AFTER A MOMENT, I cleared my throat. I didn't like knowing that the government was essentially corrupt and taking bribes to allow a private war to continue, but it wasn't anything that hadn't happened before.

"All right, now we know. So what are the other rules? We keep things quiet, no kickbacks, no taking sides. What else?"

"Show up for work on time, let me know if you're sick, keep your nose clean, do your work, and absolutely no side jobs. No moonlighting. There will be no more private cases for you, Ember. If we even suspect that either of you have a gambling or drinking problem, we have the right to take whatever measures are necessary."

"This is serious work," Angel murmured.

Herne gave her a nod. "The Wild Hunt Agency, along with the others like it, has a heavy investment in towing the line. We make it possible for the world to keep functioning without becoming a war zone, at least between the Fae. The Light and Dark courts were here before humans evolved, and will be here long after the rest of us disappear. At one time, far back in history, they tore the world apart with their skirmishes. On an individual level, I like a lot of the Fae—both Light and Dark. But as a whole, your people are a terrifying lot."

I felt singled out. "Tell me about it. I have no connections with my own people, considering neither side considers me worth claiming."

"That was one factor that led us to your doorstep. That, and your life would eventually be trashed when they got around to snuffing you out." Talia let out an odd clicking sound, tilting her head with a grin. Her smile was more intimidating than the stare she had met us with.

"So I'm a charity case? I can live with that."

Talia let out a shrill cackle. I studied the older woman. I still couldn't figure out exactly what she was. But the gleam in her eye kept me from opening my mouth.

"What role do the vampires play in all of this?" Angel asked. "They seem to take a backseat to human affairs, but you say they rule Wall Street?"

Vampires were an oddity in the world. There were too many of them for comfort, but given they couldn't breed, and given that they were ostensibly proscribed from killing for their food, they seemed to take a backseat in the United Coalition.

"Once again, don't believe everything you hear. The vampires bear no love for any of the other members of the UC. We're all just food to them, although they keep up appearances by playing by the rules. Unlike the Fae, vampires interact more with humans. They have a great deal of power in the business sector, and they do their best to keep their members under some semblance of control. They like the power games played by nations, unlike the Fae, and they prefer to work behind the scenes. They have a discipline and self-control that surprises me."

"So what you're saying is that Fae are more like berserkers who don't give a fuck what other people think, while the vampires are manipulators." That made sense to me.

Most vampires had been human to start with. There were very few Fae or shifters who ended up being turned. So vampires *would* have more at stake in the human community.

"So to speak. I wouldn't call the Fae berserkers, they're just more chaotic." Herne let out another sigh. "We're getting off topic. You are asking about the rest of the rules? Basically what I told you. No side jobs, you show up for work, no gifts or kickbacks, keep your nose clean, no investigation into any of our cases without permission. And everything is confidential."

Talia opened a file that was in front of her, and handed us each a contract.

"Read it, and sign it. We can't start until you do." She tossed us each a pen.

I scanned my contract. All of the rules were included, as well as pay rate and job title. I blinked at the salary. One month would cover three months of my usual take. I heard Angel suck in a deep breath and realized she must have come to that part.

At the very end there was a paragraph stating that if we broke the rules, we would be subject to punishment as per decree by Cernunnos and Morgana. It was in stark bold print, and I realized they weren't kidding. We were signing away our lives. I picked up the pen and hovered over the line requiring my signature. I glanced over at Angel.

"You ready to do this?"

She gave me a nod. She signed her name, and I signed mine. After dating the contract, I handed it back to Talia. When Angel and I were done, there was a palpable sense of relief throughout the room.

"Tell me, what would have happened if we hadn't agreed, now that we know all of this?" I wasn't sure I wanted to hear the answer, but then again, it paid to know everything that we were dealing with.

"You would have been relocated to a safe place. Let's leave it at that." Talia excused herself, walking over to the copy machine that was next to the sofa. She made copies of the contracts and handed them back to us. "It's official, you're on the clock."

"Now that we have that settled, let's get right down to matters. Angel, you stay here for your briefing. Then you can go out and familiarize yourself with your desk. There is a rundown of duties in the center drawer that your predecessor left for you. It includes all the different phone extensions, the way you are expected to greet clients, everything you need. If you have any questions, feel free to ask. It's *always* better to ask rather than assume." Herne was suddenly all business. He straightened his shoulders, and opened the file folder in front of him.

"A few days ago, one of our informants brought a situation to my attention. I've double checked the information and it's valid, so I ran it by Cernunnos and Morgana and they both agree that we need to take care of this as soon as possible." He pulled out a tablet, and quickly tapped on it. "Yutani, can you get Ember and Angel a couple tablets? And they'll need work phones."

He turned to us. "Your work phones are for the members of this office only. Do not give the number out to anyone. All clients will be given the office number and your forwarding extension instead. You are not to use them for personal matters."

Yutani left the room, and when he returned a few moments later he was carrying two new tablets and two new cell phones. He handed us one of each.

"I programmed them this morning for you, so they're already. The password has been entered but you need to change it to something that you'll remember, on both devices. Do *not* use a password that you use in your personal life. Do not use a password that is under four letters. You must include one uppercase letter and a number in your password. Do not try to use any non-alphanumeric symbols. Please take care of this now, and be sure to write down your passwords because I don't want to have to hack into them."

He tossed us each a packet of sticky notes. I felt rather conspicuous poking around while we were being watched, but it was part of the job. Finally, I decided on two passwords that I was pretty sure I could remember, although I did write both of them down. The first, for my cell phone, was *gnasHer1*, and for the tablet I chose *sKillet2*. The former was what I was feeling toward my situation, and the latter no one would ever guess considering how little I cooked. When we were finally situated, Herne airdropped the information files to everybody.

"Please open the document titled 'Kuveo,' and navigate to the first page."

"Which side are we dealing with?"

"I believe the Dark Court," Herne said. "Here's the rundown: Eight unexplained homicides throughout Seattle, all human. Four unexplained deaths among the shifters."

"The cops?" Talia asked.

"Turning a blind eye. Rumors are going around that the vampires are to blame, but I traced them back to two officers, both of whom have strong ties to TirNaNog, so I'm pretty sure Dark paid them to fan the flames."

"Why would they want to blame the vamps?" I asked, confused.

"If people believe the vampires are responsible for the deaths, they'll focus on them and not the Fae. Humans are uneasy around vampires. And since shifters and vampires don't get along, chances are likely that they'll believe the gossip. No disrespect to your people, Yutani."

Yutani laughed. "I know as well as you do, most

shifters are a little hotheaded. I don't care whether they're Raksashas, Weres, Selkies, or coyote shifters like me, we're all a little bit on edge."

"That's the truth," Talia said with a laugh. Her voice was scratchy, and low pitched. She sounded like a smoker who had had one too many packs for the day.

"I don't see your people winning any awards for being the most patient," Yutani said, winking at her.

Talia snorted. "Touché. Your volley."

"Back to the matter at hand," Herne said, "the fact is we have twelve mangled corpses and no perpetrator in sight."

"Is there any evidence other than the cops' connection to TirNaNog that makes you think the Fae are part of this?" I asked, wincing as pictures of the mutilated corpses showed up on my tablet. The bodies had been mangled, all right, torn to shreds and large chunks of flesh were missing. Angel let out a gasp, closing her eyes.

"Angel, I'm sorry. I forgot you might not be used to this." Herne motioned to Viktor. "Get her a glass of water."

Viktor hurried over to the sink, where he filled a glass, adding ice from the refrigerator dispenser. He carried it over to Angel, who gratefully accepted it, sipping as she tried not to look directly at her tablet.

"Well, I'm not. I'll do my best, but please give me some warning next time." She squinted, scrolling back to the first document.

"I'll try to remember. As to any other connections with the Fae, yes. That's what brought our informant in. He was in a bar where he overheard a conversation between two TirNaNog guards. They were drunk off their asses, and talking about the news stories about the bodies. Since there had only been a bare-bones story in the news, our informant decided that he should listen in. He bought the guards another drink, and they were just drunk enough to keep talking. One of them mentioned that it shouldn't be long before people blamed the vamps, and then he elbowed his compatriot and winked. When our man asked what he meant, they abruptly shut up and turned away, after muttering a warning to steer clear of the catacombs."

The "catacombs" was the name for a series of underground tunnels below the city of Seattle. At one time, they had simply been called "underground" Seattle. But ever since the space had been taken over by vampires and other nefarious undead, they had been nicknamed the catacombs. No longer a tourist attraction, they were now a place to be avoided at all costs if you weren't welcome.

"But that would lead to the vampire connection. Did he hear anything else?" Viktor asked.

"Yeah, the most damning. As the guards were walking away, one of them said to the other, 'That will teach the bloodsuckers to mess with us,' and then they disappeared. That's enough to tell me that there's something going on between the Fae and the vampires. Now, whether the Fae are trying to use the vampires as a scapegoat to hide their own machinations, or whether they're deliberately trying to get them in trouble, I don't know."

Herne frowned, putting down his tablet. "That's one of the things we have to figure out. But we better do it quick before the body count rises, because the police have taken the stance that these attacks are wild animal attacks. Given the reports are coming from cops who are on the take from Névé, my guess is that the Fae are up to something and just trying to deflect blame."

"Surely the Fae don't want to start a war between the vampires and everybody else?" I asked.

Herne shook his head. "No, I doubt that's their motive. My guess is they just want to continue whatever they're up to without interruption. If they can deflect attention, maybe we won't be tapped on the shoulder to step in."

"What do you think their end goal is?" Yutani asked.

"Given that TirNaNog seems to be behind this, my guess is they're looking to strike a blow at Névé and the Light Court. Trouble is, if they're raising havoc down in the catacombs, there are things far worse than vampires lurking down there. Originally, a small group of explorers found a subterranean level that was there before Seattle burned, and when they broke through, it became apparent that there were other creatures beyond vampires and humans that tended to go creeping around in the dark. At that time, the catacombs were walled off and forgotten."

"So what's the bottom line? Where do we start?" Yutani scrolled through the pictures, raising his eyebrows. "This is heavy-duty mutilation."

"Yes, it is. I want to move on this before the police spread the rumor that there is a vampire serial killer running around. If you'll notice on some of the pictures—Angel, don't feel you have to examine the photos, at least not right now—there are chunks of flesh missing from the bodies. I pulled some strings and got the coroner's reports. The fact that something took a bite out of the bodies gives the coroner leeway to label the attacks as wild animal attacks. But no wolf or puma did that." Herne set his tablet down.

"So officially, the call is wild animal attack. Unofficially, the Dark Court is spreading the rumor that vampires are to blame." I rolled my eyes. "And when you think about it, you could almost chalk up the bites to a werewolf or the like. The waters are so muddy on this it's hard to tell what's true."

Herne poured himself another cup of coffee. "And that is exactly the MO of the Fae courts. Stir up enough muck till everybody loses their way. So, brainstorm. Where do we start?"

Talia cocked her head to the side, then said, "Talk to the families and find out what their loved ones were doing down in the catacombs. Visit the catacombs themselves and see what we can find. What do you need from me?"

"That's a start, though not all the bodies were found near the catacombs. Why don't you run a background check on all of the victims? Try to pinpoint if they have anything in common. We have eight humans and four shifters, and that's a broad spectrum. Did they know each other? Did they frequent the same establishments? Whatever you can find. Yutani, you and I will visit the families."

"What about us?" Viktor asked.

"You take Ember and go take a look through the catacombs. Six of the bodies were found outside, near the secret entrances, but go through from the inside. See if you can find anything that might give us a clue as to what's going on. Then head over to Seward Park where the other six bodies were found."

I was glad that I'd worn jeans and a good jacket.

"Angel, you get the layout of your desk and duties. It's two P.M. now. We'll meet back here at six. Okay, that's about it." He paused. "Oh, Angel? Can you make another pot of coffee?"

"It figures." She laughed. "I always get to make the coffee." She picked up her tablet and phone and headed out to her desk, giving me a little wave.

Viktor turned to me. "You ready?"

Ready or not, I didn't have a choice. "Sure, lead the way." And we headed out into the blustery afternoon.

I FELT AWKWARD getting into the car with Viktor, given how little we knew about each other, but he tried to put me at ease.

"Please fasten your seatbelt. I try to drive as carefully as possible, but you never can tell with some of the road conditions out there. No smoking in the car." The rain was coming down in a heavy, steady stream by now. "Are you cold? I can turn the heat up if you are."

YASMINE GALENORN

I realized I was shivering. "A little, if you would. I think I'm still in a bit of shock over everything that's happened since yesterday. I'm feeling a little shaky. Oh, and I don't smoke. Neither does Angel."

"Do you need to drop by a Fast 'N Go? We can pick up a burger on the way. I could use some food."

I realize that I hadn't eaten lunch. And pancakes and bacon only went so far.

"Thanks, I'd like that. Breakfast seems like it was a million years ago." I paused. "How long have you been working for Herne?"

"I started with the Wild Hunt Agency fifteen years ago. For a long time I worked as a bouncer in a bar, but then Herne approached me about taking a job with him. It sounded a dozen times more interesting than what I was doing, and I've never regretted it." He hesitated, then added, "I think you'll really like it. I don't know about your friend, but it's a good job, and good pay. And Herne is... Well, he's *Herne*. Don't let Talia frighten you off. She's crusty, and she's a dangerous old coot, but she knows what she's doing and she'll have your back."

"I didn't want to ask because it seemed like prying, but she's not human, is she?"

Viktor snorted. "Human? She's about as human as a rock. She's a Crypto, one of the rare ones."

"Oh? Are you going to tell me, or do I have to ask?" I flashed Viktor a smile, suddenly liking the half-ogre. He seemed good-natured, and he also had brains. And I liked intelligence.

"Talia isn't in the habit of talking about her past,

124

especially given what happened to her. I'll tell you, but don't mention it to her unless she brings it up, which she eventually will. Deal?"

"You have my word." I was more curious than ever.

Viktor changed lanes, easing over into the less-congested left lane. We were heading toward the docks. As he stopped at a red light, a brilliant flash of lightning shattered the sky, followed by an ominous rumble.

"I hate thunderstorms," Viktor said. "Anyway, Talia was a harpy when she was born. A number of her powers were stripped from her during an altercation with a liche."

"What's that?" I had heard of a lot of creatures, but never a liche.

"It's an animated corpse that feeds off life energy. Often, the person was cursed before death, and when they die, they rise again. But their spirit's changed and they're driven by a thirst for magical energy. They feed off just about any life force, but Cryptos provide an incredible amount of energy for them, and they can permanently drain abilities." He shuddered. "They're terrifying, desiccated corpses with fiery eyes."

I shuddered. "And one attacked her?"

"Yeah, when she was younger. It almost drove her mad, but she managed to reach help and even though she'll never regain her powers, she's still got an eye for detail, and an ear for conversation. Talia has a photographic memory, and a photographic auditory sense. In other words, she can remember just about anything she sees or hears. You can see how that comes in handy in our business. She never has to double check any of the research she's done, since she remembers everything."

A thought struck me. "Wait. You said she's a harpy? I thought they looked like bird women?" But then again, I had never known any harpies, nor had any contact with them.

"She used to. By the way, liches have been spotted in the catacombs. At least, in the catacombs that are still fairly desolate. So be careful."

"So how did stripping her powers change her looks?" I wasn't surprised to find out that Talia was a harpy. It made an odd sense with the energy I had felt off of her. She was blunt and abrupt, and I had a feeling she could be ruthless when necessary.

"It didn't, but she met Herne, and he took pity on her. Even without her powers, Talia was a terrifying sight, and everyone ran from her but she couldn't do much for herself. She couldn't hunt any longer and had to learn how to integrate with society in order to survive. The harpies are a solitary race, and they seldom make friends even amongst themselves. Talia had to learn to be something she's not. Herne petitioned Morgana, who gave her a permanent glamour. Talia chose the form."

I suddenly felt like my life wasn't so rough. "That must have been hard."

Harpies were a form of shifter, although they did not belong to the Shifter Alliance. They were bird women, predators of an intense nature, and their shriek could deafen anybody who heard it. Often, they would take the shape of beautiful young women, and like sirens, lure men in to their deaths with their song. Thankfully, they were solitary creatures, and rare.

"She no longer has her shriek, nor can she shift form. The only thing she retained from her time as a harpy is her ability to sing. And even that is muted, mild compared to what it once was. Mostly, she's stuck in a human body, with the ability to persuade strong young men to carry her groceries to her door. But Morgana gave her the choice of any form she wanted, and Talia chose her looks."

I felt sorry for her, but knew immediately she wouldn't want that. "For all that she's been through, I see why she'd be crusty."

"Oh girl, you haven't even begun to see just how *crusty* she can be. She was downright polite to you and Angel. That's why she's not up front at the receptionist desk. But she's good at her job, and we rely on her. I think it makes her feel like life isn't a waste."

"What's Yutani's story? He's bound to Great Coyote?"

"Native coyote shifter. The native shifters have their own branch of the Shifter Alliance. Unfortunately, the universe seems to be geared on making Yutani the butt of its personal joke. But that's what Coyote does. He teaches through laughter and ridiculous situations, and he's a dangerous trickster, although not malignant."

"I don't know a whole lot about the shifters, to tell you the truth. Are all coyote shifters bound to Great Coyote?"

Viktor shook his head. "No, in fact the majority aren't. Yutani was asked to leave his pack because the Trickster led him a merry chase and the whole mess ended up with a good share of his town being burned down. It wasn't Yutani's fault, and nobody was killed, but he was deemed a menace. Coyote shifters who are bound to the Trickster usually find themselves the odd man out.

"He moved up to Seattle from the Southwest and Herne brought him into the business about three years ago. Yutani was on his way to becoming a pretty bad alcoholic, and he was sleeping in one of the tent cities on the side of the freeway."

I didn't say anything, but I couldn't help but think that Herne seemed to gather the strays and misfits. I wasn't accepted by my people because of my heritage, Yutani had been drummed out of his pack, Viktor was an ogre who didn't look big enough for his father, and Talia was a harpy without her powers. As far as Angel went, well, she kept to herself a lot because of her empathic abilities.

We pulled into a Fast 'N Go, and Viktor ordered a double cheeseburger with large fries, while I ordered a bacon cheeseburger and a strawberry shake. I really wanted a mocha, but I could wait. We ate in the parking lot, chatting about the weather and getting to know each other a little bit, before heading down to the docks.

At one point Pike Place Market had taken up most of the area around the docks. Now called the Viaduct Market, it was still a mishmash of vendors, hundreds of stalls selling food and handcrafted goods, and services. Tattoo shops abounded, as well as fetish brothels.

"The entrance to the catacombs is on a subfloor level of the Viaduct Market." Viktor glanced at me, his gaze traveling down to my dagger strap on my thigh. "Do you have a conceal license? What about a blade-carry permit?"

"Both. I don't pack a gun. They don't set well with my bloodline. Gunpowder makes me queasy, since even the smell of it can set me off. But I do have a permanent blade-carry permit. I pulled some strings with a client who worked for the city and he was very grateful for me eliminating a problem he and his wife had on their property. He wrote me out a permanent permit."

Long blades were allowed in public if you had a permit to carry. Guns were highly regulated, and between the various permits and licenses needed to own one, and the fact that gunpowder was as good as an allergen for me, I no longer bothered with the idea of one. But my dagger, I couldn't imagine being without.

"I have a pistol grip crossbow at home, I can use nunchaku, and I'm pretty good with throwing stars. I can fight double bladed if necessary." I prided myself on my abilities, and it felt good to know they were actually going to come in handy. While I never liked finding myself in an altercation, I was damn glad I could take care of myself.

"That's all good to know. What about martial arts? Parkour?"

"I train five days a week, strength training, agility training, parkour. While I'm not conversant with any particular martial art, I'm good with basic hand-to-hand." I thought for a moment, then added, "I threw myself into my training when my parents were murdered. I lived with Angel's family from the time I was fifteen until I turned eighteen. Mama J. was really good to me, and she supported my decision to become a bounty hunter."

"You found them, didn't you? Your parents. Herne told us about it when we were discussing whether we should bring you into the agency or not."

"Yeah, I found them." I closed my eyes, not wanting to flash back to the scene, but it was still as vivid as the day it had happened.

I had come home from school late to find the back door open and my parents brutally murdered. It'd all been a blur after that. When I realized that the police weren't going to bother finding out what happened, I swore that one day I would hunt down the murderers and they would pay. I had always been athletic, but that's when I threw myself into training and for over fifteen years I had kept at it. I was proud of my strength.

"I'm sorry," Viktor said. "I didn't mean to bring up bad memories." He opened the door to the Market, standing back as I entered. "We need to head to the west end. From there we can find the entrance to the catacombs."

I shook away the images that were playing out in my mind, bringing myself back into the present. "I never knew there was an entrance to the cata-combs near the Market. All I knew about were the entrances downtown—the main entrances."

"Vampires don't like it when people know too

much. A number of the entrances that exist now weren't around when underground Seattle first came to be. But remember, the catacombs were there beforehand and as the vampires took over the subterranean level, they found older entrances, and created more. I get it—it's self protection. The bloodsuckers never know when some yokel is going to go stake-happy on them. Not that it ever ends well, and they're well within their rights to defend themselves. It's just sad when some cock-eyed teen who wants to make a mark for himself."

I glanced over at Viktor. He seemed a lot more philosophical than I expected an ogre to be. "Tell me more about you. Your mother was human?"

He nodded. "She's a good woman. She and my father split up, of course. It would never have worked in the long run. I'm not sure why they even got together. She never told me and every time I asked she just said, 'Later, son.'

"After they broke up, Da went back up into the mountains, back to his people. I stayed with Mom. She accepts me for who I am. She's never once said she was disappointed in me. But Da, he's another matter. I was too short, too weak, too soft-hearted, too much like a human. I haven't seen him in over a hundred years."

I clapped Viktor on the back, feeling an odd ca-maraderie with him. "He's the one who's missing out, Viktor."

"Call me Vik, all my friends do." He pointed down the main corridor leading to the west. "There, we need to go down that way."

The Viaduct Market was awash with customers

and clients, bustling like a street fair. The stalls
were filled with fresh spring vegetables—lettuce
and radishes, carrots and early greens. Large vases
held dozens of daffodils and tulips, a veritable ar-
ray of spring colors blazing through the building.
The smells of smoked meat and hot sandwiches
filled the air, and I wished we had waited to eat
lunch. The food courts were astounding. The fish
market hadn't changed much, still boasting fresh
fish right off the docks. My mouth began to water,
even though I wasn't hungry. We passed a fortune-
teller's stall, the woman reading cards for someone
who was crying on the other side of the table. I
glanced at a tattoo studio.

"Everybody always thought my mark was a tattoo," I said.

Vik laughed. "Trust me, you're going to have
an actual one sooner than you think." He pulled
up his sleeve and showed me an intricate tattoo
of a dagger with vines around it. "Everybody who
works for Herne gets marked with this tattoo. It
identifies us to anybody who might question our
right to be where we are. Especially *your* people."

"They're not my people. I may carry their blood
in my veins, but they disowned me."

I took a long look at his tattoo. It was pretty,
I had to admit. The thought of being marked as
somebody's property—that's what it felt this was—
didn't set well, but I'd already crossed that bridge
and burned it to the ground. Apparently I had been
born for this, and marked at birth by Cernunnos.

We wound our way through the stalls, assaulted
by the clamor and smells of the market, until we

came to the west wing exit. I looked around.

"So where's the entrance to the catacombs?"

Vik smiled and pointed toward the floor. "We have to go down for that."

And with that, he pushed open the janitor's door, and motioned for me to follow him. I frowned as we entered the closet. I didn't see a staircase, just buckets of bleach, and floor wash, and mops and brooms and all sorts of mainte-nance tools.

"So where are the stairs?"

Vik reached up and pulled the chain on an overhead light. As a cold fluorescent light filled the room, he led me toward one of the side walls. Once there, he slipped his finger through a hook on the wall and pulled. There was a groaning sound and a panel began to slide back on the opposite wall. I turned quickly, expecting somebody to be there waiting, but there was only a dim light in the re-cessed alcove. As I peeked in, I saw that the nar-row nook was basically a landing, leading to a very steep spiral staircase. I shuddered when I realized it was wrought iron.

"I'm going to need some gloves before heading down that staircase."

He gave him a puzzled look.

"I'm Fae."

He still looked bewildered.

"Cast iron and wrought iron? We don't get along so well."

A look of understanding swept over his face. "Oh that's right. Hold on, I'll get you something to wear." He slipped back into the closet and returned, carrying a pair of heavy work gloves. They swamped my hands but at least they would protect me from the feel of the iron. It set me ajar, still, to be so close to the metal, but I'd be all right as long as I didn't touch it with bare fingers. If I stayed too long on the staircase I'd end up with a massive headache, but if we weren't on it more than a few minutes, I'd be all right. The animosity between iron and Fae was often overexaggerated, but it was based on fact. The elementals belonging to the iron ore had a grudge match with us, while the silver elementals actually liked us.

"Ready?"

I nodded. "They actually discovered the bodies down here?"

Vik shook his head. "No, but we're headed to where they did. I know where the entrance is located, but Herne wanted us to trace the route and see if we find anything along the way, which is why we're taking the long way around. Come on, let's move." And with that, he started down the staircase. "Shut the door behind you. There's enough light to see by here."

Not exactly jumping for joy, I shut the door behind me and followed him onto the staircase.

set off alarm bells in my stomach, yet I found it hard to look away. Even standing behind Vik, I felt exposed and vulnerable.

Vik puffed up, looming larger than he actually was, and I wondered if ogres had their own form of glamour. I realized that I could hear Vik breathing, and my own breathing, but the two men who were facing us were still as night.

"Looking for anything in particular?" one of them said, in a slow languorous voice. "Any help we can offer?" The question was suggestive, fraught with opportunity and danger.

Vik stared the men down. "Thanks, but we're fine."

"Are you sure? What about the pretty lady? She looks like she could use some...*help*."

"I'm going to reach in my pocket now, for my identification."

Vik held his hands out, as though he were facing the police, and then slowly reached for his pocket, easing his wallet out. The vampires watched him closely as he opened it and held out his agency identification. There was a pause, and the men suddenly became all business. Their hypnotic energy withdrew, leaving cold, ruthless expressions on their faces.

"We won't detain you. Be careful, though, there have been a number of unexplained deaths around here." The one with the buzz cut gave me another look. "She with you?"

Vik nodded. "She also works for the Wild Hunt."

"You know, our community would be extremely grateful if you could find out who's behind the murders. I assume that's what you're looking into."

It sounded like a warning. Then, the longer-haired vamp turned away and, followed by his friend, they headed down the corridor in the direction from which we had come. Vik waited until they vanished from sight, motioning for me to stay quiet. When they had disappeared around the corner into a side passage, he let out a long breath.

"Well, we dodged a bullet there." He leaned back against the wall. "You okay?"

"Yeah. But that was one of the most uncomfortable interactions I've had in a long time. If those are vampires, I could do without them."

"As Herne said, all four factions of the United Coalition know about us. Well, about all the agencies like us. Word spreads, especially to those in higher positions. My guess is that our two vampires have some clout down here. Otherwise, they might not have recognized my identification. I took a gamble and it paid off. Come on. I want out of here as soon as possible."

I seconded his sentiment, and we began to jog down the corridor at a faster pace. Another twenty minutes brought us past a number of other side corridors, and to a shaft with a ladder leading upward. Vik began to ascend. I still had my gloves on and swung onto it without hesitation. About fifty feet up, Vik reached up to the ceiling and slid a panel back. A moment later, a shaft of light broke through. He scrambled out of the opening, then reached down to help me out. As soon as I was standing on the sidewalk, he shut the panel again.

I looked around, blinking in the relatively bright

light. We were in a parking lot, right next to the docks. Another hundred yards and we would have ended up in the water.

"Why couldn't we just drive down here in the first place?"

He gave me a sour look. "Two reasons. Herne told us to take the long way, for all the good it did. As to the second reason, look around and answer your own question."

I glanced in the direction he had indicated. The streets were all blocked off, with heavy road work being done. In fact, I couldn't see the end of the detour.

"Where we parked at the market is about as close as you can get to this area without walking all the way. And if you look at the pavement here? At the panel we came through?"

I glanced down and realized that I could no longer see it. "Illusion?"

"I don't know if it's magic or whether it's just damn good engineering, but it's almost impossible to find the entrance from the outside unless you know exactly where it is. The vampires have managed to make it almost impossible to enter the catacombs unless you know their secret handshake, so to speak."

I folded my arms across my chest, turning away from the blowing rain. In Western Washington, it rained about nine months out of the year. Not every day, of course, but we had enough drizzle and sputter interspersed with the driving rain that our reputation for cloudy weather was well-deserved.

Puget Sound extended deep into Western Washington, coming in off the Straits from the Pacific Ocean. The waves were choppy today, whipped by the wind into a frothy mix of water and foam. I noted that the dock we were standing on was on Pier 67C. There were no boats currently at the dock, though a reader board said that a barge from China was due in later in the evening. Dockworkers were scrambling, getting ready for the impending offload.

"So where were the bodies found?"

Vik nodded over his shoulder. "Follow me." He led me to a place about three yards away, behind a series of dumpsters. "They were found here, sprawled on the ground."

I looked down. Although the rain had washed a great deal of the chalk away, I could still see the outlines of where the bodies had been. Apparently the police had started an investigation, even though the medical examiner had nixed the idea of homicide. There were dried stains on the pavement, and I knelt, placing my hand in a puddle next to one of the splatters. I tuned in to the water as it caressed my fingertips.

Tell me, I thought, reaching out to touch the essence of the rain. *Tell me what you taste.*

The wind picked up, gusting around me, as a large wave crashed over the side of the dock, spraying both Vik and me. I could feel the nature of the elemental behind it as it responded to my call. The ocean was a goddess, and Puget Sound a part of her. She surrounded the world, massive and huge, older than the land, older than humanity, older than most anything on the face of the planet. I slid into her cadence, feeling the way it rocked back and forth within me, within my veins, my tears, my soul.

A moment later, the image of blood spread through my mind, and I caught a visual of the mangled bodies as they were dropped onto the pavement, the rain washing over them and onto the ground below. I tried to see what was holding them, but the rain hadn't noticed their attacker, only the bodies as they fell into the puddles.

"I think they were dead when they were dropped here. They weren't killed here." I glanced up at Vik, wishing I could have seen more.

"How do you know?" He cocked his head, watching me.

"I'm one of the Water Fae by blood—half, anyway. My mother was Water Fae. She was pledged to Morgana."

"So you're a siren? One of the undines?"

"No, the sirens and undines, along with the naiads, are actually elementals. The Water Fae are connected with the element of water, but we aren't actually *part* of it. I can tune into rain and lakes and rivers and oceans—and I can use some of their inherent magic, but I'm not actually a part of them, like an elemental is. But if there are any water elementals nearby, I can usually contact them as well."

"Good to know," he said. "So you think the bodies were just dumped here?"

"I *know* so. They were dead when they hit the ground. If there had been a struggle, I would have sensed it through the moisture that's still on the ground here. I'm not sure where they were killed, but it wasn't right here."

"The dockworkers are leery. You can tell by the way they're moving." Vik pointed to a couple of the nearby men, who were working quickly, glancing over their shoulders at us. "They're nervous."

"If I knew three bodies were found, mutilated, near where I worked, I'd be nervous too. Has the garbage been emptied since the bodies were found?" I was thinking we might find something in the dumpster.

"Yeah. In fact, my notes say that the garbage men made a special run the next morning. Which tells me that there may have been something in there they were trying to cover up."

"Is there anything else we can learn? Should we question the workers over there?"

Vik shook his head, staring at the men. "If they know anything, they aren't going to tell us. Come on, I think we'll have better luck at the park."

"Do we have to go back through the tunnels? I'd almost rather walk in the rain than do that."

"From your mouth to my legs. Let's go. We've got a bit of a hike given the slope of the streets. But I'd rather walk too."

As we headed back to the car, hiking up the steep city streets, I thought about the catacombs. I had never known they were so extensive; it was simply a fact that had never crossed my radar. But now it made me nervous to think about the vampires roaming beneath the city streets. And if there was one entrance secreted out of sight, how many more were there, and how far did the network of catacombs run?

RATHER THAN BOTHER with the freeway, we took Holgate Street over to Beacon Avenue, which we followed until we could turn left onto Orcas Street. From there it was a straight shot all the way to Lake Washington Boulevard, which led into Seward Park.

Adjacent to Lake Washington, like a mini peninsula, the park housed three hundred acres of forest. Sheltering wildlife and waterfowl, it offered easy access to the shoreline. Directly across from the park, attached to the Eastside by a bridge, Mercer Island loomed in the middle of the lake. An exclusive neighborhood, the population was mostly human—nouveau rich. The I-90 freeway ran through Seattle, over a floating bridge to Mercer Island, and then over another bridge to the Eastside.

I had been to Seward Park a number of times. It was soothing to walk among the trees, out of the city grit.

"How many bodies were found here?" I asked, hating to think that violence had spread into a place that I loved.

"Six. Half of the victims. According to Herne's notes, they were found *after* the other six, which tells me that whoever killed them decided he needed a safer dumping ground."

"Yeah, because by then, the other dump site was

being watched."

"All the bodies here were found down near Seward Park Road, on the Cutlass Trail. It's one of the lesser-used hiking trails—"

"I know it. I've walked it many times. I come here a lot, Vik. I can think here."

We took Seward Park Road, parking in the lot near the center of the park. The rain had eased off by the time we arrived and I was grateful that we wouldn't be bombarded by the weather.

"We'll have to walk a little bit. I hope you don't mind." Vik locked the car and motioned for me to follow.

"I'm used to it." I jammed my hands in my pockets, following him across the trail into the forest. We passed the Broken Tree Trail, finally coming to the Cutlass Trail. It was steeper than the others, and it wasn't kept up. Well, compared to the rest of the park.

Once we were on the trail, I realized that my size was a definite benefit. While Vik was strong and muscled, he was definitely not light on his feet. I scrambled up the steep trail well ahead of him, not realizing I had left him behind till I got near the top. I turned around, and saw him struggling up between the trees. By the time he reached me, he was panting.

"Ogres don't make good climbers," he said.

"I thought ogres mainly lived in the mountains and that's what they do—climb with the goats."

"You're thinking about giants. Ogres are not the same. People mix us up all the time and it annoys the fuck out of me."

"All right, you're not a giant. But don't ogres live in the mountains?"

"Ogres tend to live underground. Or in caves. My father's family happens to live near Mount Rainier, but not way up the mountain. There's a trail up to the cave system they live in."

He seemed rather touchy about the subject, so I decided to leave it alone. I wasn't sure what the difference between ogres and giants were, but it might be a good idea to find out so I didn't make the same mistake twice.

I looked around. We were near the trailhead, and like most of the woods around Western Washington, the ground was a mass of forest detritus: fallen leaves, fir and cedar needles, old pinecones, mushrooms, sodden bark, as well as the burgeoning plants of the spring. All in all, our forests were a tangle to get through and it was easy to sprain an ankle if you weren't watching where you are going.

"So, you said there's an entrance to the catacombs near here?" I was doing my best to look for anything that could be construed as an entrance, but I had no clue what to look for.

"This way."

Vik led me across the trail to where a small stream burbled along through the forest, curving to flow parallel to the trail and down to the lake. Before the stream turned, it was buttressed by a narrow walkway that led to an outcropping of boulders.

Vik scrambled across them, doing his best to avoid falling in the water.

I followed. Just beyond the boulders, I saw what

looked to be a lightning-scarred tree trunk. It was a good five feet wide.

Vik stopped beside it. He reached into one knot-hole that was as big as his fist, and I heard a small click. The front of the tree trunk split open as a small door on hinges slowly swung back. He nodded for me to look inside. Hesitantly, I crept forward and peeked down into the tree trunk. A ladder led down, on a slant, in a narrow metal shaft.

"Wow. They really go out of their way to make these things invisible. So this shaft leads... Where?"

"It leads to a tunnel that goes beneath the stream, and that tunnel leads to a passageway that goes all the way back to the catacombs. It stretches under South Seattle, with a number of offshoots leading into other areas that the vampires have mined out over the years."

"Just how many vampires are in Seattle?" The amount of work gone into creating the catacombs seemed monumental.

"Probably not more than five or six hundred. However, you have to remember that vampires are extremely strong, their stamina is amazing, they don't need to breathe so they don't have to come up for air, and they have a lot of time on their hands when they're underground. Think about it. They have the entire day to work belowground. Just because they can only come out at night doesn't mean that they sit around playing poker all day."

"I can't imagine that the city officials approve."

"The city officials don't have much to say about

it. I'm sure the vampires use their financial connections as leverage. The mayor's not going to argue with the people who pay for his campaign."

I was beginning to realize just how little control humans had in this world. It seemed like everybody had their fingers in the pie. Pull on one end and you'd find another.

"So where were the bodies found?"

"Just below the trailhead, over beneath that cedar." He pointed over to a large cedar near the stream. "They were found over a period of twelve days, one every two days. Before that, the other six bodies were found one every three days."

"So whatever it is, it's escalating. When was the last body found?"

"Last night. That's when the informant talked to Herne and we got called in. Didn't you read the dossier?" Vik gave me a look like I had farted or something.

"I looked it over, but I was kind of busy figuring out what the hell I'm supposed to be doing." I glanced around. "Why haven't they closed off the trailhead? If the last six bodies were found here, you'd think they would steer people away from the area." I paused, suddenly aware of a faint scent that seemed out of place. "Hold on, I smell something."

I closed my eyes, raising my nose to the wind. There was a scent of something boggy, almost fetid, like vegetables left too long in the refrigerator. It made me nervous, and I realized that I had goose bumps all over my arms, even though I had my jacket on.

"There is something here that makes me uneasy. I'm not sure what it is, but alarm bells are going off really loud right now."

"Is it near here now? Are we in danger?" Vik glanced around, his hand on his dagger.

I tried to tune in as best as I could. The scent was cloying, but it was fading rather than growing stronger. I realize that the wind had blown a gust past me from the south, beyond the stream. I shut the door on the trunk and scrambled over the top of the blasted tree.

Once on the other side, going was more difficult. My footing was precarious, the rocks covered in slippery moss. I was holding on to the side of the embankment as I jumped from stone to stone, trying to keep from falling into the stream. The slope was getting steeper, and the rocks fewer and farther between. I would either have to follow from the cliff above, or jump down into the water and wade upstream. I glanced back at Vik, who was watching me carefully.

Turning back to the water, I tuned in, listened to it as it cascaded along.

It whispered to me, asking me if I would follow it upstream a ways. There was a sadness to it, a melancholy feeling that made me want to cry.

Finally, I eased my way down into the water and, knee-deep, pushed against the current, slogging over the slippery rocks in the streambed. I had only gone a few feet when I noticed something ahead, lodged against the side of the embankment. Whatever it was, it sparkled in a sudden spate of sunlight that burst through the forest, slicing through the clouds.

Taking a good look around to make certain nothing was waiting to pounce on me, I followed the water over to the sparkling item. I found myself staring at a necklace, the chain of which had been broken. I slowly reached for the pendant, and as my hand met the water to scoop up the necklace, a shriek ran through me as sure as if I had heard it aloud. I let out a shout and stumbled back, surprised by the sudden pain that accompanied the cry.

"Are you all right?" Vik called.

I glanced up. He had followed me along the top of the embankment, and was leaning over to look down. About eight feet above me, he looked ready to jump over the edge if I needed help.

"I'm okay. I found something and I think it belonged to one of the victims." I pocketed the necklace, then looked around to see if I could see anything else. There was nothing in sight, and the odor I had smelled earlier had vanished.

I looked upstream, wondering how far the creek actually went. Twenty yards ahead, it seemed to disappear into the side of the slope. I closed my eyes picturing where we were in the park and figured that the stream must feed into the park from one end of Lake Washington and then trickle down back into another part of the lake. Wondering what we were getting involved with, I turned around and headed back toward the trail, motioning for Vik to meet me there.

Chapter 8

BY THE TIME we got back to the Wild Hunt, it was nearing six. Angel had settled into her station. She had bought a bouquet of flowers for the end table, the magazines were all new and up to date, neatly stacked on the end table. And her desk looked like somebody was actually working there. She was poring through a file when Vik and I trailed into the room. When she saw us, she looked relieved.

"Herne and Yutani got back about ten minutes ago. Herne asked me to tell you to go back to the break room when you got here. I'll be there in a minute." For the first time in a while, she seemed relaxed.

"Getting familiar with your job?" I asked, heading down the hallway.

"Actually, I am. And I think going to enjoy it, sans the part where we look at pictures of dead bodies." She picked up her tablet and a notebook and put out the sign that said, PLEASE RING FOR SERVICE.

Viktor motioned for us to go in without him. "I'm going to stop at the bathroom first."

Angel and I headed into the break room where Herne and Yutani were discussing something. Talia was tapping away on a laptop. They all looked up as we entered the room.

"Viktor will be here in a moment. He stopped at the restroom." I realized suddenly how I looked, soaked up to my thighs from the stream and grunged up with mud, dirt, and dust. But there was no time to change.

Herne stared at me, his lips crooked into a smile. "You look like you've seen some action today," he said, arching his eyebrows. There was something sensuous about the way he spoke, and the way he looked at me. Either that or it had just been way too long since I'd had sex.

"I decided to go swimming. The water's nice and cold, if anybody wants to know." I pulled out a chair and slid into it, shivering. I'd kept warm while I was on the move, and in the car the heater had dried me out some, but now I felt chilled. "Any way to turn up the heat in this joint?"

Herne shook his head. "I got the rent so low on this building because I agreed to keep utilities within a certain range. But if you're cold, we do have a shower and you can heat up that way. I don't think we have any spare clothes that will fit you, though."

"I'll pass. I can manage until we go home." At

least my butt and thighs weren't wet.

Talia snorted, letting out a harsh laugh. "Or your boobs."

I gave her a questioning stare. "What?"

Herne laughed, slapping the side of his thigh. "Talia didn't mention it earlier, but she has a way of catching random thoughts. Usually the ones we don't want anybody hearing." He gave her a reproving look. "Be nice to the newbies."

She winked at me. "I don't tease people I don't love, girlie. Or at least, that can't handle my sense of humor." With a shrug, she added, "Herne's right. I'm not psychic, but I'm able to catch random thoughts. Trust me, I don't deliberately pry."

Oh great. A harpy who could randomly read thoughts. Just what I needed in my life. She gave me a long look, and I wondered if she had heard what I was just thinking. Feeling paranoid, I cleared my throat.

"So how often does this ability of yours kick in?"

She chuckled. "Only now and then. Usually when I'm not paying much attention. Don't worry, I can't hear everything you thinking, nor would I want to. No offense intended."

"No offense taken," I said, glancing at Angel, who rolled her eyes. But oddly enough, the interplay was comfortable, and I realized I might actually enjoy being around these people.

Viktor entered the room, looking at the coffee pot. "Coffee?"

Angel jumped up. "Let me get you some. Ember, do you want any, or do I even need to ask?"

I stuck my tongue out at her. "Lots, and you

know how I like it."

"Oh babe, you know I do." She blew me a kiss as she went to fix our coffee.

I placed the necklace on the table in front of me.

Herne looked at it expectantly. "What's that?"

Viktor let out a long sigh. "Ember found it on our scouting mission today. We think it belonged to one of the victims."

"I *know* it belongs to one of the victims," I said. "That's how I got soaked. It was down in Seward Park, in a stream."

"Why don't you to go first?" Herne leaned back in his chair and crossed his arms, listening.

Angel brought our coffee to the table. She motioned to Herne and Yutani, but both of them shook their heads. Talia already had tea in front of her, so Angel sat down.

I let Viktor take the lead. As he ran down what we had found, including our encounter with the vampires, I glanced over at the window looking out of the break room. Outside, it was starting to hail.

I glanced back at the clock. It was only five-thirty. We had only been working since noon, but I already felt like I had done more than a day's work. Working for myself, I set my own schedule, and even when I was tired, it didn't seem quite so intense. It'd been a long time since I had worked for anybody else.

When Viktor got to the part about the stream, I took over. "And then I saw the necklace. The water led me to it."

"So Morgana is right, you *do* have a way with the water element."

"Of course I do," I said, glancing at Herne. "My mother was Water Fae. That's why I honor Morgana, because my mother was bound to her."

"We're probably going to make good use of your abilities," Herne said. "Go on."

I finished telling him what it happened. "I was thinking, maybe we can get more off of this necklace. I'm not gifted with psychometry, but Angel has the talent." I glanced over at her. She gave me a dirty look.

"Do you think you can give it a try?" Herne turned to her.

"I can try," she said. "I'm not sure what I'll pick up, but I'm willing to give it a go."

I pushed the necklace across the table to her. She picked it up, wrapping her hands around it, and closed her eyes as she leaned forward, bringing her forehead down to rest on her closed fists. A moment later she jumped, letting out a small cry.

"Oh my God, I can feel her fear."

She began to breathe heavily, letting out a small moan. "*It's after me. It's after me and I can't get away. What is that thing? I've got to run. Maybe I can hide somewhere. How do I get away? The old house—I need to find my way up to the house. Maybe I can hide there.*"

She paused, her shoulders shaking. A moment later she let out a strangled cry. "*Stop! Please stop. Stay back—stay back or I'll scream.*"

Turning her head to the right she suddenly said, "*Why are you doing this to me?*"

With one last cry, she threw the necklace across the table at Herne and launched herself back in her chair, tipping herself over with a thud.

I was around the table in seconds, kneeling by her. "Are you all right?"

She groaned and I helped her up and righted her chair. Tears were streaming down her cheeks, and she started to hyperventilate.

Viktor immediately raced around to her side, slowly brushing his hand across her back. That seemed to calm her down immediately. Angel let out a ragged cough, thick with tears, and then shook her head.

"Angel? You okay?"

She nodded, taking her seat as she winced. "Yeah, I just got the wind knocked out of me. I'll be all right. It was freaking terrifying. I couldn't get away, and I knew it was going to kill me."

"Do you know what was chasing you?" Herne asked.

Angel shook her head. "No, I wish I did. But it was huge and dark and like a shadow that was moving toward me. I do remember sharp brilliant white teeth flashing in the darkness. And a hunger... A hunger that seemed to engulf everything, and I knew it was after me."

"You mentioned a house," Talia said. "Did you get any visuals?"

"It seemed familiar. I think I've actually been near it. My sense is that the house is old. And *empty*. Mostly, I just sensed the need to get away from whatever was chasing me, but it was quick. And... I'm not sure what else. Surprise. Being taken by surprise?" Angel shivered, taking a long swallow of her tea. "Whatever that thing is, I hope to God I never encounter it. All I could feel there at the end was absolute terror."

The room fell silent as we took in what she said. She had been so terrified, so frantic that her emotions were palpable in the room.

"Well, that gives us a little more to go on," Herne said after a moment. "I'm sorry you had to go through that. I wouldn't have asked you if I would have known it was going to be so traumatic. But I'm glad you did, to be honest."

"I can tell you this," Angel said. "No wild animal attacked her. She wasn't killed by a bear or a wild dog or anything of that sort. This was a creature, some form of monster." She set her lips, staring at the pendant on the table. "I want to find what killed her. That much fear, it's not right."

"I'm not sure we can bring them to justice if you're talking about the cops. But we make our own justice." Herne gave her a sad smile. "The truth is, a lot of people get away with very evil deeds. It's something we have to accept. The universe isn't fair, and not everything balances out. But we do what we can." He looked over at me, then Viktor. "Is that everything?"

"Yeah," Viktor said. "Ember, can you think of anything else? Anything we left out?"

I shook my head. "I think that's all."

"Then I guess it's our turn," Herne said. He glanced at the clock. "Everybody good for staying another hour? We can order pizza."

I looked over at Angel, who shrugged. "Neither one of us have any hot dates going on."

Herne caught my gaze and again, the slow smile

spread across his face. "More's the pity."

"I have to agree." I held his gaze for a moment, then dragged my eyes away. Angel was right. It was dangerous to flirt with the boss, but I couldn't seem to help myself. There was something about him that pulled me, something that told me he wouldn't meet with the end that my other boy-friends had.

"Well," he said, straightening. "We visited all the families, all that we could find. Four of the victims were so mangled they still don't have an ID on them. And two didn't have any family in the area. So we're going to have to call them later on. But of the six we do have information for, we managed to visit four of their families. We got all the information we could, although I'll tell you—one of the victims has a family that I wouldn't wish on my worst enemy from hell."

"Before we get into that, I haven't had enough time to look over the dossier," I said. "If I remember right, you said eight of the victims were human and four were shifters?"

He nodded. "Right. And the shifters were all Wulfine, but that's not uncommon, given how many wolf shifters are around the area. All the local packs are from Mount Rainier and the Cascades, you know. We also have a fair number of cougar shifters and bear shifters too. There are a smattering of others, including a number of Selkie, but mostly the first three."

"So the families you talked to today, were they human or shifter families?"

"Two shifters, two humans. The family from hell

was human. We might as well start with them because they were the shortest visit." He looked over
to Yutani. "You want to take over?"

The lanky coyote shifter let out a short laugh
and pushed his glasses back up on his nose. "Gee
thanks, boss. Leave the dirty work to me, why
don't you?"

"Somebody's got to do it." Herne arched his
eyebrows.

Yutani leaned forward, consulting his tablet.
"Okay, here's the rundown. We talked to the
mother and father of Marilyn Reginald. She was
one of the first victims to be found—down by the
docks. Marilyn was an office worker for Psitech
Corp. She was a low-level office worker, basically
went to her job and home again. She wasn't dating
anybody, but was active in several amateur ghost
hunter organizations. She was active in a couple
local groups that take trips out to haunted houses
to check them out."

"Her family, however, basically can be summed
up as trailer trash to the max," Herne said. "According to her father, Marilyn thought she was
better than the rest of them and had moved out
about three years ago, never talking to them after
that. They wouldn't tell us anything about her—or
couldn't—and all her mother said was, 'Who's going to get her money?' Which pretty much sums up
our visit."

I grimaced. Greedy next of kin were on my list of
lowlifes.

"So you got no useful information out of them?"
Talia was taking notes on her laptop.

"Nada. As I said, we learned more about her in our background check than anything else. Basically, Marilyn was a good-hearted person who was interested in ghosts and the paranormal. She had an uneventful career, and was saving for a trip to England. I sincerely hope that her family doesn't get their hands on what little she had." Herne shook his head, looking disgruntled.

"So who's next?" Viktor was also taking notes and it occurred to me that maybe I should be as well.

I glanced over at Angel who was scribbling things down on her notepad. I mimed writing to her, trying to get her to give me some paper. She looked perplexed, tilting her head.

"If you want something, just ask for it." Herne looked like he was restraining a laugh. At that moment I wanted to smack him.

"Fine, thank you. I need a notebook and pen, please."

Flashbacks of my high school years flooded my mind. I hadn't been the best student, although I had been near the top of the class in terms of my test scores. Angel was always bailing me out because I forgot my notes, forgot my books, and I would have forgotten my head if it hadn't been attached to my shoulders. I just couldn't muster up the enthusiasm for school, given how much the other students teased and picked on me. Luckily, once I started training in the gym, they shut up.

Angel jumped up. "I've got extras in my desk."

"Why don't you show Ember where the store-room closet is. Any time you need something, just go ahead and get it, but make sure you mark it down on the inventory sheet. And no stocking your home office from our supplies." Herne leaned back, crossing his arms as he waited for Angel and me to return.

The stockroom was a small closet packed to the gills with office supplies. As Angel and I rummaged for steno books—which made wonderful notepads—I glanced at her.

"Are you doing okay? I know that took a lot out of you to read that pendant."

"I'm all right. But I can tell you right now, I'd like to put a stop to whoever or whatever killed that poor girl. I'm still terrified. If the Fae are able to rustle up creatures that can do this much damage, I'm grateful that DJ's out of harm's way."

I gave her a nod. "I understand. We'd better get back." Clutching my notepad and a pen, I returned to the break room, Angel following me.

"Our second victim, René Johnson, was also human. She also led a solitary life, although she did belong to—and you'll notice a similarity here—a paranormal investigations group. This one wasn't just a ghost hunting group, though. They study a number of things, including UFOs and Bigfoot."

"Did René and Marilyn ever cross paths?" Talia looked up from her laptop.

"We're not sure about that. To cut to the chase, all four of our victims were involved in various groups studying the paranormal or ghosts or things of that nature."

"All of the victims identified were, actually. I discovered that today," Talia said.

"Do we know if they were involved in the same organizations?" Herne asked.

She shook her head. "There are dozens of groups around like that, and the information isn't required for your work resume or anything of the sort."

"Well, it's something to go on, at least. Talia, tomorrow would you do your best to cross-reference the names of all the paranormal groups with our victims and see if any of them overlap in the same group?" Herne checked something off his list. "The other families didn't give us much to go on, either, though they weren't nearly so objectionable."

"I can do that," she said.

Yutani frowned. "If the pattern holds true, the next victim should surface tomorrow night. So we have one day before another murder takes place."

"Unless something breaks the pattern, but I'm not holding out hope." Herne glanced up at the clock. "It's a quarter after six. Time to call it a day. See you all bright and early tomorrow morning at eight."

"You were going to have my car and things here?" Angel asked.

Herne slapped his forehead. "Damn it, I knew I was forgetting something. All right, Viktor and I will take care of things tonight. I promise, your car will be here tomorrow morning."

"Great. I really could use it." Angel stopped as her phone rang. She pulled it out, frowning as she looked at the Caller ID. "It's my landlord." She answered, speaking in low tones before she let out a loud yelp.

"What? You've got to be kidding me! No... No, he wasn't home." She paused, then said, "To the ground? Why didn't you call me earlier?" A moment later she let out a long, shuddering breath. "No, I understand. I'm away from home right now so I can't make it over there. I'll talk to the police." As she hung up, she started to shake.

"What's wrong?" I took a step toward her.

Angel sank down into a chair again. "My house... It burned to the ground this afternoon. And my car was trashed. Everything I own is gone. The landlord just called me. He's hopping mad, wanted to know what the hell I was doing. At least he calmed down when I told him I was away from home." She looked up at Herne. "If DJ and I had been there..."

"Viktor and I'll go over there right now, but I guarantee you this has a Light Fae signature on it. Retaliation for their men, probably planned out before your name filtered through as being on the protected list. We'll look for anything that can be salvaged. In the meantime, you and Ember be careful. Word needs to circulate that you're under our protection."

As Angel and I left, Viktor escorted us to my car, checking it over before he allowed us to get in. He leaned in at the driver's window, and I rolled it down.

"If you need me, for anything at all, just call. Herne, too. We'll watch out for you girls until this is all settled."

And with that, he headed back toward his car and I turned on the ignition, easing out of the parking garage. As we headed home, all I could think about was how our lives had changed within the past twenty-four hours. And if it had changed this much in so little time, what would it be like within a couple more months?

ANGEL GLANCED IN my cupboard, shaking her head. "Do you realize the only food we have here is the food that we brought from my place? Don't you ever eat, woman?"

"I told you, I don't cook. I can make boxed macaroni and cheese, I can open a can, and I'm pretty good with frozen dinners. Sandwiches are my forte. But you know as well as I do that I've never been good in the kitchen." As a matter of fact, I hated to cook.

Loved to eat, hated to cook. They'd write that in my obituary.

"I'm surprised you managed to get this far living on what you do. What do you want for dinner? We have some ground beef, cheese, chips. I can make either patty melts or we can have nachos."

"Nachos sound fine with me. You know I'm not that picky. As long as I get my caffeine, whatever food you put in front of me I usually eat." I pulled out my laptop, firing it up on the table so I could talk to her while I was doing my research. The cat began winding around the keyboard until I gave him a good petting and set him down on the floor.

"What are you looking up?" She pulled out a pan and a spatula.

"Ghost hunting groups in the area." Even though Talia was going to be doing some research, the connection had piqued my interest. I just wanted to see how many groups were out there.

"You should leave the office at the office," Angel said, but she didn't sound all that convincing. "Remember, no investigating without permission."

"Don't *you* talk. I know you're thinking about her too. The girl with the pendant. Besides, I'm just looking up stuff on the internet. I'm not talking to anybody." I glanced over at her, where she had started chopping tomatoes and peppers.

Angel set down the knife. "Yeah, I am. I just can't get the fear and pain out of my head. Whatever was after her is terrifyingly huge. I'm not sure if I mean in stature, but big and powerful and violent. And it's so hungry, and everybody looks like food." Angel leaned against the counter, staring at her knife. "Everything I own is gone, Ember. My brother, my home, my car, my things... It's as though my entire life has been ripped away and I feel like I'm in freefall." The bravado of the day vanished and she burst into tears, leaning over to rest her elbows on the counter as she cried into the pile of tomatoes.

I pushed back the laptop, uncertain of what to say. We had always been there for each other. When my mother and father were killed, Angel and Mama J. kept me going. They had been my anchors and rocks. Now, Angel was the one who was adrift. DJ might still be alive, but he wasn't around. And though Angel didn't own anything worth a great deal, what she did have represented home to her and a connection to a mother who had cherished and valued her.

I wrapped my arms around her shaking shoulders. There wasn't anything I could say to make it better, but I could feed her my strength, remind her that I would always be at her side.

After a few moments, the tears slowed and she let out a long sigh. I handed her a tissue, and then another, and she wiped her eyes and blew her nose. Then, washing her hands, she turned back to the vegetables.

"Thanks. I just needed..." Her voice drifted off as she stared at the cutting board.

"I know. I understand."

"I hope you don't mind a little extra salt in the food." She attempted a smile, and I laughed.

"You know me, the saltier the better. Maybe Herne and Viktor will find something left." I wasn't one for holding out false hope, but right now, she needed something to cling to.

"Maybe they will. Anyway, at least I've got a job now that I like. That's something. And DJ—I meant it when I said he'd be better off where he's at. He'll have a good role model. Cooper had such an even, steady energy. I hope to get to know him better. I don't want to intrude on his life, but I'd like to learn more about the person who's taking care of my brother."

She began chopping vegetables again and, following her lead, I began rinsing the dishes as she finished using them.

I was setting the table when the doorbell rang. As I glanced out the peephole, I saw Herne standing there, holding a large bag. I opened the door.

"I told Viktor to go home, but I thought I'd bring these things over now. There wasn't much left, I'm afraid, but they should make Angel feel better." He paused, staring down into my eyes. "You two have a friendship that I envy. I have a lot of friends, but I don't have anyone I can call my best friend."

Taken aback by his admission, I sought for words. "I think sometimes the word 'friend' is overused. I don't have many friends, but the few that I do have, I cherish."

Standing so near him made me weak-kneed. He smelled like cinnamon and honey, smoke and musk, all yummy things rolled together. His hair flowed down his shoulders, out of the braid he had worn it in this morning. I noticed how broad his shoulders were, and how straight, and his jaw was firm but he held it soft, as though he didn't need to prove anything to anybody.

Suddenly realizing that I had been standing there staring at him, I stuttered, reaching for the bag. "I can take this, unless you want to come in and tell her what you saw. Maybe that would be good." The rush of words sprayed out of my mouth, like a garden hose gone wild.

"That would be nice, but you're standing in the way." He moved closer, staring down at me with a questioning look in his eyes. "Ember?"

"Yes?" I could barely breathe.

Angel peeked around the corner. "Who is it?"

Feeling like an idiot, I flushed and took a step back.

Herne blinked, looking startled. "Just me. I

come bearing gifts. I hope that they help. I know you suffered a great loss." He set the bag on the coffee table in the living room.

"I'm just finishing up dinner. Would you like to stay and eat with us? There's enough."

I tried to flash her the message of *Don't ask him don't ask him*, but apparently she was ignoring me.

"Don't mind if I do. I'm pretty hungry, and we never did get the pizza at work."

As he settled onto the sofa, I gave Angel another look, this one saying, *I'm going to kill you later*. Wrinkling her nose at me, she smiled and motioned for me to join her.

"Why don't you give me a hand in the kitchen, Ember?" As she headed back into the kitchen, I followed, swearing that I'd get even with her later.

Chapter 9

THE NACHOS WERE good, as usual. One thing Angel had inherited from her mother was the ability to work a stove. Mama J. had been an incredible cook, and she had made the best pie in the world. Everybody had come to her diner, first out of hunger, then the food kept them coming back. During dinner, Angel kept looking over at the bag that Herne had brought, and I could see that her thoughts were focused on whatever lay within.

"Are you sure you don't want to open it now? We can eat afterward."

I was over my snit about her inviting Herne to stay. It felt comforting to have him there, actually, once I got my hormones under control. I was amazed that Angel didn't have the same reaction to him that I did. A lot of times we tended to gravitate toward the same type of men. It hadn't proved an issue, however, given Angel only dated men who were taller than she was. I was short enough that it was never a problem.

"I'm almost afraid to," she said. "When I think about everything that went up in flames, it breaks my heart. It's like, there's this hope that maybe something survived—my photos or DJ's baby blanket, or something important. If I look, and they aren't there, then I know they're gone forever."

I could understand her fear. Sometimes it was easier to hold onto the hope of what *might be*, rather than face the reality of what *was*.

I glanced over at Herne. He had a sober look on his face, as he set down his plate. He had practically licked it clean, and now he wiped his hands on his napkin.

"If you want, I can open it for you, and Ember and I can bring out what survived. It might be easier to watch us unpack it." He stood up, motioning for me to join him.

Angel nodded, biting her lip. She was holding her stomach as we walked over to the bag. She looked like she might throw up. I nodded for Herne to move out of the way as I sat cross-legged on the floor beside the bag. It would be easier for her to watch me unpack it than a stranger.

"Ready?" I asked.

She nodded.

I slowly opened the large garbage sack. As I peeked inside, the scent of soot and ash blew up in my face. My nose tingled and I coughed. I rolled the plastic down, gingerly reaching in to pull out the first object I could find. As I lifted it out of the bag, a fine layer of ash covered everything, falling to the floor as I shook it off.

"The carpet—" Angel began.

"That's what vacuums and carpet shampooers are for." My hands black from the soot, I realized that I was holding a photo album. "Look! Pictures!"

Angel had squeezed her eyes tight and now they flew open. I motioned for Herne to hand me the paper towels, and I wiped the cover of the photo album off, cleaning it as best as I could. I handed it to Angel and she laid it on her lap, opening the cover. She gave a cry of relief.

"They're intact. Mama J. had three photo albums, and this is the one that has a lot of DJ's baby pictures in it. Thank you, thank you so much for finding this." She looked over at Herne, tears in her eyes.

"I just hope I found other things of value as well. I'm so glad that I was able to sift through the rubble. The cops didn't like it, but I told them to back off."

"You're a good man," I said under my breath. But he caught my words and flashed me a genuine smile.

I dug deeper into the contents of the bag. Another photo album containing pictures of Angel when she was young, and of Mama J. and her relatives, had survived the fire. Two rather ratty stuffed animals—both bears—and a few outfits had also made it through. There were also some pots and pans, and about thirty books that had somehow escaped the flames, along with Angel's jewelry box, which held her mother's wedding ring and her grandma's necklace.

"I wish we could have found more, but everything was pretty much burnt to the ground. The entire house is gone. I talked to the landlord while I was there and he said that he's just grateful you and your brother weren't at home. There was a smell of gas in the air, and I think it's likely the fire marshal will blame a gas leak for the fire. But don't believe it," Herne said. "I'm pretty sure the Light Fae were up to no good."

"What will they do when they realize they didn't kill her and her brother? It'll come out that they survived."

"By then, word will have filtered through that Angel and her brother are under our protection, so it should be all right. But we need to keep DJ safe and out of the way, just in case."

"If you'll excuse me, I'm going to take these things into my room. I'll be back in a few minutes. There's dessert if you want—I found some more cookies in Ember's cupboard."

As she dragged the bag into the guest room, I let out a long breath. Grateful that Herne and Viktor had managed to find enough of her sentimental belongings to make a real difference, I dropped onto the sofa, leaning back against the seat as I closed my eyes. A moment later I felt someone next to me and when I opened my eyes, Herne was sitting there, curled up beside me, staring at me. I slowly blinked, and once again, felt my breath quicken.

"You and Angel are tighter than sisters, aren't you?" His voice was soft, and he was too close for comfort, but I didn't want to scoot away.

"Angel and I have been soul mates since we were kids. I think we've been around several times on the wheel before."

"Sometimes, you just know when you've lived lifetimes together." He reached out slowly and pushed my hair back away from my face. "I hope that you enjoy working with us. If you ever need anything, just say so. I'll do my best to help out. I know this is a difficult transition, but I'm glad that I'm part of it."

I could barely breathe. The feel of his fingers on my face sent ripples through my body, quickening my pulse. I wanted his hand to drop down, to trace along my breasts, new boss and stranger or not. But it felt like I knew him from somewhere, like our energies meshed together in a way that was familiar and soothing. His lips bowed with a gentle sway, making me want to lean in and press my own lips to them. But I caught myself before I could blunder, and—shaking—straightened.

"I'll remember that." I felt like my words were hanging in midair, but then Angel returned and I abruptly pulled away. I pushed myself to my feet, almost tripping. Angel flashed me a knowing grin, but I looked away, not wanting to display my emotions on my face.

"I suppose I'd better go," Herne said. He stood and put on his leather jacket, zipping it up against the rain. "See you both at eight tomorrow morning."

As he headed for the door, he caught my gaze and held it for a moment. I stared back at him.

There was so much going on unspoken between us, but I didn't want to assume anything, and so I just showed him to the door, giving him a little wave as he headed toward the elevator. Shutting the door behind me, I leaned against it, letting out a soft groan.

"You like him," Angel said, a wide grin on her face. "Don't try to wiggle out of it. There's something between the two of you. I can feel it from a mile away."

I wanted to believe her, but the fear was still there. While I doubted that Herne would end up dead like my other boyfriends, there was enough uncertainty that I was afraid to chance it. And there was still the fact that he was my boss, and also the son of a god.

"Don't even start," I said. "Did you have a chance to unpack?"

"Yeah, I'll clean it all off later." She crossed to the kitchen, holding up the box of cookies. "How about I make you an espresso, and we watch some TV? I need to unwind, and I think you need to cool off."

I couldn't argue with her there, so for the next hour we watched a documentary on penguins in the Arctic. But all the while, I could still feel his fingers tracing my face, and the fire that they had left behind.

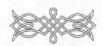

WHILE ANGEL WENT through her things,

I returned to my search. I had jotted down the names of some of the parapsychology groups that I knew our four victims had belonged to. As I began searching through the websites, looking for anything that might stand out to me, I began to notice a common theme. Each of the groups met at least once a month, and had at least three or four field trips per year. Several of them had member lists posted on their sites, and I was able to find the names of our victims included in them. While not every victim belonged to every group, there was some overlap, so at least some of our victims must have known each other.

"Find anything?" Angel asked as she returned from the guestroom. I had a daybed in there, and I had moved some of my weapons and gear out of the way for her.

"I think so," I said. "There's something here and I can't quite seem to put my finger on it. But I know there's some connection. I think at least a couple of our victims had to know each other. At least a cursory acquaintance. Wait a minute." I paused. I leaned forward, staring at the screen. And then I realized what looked so familiar. "*Here.* I've seen this on several of the groups I looked up." I pointed to a picture on one of the field trip pages. "This group, the Faustians, recently took a field trip to look over the Castle Hall area. At Under-Lake." I glanced up at Angel. "I think..."

I rapidly switched between tabs, searching on the various websites.

"What?" Angel sat down beside me, craning her neck to see the screen.

"Four of these groups recently took a field trip to Castle Hall." I looked at her, my mouth dry. "Besides the fact that DJ overheard the Light Fae there...the fact that several of our victims probably visited the area recently seems like there's got to be some connection. Either that, or it's a massive coincidence."

"I don't believe in coincidence," Angel said.

"I know you don't. I do, but this seems too co-incidental to be a fluke. Do you think I should call Herne?"

"I think you just want to hear his voice. Maybe you should wait till tomorrow." Angel gave me a long look. "You need to walk softly around him, Ember. There's so much energy between the two of you that it could spontaneously combust. Find out a little more about him first." She reached out to pat my hand. "I want you to be happy. I want you to find the right guy. I *don't* want you to get hurt."

"And you think that I will, if I go for it with him?" It wasn't a rhetorical question. I trusted Angel's instincts.

"I don't get a feeling on that either way. I just know there's more to him than meets the eye. They brought you into the agency for more reasons than just because of me. I think you need to find out what those reasons are before you jump into any-thing else." With a yawn, Angel stood. "If you don't mind, I'd like to take a shower and go to sleep. It's been a long past couple of days." She paused, and with a sad voice, added, "I miss DJ. I miss that little guy so much."

"I know you do. And I wish things could be other

than what they are. But like you said, there's so much on the line right now, for both of us. Go take a shower and go to bed. We both need sleep."

As Angel headed into the bathroom, I crossed to my own room. I was too tired to do anything but fall under the covers and sleep. But my dreams were filled with screaming victims, and dark shadows chasing them, and at one point I turned around and felt Herne's eyes on me, watching me closely, like a hawk. And then he turned into the silver stag and dashed through the woods, and I found myself alone again with a growing shadow threatening to gobble me up.

COME MORNING, ANGEL had toast and eggs ready. I fed Mr. Rumblebutt, then made my latte, and fixed her a cup of tea. We gobbled down our breakfasts, and carrying our travel mugs, headed for my car.

"I need to buy a new car as soon as I can," Angel said. "I got a call this morning while you were showering. Sure enough, they're chalking up the fire to a gas leak. They say that it managed to travel to my car as well, because they said my car was in the garage. But I didn't leave my car in the garage. I didn't tell them that, though, given what Herne said would happen."

"Did you have renter's insurance?"

She shook her head. "Are you kidding? Who can afford that? But I did have car insurance, and while it won't pay for a new car, I should be able to get a decent clunker that will last for a while."

"With your new job and pay rate, you should be able to get a loan for a new one." I still couldn't get over the fact that we were both making so much more money than we had ever seen in our lives.

"I suppose so. It seems like we have job security. Maybe I'll go talk to the bank later today."

The city streets were slick with rain as it sputtered out of the heavens. It was a gloomy day and I longed for a sun break, just a few days of balmy weather. The wind picked up at that moment, and I shivered as the car rocked. I'd hate to be dealing with buses right now.

"Well, here we are," I said, pulling into the parking garage. "Are you ready for the day?"

Angel nodded. "We don't have much choice, so we might as well make the best of it. And it could be worse. I could still be at my old job."

"Yeah, I suppose you're right about that."

WE FOUND OUT that every morning at the Wild Hunt Agency, we started the day with a brief meeting to bring everybody up to speed. Talia was there, carrying a box of doughnuts. Yutani had a sheaf of papers in his hand, and he looked like he'd been up all night. Viktor was entirely too bright and perky for eight in the morning, and he gave me a two-fingered salute as we entered the room.

Herne was the last one to straggle in. He was

talking on his cell phone. Talia had made coffee, and I thought about refilling my cup, but the fact that I'd already had four shots of espresso made me hesitate.

Angel gave me a sardonic look. "You know you want to. Go ahead. It never seems to affect you, anyway."

"That's because I live on the stuff. I think the mix of the Dark and Light Fae scrambled some of my brain cells." I was joking, kind of. There weren't enough of us half-breeds between the two Fae courts to do any studies on.

"Excuse me," Herne said, waving for us to be quiet. "I'm sorry, I couldn't hear you. My staff was joking around." He flashed us a warning look, then turned away. "I know what you said. There's not much I can do about it." He paused, then let out a huff of irritation. "I don't think you're going to find it of much use now, but go ahead and knock yourself out. Call me when you have an answer." He stared at us for a moment, then slipped the phone in his pocket.

"Anything the matter, boss?" Talia put a doughnut on the plate and shoved it his way.

Pulling the plate in front of him, he picked up the cream-filled bun and took a big bite out of it. A moment later, he wiped his mouth on a napkin.

"Yeah, there's plenty the matter. Just a run-in with Névé's court. You know how it goes." He turned a long look to Angel and me. "They've got you on the rosters now. They weren't happy about it, either. Apparently you really did interfere with their plans by killing those two Light Fae. And apparently I interfered with their plans by making sure you were taken on here."

"So they're pissed?"

"Mightily. Anyway, they have no choice but to agree to our terms. Morgana made it clear to them. And yes, before you ask, they petitioned her about it. She not only made it clear that they have to abide by rules we already have set up, but that you are under *her* protection as well."

My stomach lurched. That they had gone all the way to the goddess to try and get permission to retaliate left me feeling rather weak-kneed. And then to know that a goddess was taking a personal interest in me was almost just as disconcerting.

"I guess they take things seriously." Thoughts of my parents flashed through my head again. "I had a thought last night. I'm not sure if now is the right time to mention it, but I did a little research on my own."

"You didn't go out anywhere by yourself, I hope?"

"Not at all." I tossed a printout on the table that I had made of several of the ghost hunting sites agendas. "I remember what you said about that. No, it occurred to me that there might be some connection between some of the activities on the various paranormal groups. So I took a look at their recent field trips. At least four of them recently visited the Castle Hall area of UnderLake."

Herne glanced over at Talia. "Did you notice this connection?"

She shook her head. "No, but I wasn't finished with my research either. What about you, Yutani?"

Yutani cleared his throat. "I've been running algorithms, trying to find connections between the victims and anything that might be part of their lives. I did connect all of the victims that have been identified with paranormal groups. And I also made a printout of the connections I found between the groups. There's probably something about Castle Hall in some of them, but I haven't had the time to go through it yet. That's what I was planning on doing this morning."

He brought out twelve printouts, and placed them on the table. "Here are spreadsheets of the different victims and the groups they belonged to. We could start combing through them, or I can run a query asking about Castle Hall, now that I've got all of this information gathered together. That would probably be a lot quicker."

"Go ahead. Meanwhile, Talia? What else have you found out?"

Yutani gathered up his papers and left the room. I caved and poured myself a cup of coffee, stirring sugar and cream into it.

Talia polished off a maple bar, licking her fingers. "I did a little digging into bank accounts. As far as I can tell, there doesn't seem to be much of a connection that way. Some of the victims were middle class, some were poor. None were rich, and none belonged to influential families."

Herne turned to Angel. "How are you finding your desk? Do you need anything? Are the ergonomics all right?"

"Everything's fine, although the chair could use replacing. If you don't mind, I'd like to do some reorganization of the filing cabinets. Whoever had the job before me did an adequate job, but I think there are more efficient ways to organize all of the files."

Herne slowly nodded. "I don't have a problem with that, but remember that all the files are confidential, and any that are filed in blue folders need to stay in a locked drawer. As for a chair, find one you like and put in a requisition slip with me. Try to keep it under $400 if you can, but if you need to go above that, just talk to me and we'll work it out."

Angel gave him a nod, jotting down notes on her pad. I had at least remembered my notepad and pen today.

Just then, the office phone rang twice. It stopped then rang three more times. Talia glanced at Herne, then walked over to the phone on the counter and answered it.

"I forgot to tell you both, that's the emergency code. If it rings twice, then stops for a moment, then rings three more times, answer. It will either be my father, Morgana, or one of their representatives," Herne said.

I blinked. "Cernunnos and Morgana use a phone?" Somehow, I hadn't counted on the gods being part of the tech generation.

"If you live in this world, you kind of need to. Whether you're a god or not." Herne glanced at Talia as she handed him the phone and mouthed "Morgana."

"Herne here." He listened for a moment, then let out a long sigh. "Yeah, I've got it. Hold on."

He pulled out his cell phone, and glanced at the screen. "Yeah, the text came through. We'll get right on it." He paused, then added, "*Yes, Mother*. I said we'll get right on it." As he handed the phone back to Talia, who replaced it back in the cradle, the tension in the room seemed to rise.

"What's up, boss?" Viktor asked.

"Wait till Yutani comes back, please. Can somebody get me a cup of coffee, three sugars, and about two spoons of cream?" Herne just stared at the screen of his cell phone, shaking his head.

I glanced at Angel, who gave me a little shrug. I picked up a chocolate-covered cake doughnut and bit into it, blinking as I realized they were from Ray's shop.

Talia must have noticed my surprise. "Good, aren't they?"

"Yeah," I murmured. "I know all about these doughnuts, and the guy who makes them."

Talia looked like she was about to say something, but stopped when Herne shook his head at her. I wondered what was going on, but didn't feel comfortable asking. At that moment Yutani came back through the door, clutching a whole bunch more printouts. He pulled out a chair and slid into it.

"Well, you're right. Every single victim—of the ones identified—belonged to a group, different ones, that recently visited the Castle Hall area of UnderLake. And every victim seems to have visited the park the day they disappeared." He tossed the papers on the table and leaned back.

"How long did we figure we have between victims?"

Viktor consulted his notes. "Another day, at least. It looks like they're down to one every two days."

Herne sighed. "The pattern has escalated. There was another murder yesterday afternoon, but they didn't find the victim until this morning. Same MO. Victim mutilated to pieces. Morgana just let me know."

"How does she know? I thought the gods weren't omnipotent?" I wasn't quite clear on how much the gods actually *did* know.

"She has spies all throughout the police department. You'd be surprised how thorough Cernunnos and Morgana's network is. One of her informants notified her as soon as they found the victim this morning." Herne stared at me. "You don't think my father and mother would leave this all to chance, do you? They are trying to prevent an all-out war down here, so they've got to have people on the inside."

It made sense when I thought about it. I just hadn't expected it for some reason. Then the reality of what he had said hit home.

"A thirteenth victim? That's a lot of dead bodies. What the hell are they doing?"

"I don't know, but with regards to the rumors that the vampires are behind the killings, what better way to deflect suspicion off yourself by finding a scapegoat?" Herne looked puzzled.

"Do you think one of the Dark Fae is a serial killer? That he's gone off the deep end and his people are trying to protect them?" Angel asked.

He considered her question for a moment. "Actually, I don't. If that were the case, they'd take him out. Neither side wants the sort of chaos a serial killer brings into play. No, there's something else going on. I'm just not sure what."

I raised my hand.

Talia laughed. "You're not in school, honey. If you have something to say, just come out and say it. We're all part of this agency, and even though you're new, that doesn't mean that you can't have an opinion."

I flashed her a grateful grin. "Thanks. I just wanted to remind you all that the shadow that Angel felt when she was inspecting the pendant seemed to be some sort of a monster. Could the Dark Fae be summoning up some sort of demon?"

Herne gave me a thoughtful look. "That's not out of the question. Both sides have made deals with not only the sub-Fae, but their underlings. We can definitely investigate that angle."

"So who's the new victim?" Yutani asked.

"I sure don't want to tell you this," Herne said, giving Angel a sideways glance. "Hang tight. This time, it was a fourteen-year-old boy. Apparently, neither sex nor age are factors when it comes to victims."

I closed my eyes, trying not to think about the age of the boy. There was nothing I could do for now, except help to find his killer. "Where was he found?"

"Yeah, was it in Seward Park?" Viktor asked. "And was he human or a shifter?"

"Human." Herne let out a long sigh. He consulted the text on his phone. "And he was actually found on the Eastside."

"In the UnderLake District?" I began to jot down notes on what he was telling us. I glanced over at Angel. She had a sick look on her face. I wanted to comfort her, to remind her that DJ was safe, but this wasn't the time or place.

"No, actually he was found on Mercer Island." Herne held up his hand. "Before you mention it, I know perfectly well that Mercer Island is directly across from Seward Park. We seem to have a trail of bodies leading from the docks to the catacombs, to Seward Park, and now Mercer Island. Heading east."

"If the murders are now one day apart, that means there'll be another one today, probably found tomorrow." I swallowed hard. Whatever we were facing seem to have an insatiable appetite. But what was it feeding on? Oh, there had been bite marks on the victims, and chunks of flesh taken out of a few, but not enough to feed a big hungry monster.

"So what's next?" Viktor asked, looking as queasy as I felt.

"You, I, and Ember will go examine the murder site. Or rather, the dumpsite. We still don't know where all the victims were murdered. Talia, get on the phone to those organizations and ask for full member rosters. See if our newest victim was a member. Yutani, run all the names through whatever computations you do, see if there are any connections between any of the other members that might link them to the murder victims we already have. Angel, you help Yutani and Talia however they need."

"Of course," she said, still holding her stomach. "What do I do if somebody comes in about a case? Do you even take cases that aren't related to the war between the Fae? I'm not clear on that."

Herne stood up, shrugging into his jacket. "Yes, we do, between cases that my father and mother send to us. And if anybody comes in wanting information, take their name and number, and set up an appointment for Wednesday or Friday afternoon. That's when I offer consultations for other cases. From two until six P.M." He motioned to Viktor and me. "Get your coats and let's get a move on. We'll take my car."

As we hurried out of the office, I realized that I actually cared about what we were doing. I cared about the murder victims. It'd been a long time since I was this interested in my work, and that was a good feeling, even though it came at the expense of others.

Chapter 10

HERNE DROVE A black Ford Expedition, and he motioned for me to get in the front seat. Viktor scrambled in the back, looking like he didn't care one way or the other. As we buckled up, Herne gassed the SUV and we took off out of the parking garage. He drove a little too fast for my comfort, but he was a good driver, and it didn't surprise me that he drove a car as big as a house.

"How are we going to explain showing up at the murder site?" I asked. "Won't the police get suspicious?"

"First, the police know all about my agency. Second, they've already been there and gone. If we encounter anybody, we walk softly and maintain composure. They won't carry on an investigation once they realize this is connected to the other murders, so they're not going to interfere with us."

"Remember," Viktor said from the backseat, "the

Light and Dark Fae courts are chaotic, and they'll push the boundaries until they get smacked. I know that your bloodline comes from both courts, and I don't mean any disrespect, but it's like dealing with unruly children who have their fingers poised over a weapon that could annihilate part of the country."

"You don't offend me," I said. "Remember, my parents were killed by the Fae because they wanted to be together. From early on, the other Fae children let me know I didn't belong to either side. If it wasn't for Angel, I would have a rap sheet a mile long. She helped me steer clear of that. And her mother—Mama J.—helped keep me sane when my parents were killed. I know they sent the sub-Fae to do the job. Why get their own hands dirty when they can pay off a mercenary?" I knew I sounded bitter, but I had damn good reason to.

"When my father and mother gave me the dossier on you, there was a lot of information in there. But I have to hand it to you, you've managed to stay off the radar a lot better than most people," Herne said softly.

I nodded, staring out the window. We were on the I-90 bridge already. Luckily, the morning rush hour had died down, and while it wasn't smooth going, we weren't in stop-and-go traffic, either.

"Yeah, I found them. I came home from school and when I saw the door ajar, I thought maybe my mother was cooking and wanted to cool off the kitchen. I don't know why I thought that, it just made sense in my head. I pushed open the door and bounced into the house, hoping for cookies.

What I found was my mother splayed out on the ground, butchered."

"Cripes almighty," Viktor said, sucking in a deep breath.

"I remember screaming so hard that I lost my voice. I ran into the living room only to find my father facedown on the carpet, a knife in his back. I don't remember much else after that, just that the cops came, and said it had been a home invasion. They didn't look very hard, and I saw one of them giving me a funny look, almost like he was surprised I was standing there."

"He was probably an agent for either TirNaNog or Navane." Herne sounded angry, and a cloudy look had filled his eyes.

"Probably. I just...I want to find out who did it."

I didn't like talking about my parents. It made me uncomfortable. But Herne and Viktor already knew what had happened, considering they had a dossier on me, and for once it felt good to be able to tell things from my side.

"When we get a chance, we'll look into the case," Herne said. "It's been a long time, and if they hired sub-Fae, it will be a lot harder. But we can try."

I glanced at him, suddenly grateful. While I doubted we'd ever find out the truth, just the fact that he had offered warmed my heart.

"Thank you," I murmured. "Nobody's ever offered to help before."

Viktor cleared his throat. I glanced at him in the rearview mirror area and saw him wiping his eyes. He averted his gaze when he saw me staring at him, and looked out the window.

"I know it was hard for Angel to hear about the boy. He's only four years older than DJ." Herne let out a sigh. "I hate kid killers. Just as much as I hate animal killers. It's one thing to hunt and use the food, it's another to torture or kill for trophies."

"Has anybody ever tried to shoot you when you were in stag form?" It still boggled my mind that he could turn into a silver stag. The memory of how beautiful he had been had stayed in my mind, eliminating any doubt that Herne was of divine blood.

"Yes, once or twice. It would be difficult to hit me, though. I'm not exactly in phase with this world when I'm in stag form. I want to reassure you, just in case Angel asks, DJ is in really good hands. Cooper is probably one of the best among the shifter clans. He'll take good care of the boy and give him a good upbringing. I'll make certain that Angel gets a chance to see her brother several times a year. But it wouldn't be safe for her to know exactly where he is. While most of the Fae respect the covenants that protect us, there are a few we cannot trust to abide by the law of the Fae courts."

"I think she understands. And the murdered boy will probably cement that in her mind." I leaned back in my seat, staring out the window as I fell silent.

As we passed over the water, the floating bridge seemed to go on forever. In reality, it was less than a mile long, but it was one of the largest floating bridges in the world, and the pull of the water rose up from the lake, tugging at me. I closed my eyes, drifting in the energy of the waves, letting myself flow as the wind whipped them into foamy caps.

We were midway across the bridge when I felt one of the water elementals rear up, letting out a loud roar of anger. I started straight up, catching my breath.

What's wrong?" Herne asked, giving me a quick glance.

"I'm not sure, but the water elementals are angry today. I just felt one let loose with a roar that shook my insides. I'll see what I can find out. When we're over the bridge, if you could pull off somewhere near the lake, it would help." I glanced back at Viktor. "Can you bring up a maps app and see if there's a park right near the lake?"

Viktor was on it like white on rice. A few seconds later he said, "Yeah, Slater Park. The minute we hit Mercer Island, take the first exit, then turn right on Mercer Way, then right again on Twenty-eighth Street. After that, hang a left on Sixtieth, and we'll be there in a block."

At that moment, we passed off the main part of the bridge onto Mercer Island. Herne quickly shifted into the right lane, following Viktor's directions. Within less than five minutes, we were pulling into Slater Park.

A small park, there were only room for a few cars, but we managed to find a parking space. We walked down the narrow path to the edge of the lake. Three stone steps took us to the edge of the water proper, and to our right was a long driftwood log to sit on.

The park was small, probably the size of three

lots, but it was a pretty place, with trees and benches, and geese wandering around by the water's edge. I could see kayakers out on the lake, and I wondered how they were doing amid the choppy waves. To the right, a ways down the shore past several houses, was a small mooring for boats, and a pier on which people could walk out to sit and watch the water, or to fish.

It would be easy for me to tune into the water elementals here. I knelt in the wet gravel and sand by the edge of the lake, reaching out to immerse my hand in the water. Herne and Viktor sat on the driftwood log, waiting for me.

I closed my eyes, inhaling the fresh chill air, grateful that the rain had died away. As the icy water splashed across my fingers, once again, I felt the agitation of the water elementals who lived in the lake. I tried to tune into them, forming a question in my mind, trying to shape it into emotion rather than words. I zeroed in on their anger, expressing curiosity, essentially asking them what was wrong.

One of the elementals—I believe it was the same one I had felt from the car—let out another roar and then came closer. I could feel it in the water. It rose from the waves, a frothy form frozen in spray, peeking from below the surface at me. As a tendril reached out through the waves to lap at my fingers, I felt it accept our common bond. A feeling of sadness and anger rushed over me. Anger at being used for something dark and dangerous, anger that something had crossed through it on the bottom of the lake, leaving a trail of sludge and slime behind.

It felt like the water had been tainted where this creature had crossed, and the elementals were in an uproar about it. I tried to get the elemental to form an image of the creature, and a dark shadow rose up in my mind, the picture of a massive fox filling my thoughts. But it was no fox like I had ever seen. It was cloaked in shadow and flame, with multiple tails and teeth that were needle-sharp and gleaming like diamonds. Its hunger was insatiable. The energy hit me like a ton of bricks, knocking me back on my butt, dazed. I groaned, shaking my head as Herne ran over to help me up.

"Are you all right?" He looked worried.

"Yeah, I'm all right. I just got blasted with an image that I don't quite understand. But the water elementals out there in the lake are furious. Something walked through the water, crossing across the lake, I guess on the bottom. Something that feels tainted and evil, and apparently it left a wake of that energy behind it. I'm pretty sure the elementals can clear it, but they're so angry. The wind may be causing the whitecaps, but the water elementals are helping them along. They don't like evil things in their home. And whatever this is, it feels invasive and hungry."

"Did you get a look at it? Were they able to give you a picture?" Herne asked.

I nodded. "Yes, but I have no clue what we're dealing with. It looked like a fox, but it had a number of tails, and teeth that reminded me of sewing needles. They looked like bone, rather than metal. Sound familiar?"

He shook his head. "I have no idea. But we can do some research. Was there anything else?"

I shook my head. "No, just the anger over having their water tainted." Shivering, suddenly feeling exposed, I added, "Can we leave now? I don't think I can get anything else out of them."

Herne nodded. "I appreciate what you were able to find out. Come on, let's get back to the car."

As we headed back to the parking lot, I glanced back over my shoulder. One of the water elementals rose up again, looking like a clear statue atop the water. I realized that only I could only see it, but I raised my hand and waved, and it waved back. A gentle energy washed over me, almost like an apology. I smiled faintly, wishing I could connect with them easier. In my heart, I realized that I loved the water elementals. And I wished my mother was still alive to teach me her heritage. As we climbed into the car, I fastened my seatbelt and locked my doors. The day had grown darker, in more ways than one.

"SO WHERE WAS the body found?" Viktor asked from the backseat.

Herne turned the heat up. "I hope you don't mind, it's a little cold in here."

Neither Viktor nor I objected. I warmed my hands over the welcome blast of heat coming out of the side vents.

"We're not far from where they found the boy,"

Herne said. "We just continue on Mercer Way until we reach Groveland Beach Park. He was found in the park, down near the water."

I pulled out my phone and looked up the park on the maps. "That's directly across from Seward Park. Something crossed through the water that disturbed the elementals. Want to make a bet it was our monster?"

"If so, then we know whatever this is can travel from the Eastside through the water to Seattle proper. Which means it's not stationary. And that's a problem." Herne's brow furrowed, and he shook his head. "Whatever it is, it has to be relatively new to the area. Otherwise, we would have seen victims like this for a long time now. Its hunger seems insatiable."

"Either that, or it just woke up," Viktor said. "There are a number of creatures that are asleep in the depths. Whether it be the depths of the water, or the earth, or even an interdimensional space."

"It might have come in off the astral," I said. "Wherever its origin, we have to find it and send it back, or better yet, defeat it. Trouble is, we have no idea how strong it is, or what its vulnerabilities are."

"Yeah, I thought about that." Herne nodded to a fork in the road ahead. "We turn here, onto Fifty-seventh Street. From there, it's a jog to the left and we pull into the parking lot at Groveland Beach Park."

Mercer Island was a haven to the rich, mostly human, population. The houses were kept in pristine shape, and gated communities were standard.

As we passed through the streets, there seemed to be an odd superficial feel to the place. Oh, it was pretty, but it felt very chrome and glass, almost stark even among all of the trees. The lawns were perfectly manicured, the hedges smooth and even, and nothing stood out of place as unique or different. All in all, it was a cookie-cutter community.

We pulled into the park, which was a little bigger than the one we'd been at before. Herne eased into a parking spot, and we set out on the trail, headed down to the beach.

The trail led through a small stand of trees, opening out onto the shoreline. Across the lake, we could see the hilly knoll of Seward Park, and to the northwest, the more distant shoreline of Seattle. Here, patchy grass offered a place to spread out a blanket for a picnic, and a compacted sand shore looked out into the water, complete with a walkway onto a pier. Ladders dipped into the water for swimmers to hold onto. There was a small bathhouse a few hundred yards away, as well as park benches every few hundred yards.

Near the bathhouse, a man in uniform was waiting. He looked like a cop.

"Don't say anything when we meet him. Let me do the talking," Herne warned us.

Viktor nodded, looking used to this.

We walked over to the man, who was leaning against the blue brick building. He straightened up when he saw us, and gave Herne a slow nod.

"Nice day," Herne said. "Any news today?"

"Yeah. Found it on the body. Check your stash." And with that, the cop cut through the trees to head up the trail.

Herne walked over to the trashcan and pushed back the flap, reaching in to pull out a small plastic bag. He waited until the cop was out of sight, then opened it. Inside, there was what looked like a computer jump drive. Slipping it into his pocket, he motioned to us.

I wanted to ask what had just happened, but Viktor wasn't saying a word, and I decided to keep my mouth shut until I knew it was okay to speak. For all I knew, cops had the park bugged or something.

Once we reached the car, Herne pulled out a mini-computer and powered it up. He plugged in the jump drive and a document appeared, along with a number of files.

"Well, what do have we here?"

"What is it?" I asked craning my neck, trying to see.

"Our informant found this on the body, and it looks like some interesting information here." He glanced up as Viktor leaned forward to look over the backseat. "By the way, our victim's name is Kevin Mason. Was...Kevin. Poor kid. But it looks like he's been doing some snooping around. There's a file labeled 'TirNaNog,' and a file labeled 'UnderLake,' and several others. We need to take this back and have Yutani analyze it. I want to know what this kid got himself into. Unfortunately, I have the feeling whatever it was, also got him killed."

YUTANI POCKETED THE jump drive when Herne handed it to him, a wide grin spreading across his face. "Always happy to help," he said, heading off toward his office.

Angel was wrapped up reading through the office email, and Talia was nowhere to be seen. Viktor excused himself, leaving Herne and me in the reception room.

Herne glanced at me. "Come in my office and have a talk?"

I followed him back to his office, wondering what it would look like. I got a surprise when we entered the room. I had expected form and function, but this was nothing like what I had anticipated.

The room was fairly large, the walls pale sky blue, with a white ceiling. It was filled with plants, all of which looked healthy and lush, and a pair of massive antlers was mounted on the far wall. They were polished to a high sheen. A large case against one wall held a number of weapons behind locked glass doors. I saw at least four handheld cross bows, a regular bow, a number of blades—including a sword—and some various hand-to-hand combat weapons.

To one side sat a mini fridge, and next to it, a table holding a microwave. The desk was walnut, the dark wood shone under the light, and the accompanying leather chair was black. They both sat beneath the antlers. To the right, a cot was made up with two thick pillows and a microfiber blanket. To the left, a pair of wingback chairs sat kitty-corner next to a small end table. In front of the desk was another pair of wingback chairs.

"Nice digs." I looked around, but saw no pictures of any kind other than a couple paintings on the wall that were autumn landscapes.

Herne moved around behind the desk, taking his seat. He motioned to one of the chairs opposite. "Sit down. Do you want something to drink? More coffee, or maybe some juice?"

"Water, if you have it." I wanted more coffee but I knew my body could use some water, and I felt jarred. Maybe it was the interaction of the water elementals, or the knowledge that we were looking into a fourteen-year-old's death. Whatever the case, my nerves felt on edge.

"Flavored or plain? I have lemon and berry flavors." He moved to the small refrigerator.

"Berry is good." I accepted the bottle of water and leaned back in the chair. The leather was so soft it reminded me of a baby's butt. I let out a sigh as I opened the water and swigged it back.

"Feeling overwhelmed?" Herne returned to his seat, bringing his feet up to rest on his desk. I cringed when I saw his boots touched the pristine wood. He must have noticed because he slipped his feet back on the floor and sat up, dusting off the desk.

I shrugged. "I'm not sure. I suppose 'overwhelmed' is a good word for it. So much has happened the past couple of days that I think I'm still in mild shock." I hesitated for a moment.

"What is it? I'd rather you come out and say it than hide any resentment or worry."

"It's not resentment. In fact, I think this is going to be a good gig. It sure beats scrounging up clients on my own, even though I do like working for myself."

I tried to find the right words. Finally, I said, "I think that dealing with this much death is taking a toll on me. I'll adapt, but I'm not used to dealing with murders. The last time I had to face anything so gruesome was when I found my parents. I've killed goblins and the like, but innocent victims, I haven't dealt with very much. Usually the goblins are thieves or they're causing a ruckus. They aren't supposed to be here anyway."

I wondered if he'd think I was weak and reconsider having taken me on. But he just gave me a long, considered look.

"It always takes time to adapt. I'd be worried if you didn't feel some sort of reaction. Angel's having a harder time of it, I can tell. She and I talked earlier on. She's definitely not used to this sort of activity. I suspect the fact that we had to relocate her brother to safer territory is also eating at her. But there's not much we can do about it. I'll arrange for her to talk to him on the phone soon, and that should help ease her concerns."

"I appreciate it. Angel's my blood, even though we don't have an actual family connection. And DJ's a good kid. I guess looking into a teenager's death hit home today. I keep thinking about DJ and how close he came to being killed." I paused. "In the woods, how did you happen to be around when I was tracking DJ?"

Herne leaned forward, resting his elbows on the desk. "I was following you. As I said, we've been watching you for a while now. My mother contacted me and told me to get out there and track you down. I'm not sure how she knew what was going on, but I don't question her. And I certainly don't question my father. I learned the hard way that neither one appreciates it." With a laugh, Herne picked up the stack of papers on his desk and glanced at them. "Angel certainly does her job thoroughly."

I wasn't sure what else to say. I wanted to stay, to talk to him, but I wasn't certain what to talk about. I was feeling extremely awkward, when Herne looked up at me.

"After work today, do you want to grab a burger with me?"

I blinked. I hadn't been expecting that. "Do you mean, with Angel?"

"I was sort of hoping just you and me. You could give her the keys to your car and I can drop you off after we eat. That is, if you're interested."

"I'd love to." My words came out so forcefully that I blushed. I sounded like an overenthusiastic teenager.

Herne just grinned. "I'd love to as well. All right, let's go see what Yutani's found out for us. He is brilliant, you know? The man's IQ is off the charts. And he's not just a computer geek, he's really good at seeing patterns. But he can't spell worth a damn."

As he escorted me out of his office, all I could

think about was that we were going on a date. Herne smelled so damn good when he passed by me that I wanted to just climb up him and lick him like a lollipop. Right then Talia swung around the corner, and the look she gave me made me blush even harder. I knew right then that she had caught my thoughts and all I could hope for was that she would keep them to herself.

Chapter 11

WE GATHERED IN the break room again. Angel brought her notebook, and settled down at the
table. She looked like she was feeling more comfortable, although I detected an aura of sadness in
her eyes. It didn't surprise me, since I think we all
felt the same way.

Yutani was the last to join us, and he was carrying several printouts as well as a laptop. He
opened it up and tapped away at the keyboard
for a moment, pushed it back on the table, then
cleared his throat.

"All right, I've been through his files. There are
a number of them that will take me a while to go
through, but I made a cursory examination of
everything. This kid was *brilliant*. He was also one
hell of a good hacker, and I'm not sure how he was
able to snoop his way into the information that he
did, but he had his finger on the pulse of a lot of

things. If anybody suspected what he knew, it's no wonder he was set up as a target."

"Like what?" Herne frowned. "Honestly, sometimes I wonder how kids make it to adulthood. Especially the smart ones. The dumb ones can rely on luck a lot of times."

"Well, first and probably foremost, he stumbled onto the Dark Fae during a summoning ritual. In fact, he recorded some of it on his phone. I have the video here. I think I know who—what—our killer is." Yutani hit a key on the laptop, then turned it so we could all see the screen.

Splashed across it was the image of a demonic-looking fox, with multiple tails. Its eyes gleamed with a cunning light, and there was something otherworldly about the creature. Other than the fact that it was obviously no ordinary fox. I caught my breath as I realized it was a photograph and not a drawing. And then I realized that was what the water elemental had been trying to show me.

"Is that a picture that he took? That's what crossed through the water." As I stared at it harder, I realized that the fox was standing next to a bench, making it at least as tall as Viktor. The thing was huge.

"I believe it is. It was on his camera roll. The kid took fantastic notes, so I know this is what he saw them summon. He didn't know what it was, but he heard them call it by name. Whoever the head honcho was that summoned it called it 'Kuveo.' " Yutani chewed on his lip for a moment as we studied the picture.

"Did he say where they summoned this creature?" Talia asked.

Yutani nodded. "Yeah. UnderLake Park. He was there with one of his ghost hunter groups, trying to stir up the spirits of Mr. and Mrs. Castle—the couple that disappeared from Castle Hall. He wandered off, sensing there was something going on, and he found a stairway leading to an underground temple or something, where he stumbled across this."

Herne crossed his arms. "Give us the full rundown. Did he know if they saw him? Obviously they must have, given he's dead now. Did he do any research into this creature?"

Yutani scanned through his notes. "It looks like this happened about three weeks ago. Shortly before the murders started. Like most kids, he was very cocky about how stealthy he thought he was, and how he had outwitted them. But I could tell by his notes that he was worried. He had made the connection between the *wild animal murders,* as he called them, and Kuveo. He wasn't sure who to tell, but he said he was thinking about taking the information to the authorities. Obviously, the poor kid didn't know that the Fae pretty much own the cops."

"All right, so he made the connection between Kuveo and the murder victims. Did he by any chance save us some time by researching what this creature is?" It would be logical to assume that Kevin would have done the additional research, but logic didn't always play through. And the boy had only been fourteen.

Herne motioned for Yutani to push the laptop

toward him. As he studied the image, his expression grew studied and somber.

"He was looking for what he could find on it, but hadn't had much success. He also had several other files indicating that he was researching some unsolved cases that seem to be connected with various spooks and haunts throughout the area." Yutani handed us each a packet of papers. "Here are copies of his notes on Kuveo. Mostly, it's a transcription of what he heard during the summoning. I figured maybe you could translate it, Ember. I don't speak whatever language they were talking, and it's not the common Faespeak."

There was a common language the Fae used among themselves, although there were many dialects and two distinct subsets for both Light and Dark. I could speak both to a degree, but as I glanced over the transcript of the ritual, I realized that I didn't have a clue.

"I don't recognize this at all. And I speak both Nuva and Turneth, the Light and Dark variants." The only word I recognized was *Kuveo*, and that was only because Yutani had clued us into it.

Herne turned toward Talia. "You and Yutani start researching Kuveo. We need to know what we're dealing with. I have a feeling there's going to be another murder tonight, but we don't know where it will be so there's nothing we can do to stop it. And obviously, warning the cops isn't going to do any good."

"There's something else," Yutani said. "Kevin made reference several times to the underground tunnels, but I don't think he was talking about the catacombs. He mentioned the tunnels below the lake. Now, I've never heard of any tunnels below Lake Washington, so I did a quick search and found that yes, there are apparently a couple tunnels that were made by goblins some fifty to sixty years ago, deep below the lake. And guess where they run?"

"Between Mercer Island and Seward Park?" I glanced over at him.

He nodded. "Yes, but they also lead up to Under-Lake, beneath the cities on the Eastside. Not only that, but the entire Eastside was once a hotbed for mining, so in addition to that, there are old mine shafts and tunnels all over the place. So this network probably accounts for finding our victims as far over as the docks. Because once the tunnels are on the Seattle side, it would be an easy hookup to the catacombs."

Angel grimaced. "The way the whole area is riddled with fault lines and tunnels, it's a wonder the whole damn place hasn't caved in on itself."

And that gave us a much-needed laugh.

WHILE YUTANI AND Talia did the research on Kuveo, Viktor headed out to talk to some of Herne's informants. Meanwhile, Herne asked me to meet a new client with him.

"Is this another incident concerning the war between the Fae?" I had no idea what percentage of cases he worked on were focused on cleaning up that mess. I hoped not too many, given it seemed to be a pretty bloody business.

"Well, the client is Fae, but it's not concerning an altercation with the other side. I'm not clear what it is yet, but it always helps to have another pair of ears." Herne glanced at the clock. "He'll be here in about forty minutes. Meanwhile, why don't you go read through the transcripts that Yutani gave us. Probably a good idea to comb them for any information we can get."

I looked around. "Should I use the break room?"

Herne rolled his eyes. "I can't believe I haven't assigned you an office yet. My bad. Excuse me, I really didn't mean to neglect that." He motioned for me to follow him down the hall from the break room. "The first door to the left is Yutani and Talia's office. They share the same room because they both are computer savvy and do bulk of our research. The second is empty. The one on the right end is open and better than the other."

I pointed to the door between the break room and the office he had just gestured to. "What about that one? Is that Viktor's office?"

"That's the armory. Viktor doesn't have an office. He's usually out in the field, so he makes do with the break room most of the time."

He opened the door and ushered me in. I glanced around the room. It was cozy, though not so small that I'd feel claustrophobic. The window looked out onto the street, and the hardwood floors were in good condition. A desk sat against one wall, with a standard office chair in front of it. To the left beneath the window was a secondary desk, and on the left wall was a filing cabinet and a bookshelf, as well as an extra chair. All in all, it was almost as big as my living room, which wasn't saying much. But it felt comfortable, and protected.

I walked over to the window and pulled aside the blinds, glancing out. The gloom had lifted for the moment, and I saw a rare glimpse of sun. I opened the curtains and sunlight filled the room, giving it a whole new atmosphere.

"This will be fine." I leaned against the edge of the window, staring up at the sky. "Well, blue sky. We don't see that often this time of year."

Herne joined me, closing his eyes as the sunlight hit his face.

"You're right," he said softly, as he opened his eyes again. We were standing inches apart, and he was staring down into my face. His breath washed over me like silk.

I froze, unable to move or to think, caught up in the energy that seemed to wrap around us every time we were within arm's reach of each other. I wanted to know what it felt like to have him wrap his arms around me, but I was afraid to move. I was afraid I was misreading his signals, and part of me was afraid that I *wasn't* misreading him.

"What are you thinking?" His voice was soft.

I shivered, shaking my head. "I don't seem to be thinking clearly at all."

Just then, Yutani peeked around the door. "I found something you might want to see." He paused, glancing at the two of us. "Am I interrupting?"

Herne let out a soft sigh, then shook his head.

"No, I was just getting Ember settled in her new office." And with that, he broke away, clearing his throat. "What did you find?"

"It has nothing to do with this case, but it's an answer to something we were looking at a week ago. The Harstein affair?"

Herne's expression suddenly shifted into business mode. "Oh, right. Show me." Pausing, he turned back to me. "Why don't you get settled here and arrange things the way you like. I'll see you in my office in about half an hour to meet with the new client."

As he closed the door behind him, I wondered if I had been imagining everything. Or maybe Herne just had the ability to categorize parts of his life when he needed to. One way or another, I felt like I had been doused with a bucket of cold water.

Frustrated, I sat down at the desk and pulled open the drawers. There was nothing to personalize them, but I found paper and pens, all the usual office supplies, and a laptop computer. I pulled it out and opened it up, but I didn't know the password so I couldn't log in. Restless, I crossed to the window and stared out, crossing my arms over my chest.

What did I want from Herne? I wasn't sure of the answer. I was so attracted to him, and yet —the memory of my dead boyfriends played through my mind like some deranged merry-go-round. But Herne was the son of a god, as I had noted to Angel, and somehow I doubted that whatever curse I seemed to be under would cast its deadly effect on him.

Just then my phone rang, and I glanced at the Caller ID. Speak of the devil, it was Ray Fontaine. "Hey Ray, how are you?"

"I'm fine. I still haven't figured out what broke into my storeroom, but we haven't had any trouble since I hired a witch to strengthen the wards on my building. I just..." He paused, then slowly added, "I just miss you. I wanted to talk, to ask how you were doing. I saw the news about Angel—well, her house. She okay? What about her brother? I imagine they were probably pretty shaken up."

"Shaken up is right." I couldn't tell him about DJ, so I just added, "Angel found a new place to stay." I suddenly realized that I couldn't tell him any more than that. As much as I liked Ray, I had no idea who he was friends with. The world suddenly seemed like a mishmash of enemies out there, unseen and unplanned for.

"What are you doing tonight?"

I could sense that it was more than just a casual inquiry.

"Ray, you know I can't date you. You know why. I wish I could, but you'd be in danger."

"What is it that kills your boyfriends? I know you aren't a succubus."

Surprised that Ray even knew about succubi, I laughed. "No, I'm not a succubus. Sometimes I wouldn't mind being one, but I'm not. I'm just dangerous to get mixed up with, it seems." I paused, wondering if that was an appropriate thing to say.

"How long did you see them?"

"Leland I saw for three months. Robert only

lasted two weeks."

"I know this is an indelicate question, but I wonder if it might play into things. Were they the only men you ever slept with?"

I froze. There was something off about his question. The last thing I felt like talking about with Ray was my sex life.

"Ray, I'm thirty years old. I've had my share of lovers. That has nothing to do with the matter."

"Oh." His voice was so soft for a moment I almost didn't hear him speak. Then, he added, "So how many partners are we talking?"

And there it was. The hint of judgment that somehow, I knew would be there. Ray liked to be first. First in business, first at snapping up new technology and gadgets when they came out. And I had the feeling he wanted to be first in the bed as well. I had never talked to him about my sex life before I broke it off, but I had always had the suspicion that he hoped I was a virgin.

"Do you *really* want to go there? Considering that we're no longer together?"

"Why, are you afraid to tell me? Afraid I'll think you're a slut?" He paused, then added, "I'm sorry. I'm being boorish. It's just...I've been thinking about you since I saw you the other day. I miss you. Are you sure you won't consider going out with me again? I know you consider yourself a jinx, but what if the other guys were a fluke? What if Robert and Leland were actually coincidences? That goblin that hurt me could have attacked me even if you hadn't taken me along with you."

I closed my eyes, rubbing my forehead. I didn't

want to deal with this right now. It had been a mistake reconnecting with Ray, and I should have known better.

"Ray, don't do this. Trust me, I just know that you'd be in danger. And let's face it, we're very different people. You're a baker, a damned good one—the best, even. And I'm..." I paused. I wasn't sure what to say.

"I know you think you live a more rough-and-tumble life than I do. But that doesn't mean I'm soft. Or that I can't take care of myself, if that's what you're afraid of."

I glanced at the clock. I still had another twenty minutes to go before I was needed in Herne's office, but Ray didn't have to know that.

"Listen, I've got to go. I have a meeting to attend. I have to go."

"Can I call you tonight?"

I wanted to blurt out that no, I had a date. But that would be a big mistake. So I just told him a flat no and hung up before he could say anything more. I was still sitting there, staring at my phone, when he texted me, asking me to let him know when I had time to get together. Putting my private phone on mute, I stuck it deep in my purse.

Feeling at loose ends, I left my office and went out in the waiting room, wanting to talk to someone who would understand.

Angel was at her desk, poring over the transcript, which was what I should have been doing.

"I got a problem." I leaned on her desk. "Ray Fontaine has decided he wants back in my life. As my *boyfriend*."

Angel blinked. "After the talk I had with him?"

"And after the talk *I* had with him. And I also discovered that something I suspected when we were going together was actually true. He's extremely jealous and insecure. He doesn't like the idea that his girlfriends might have slept with other men. He was actually asking about my sex life. As to how many men I've been with."

"Oh good God. That's the last thing you need to deal with right now." She glanced up at the clock. "That new client's going to be in soon. This will be the first time that I've done an intake on someone. I hope I do it right."

"I wouldn't worry too much. You seem to be getting the hang of matters pretty quickly. How are you finding the job?"

"I actually like it," she said. "Oh, I wanted to ask. Tonight, do you mind driving me around to some car dealers so I can test drive a few? I called my bank and applied over the phone, and they can give me a loan for a new car."

Well, that solved one problem. I fished out my car keys. "Here. You take my car and go wherever you need to."

"How are you going to get home?"

I blushed. She studied my face for a moment then grinned.

"You're going out with Herne, aren't you?" When I didn't answer, she laughed. "I knew it! Well, have fun and be safe, whatever you do."

"We're just going out for a cheeseburger. That's all." When she didn't say anything, I added, "I mean it. All we're doing is going out for a bite to eat."

Just then the door opened, and in a man walked in. I recognized right away that he was Fae, but I wasn't sure whether he was Light or Dark. He gave me a long look, then smiled at both Angel and me, and walked up to the desk.

"I have an appointment with Herne. My name is Barnaby." His voice was gravelly, sounding lower than I thought it would be.

Angel checked her appointment book, marking off his name. "I have a form for you to fill out," she said, handing him a clipboard with a sheet of paper on it and a pen attached. "If you'll have a seat and fill out the information, I'll let Herne know you're here."

Herne peeked out of the door, glancing around the waiting room. His gaze fell on Barnaby, then he glanced over at me and motioned for me to join him in his office. He held up five fingers to Angel and she nodded.

"That's our client. He's a clurichaun, one of the Irish Fae folk." Herne settled behind his desk, pulling out a notebook and pen. "Don't accept anything to drink from him. Clurichauns are pleasant enough, but they can ensnare others quite easily if they choose."

"Don't forget, I'm Fae by blood. Other Fae can't entrap me with their glamour." I glanced around. "Where should I sit?"

Herne laughed. "I'm sorry, I did forget. You don't carry yourself with the usual energy of the Fae, and it's probably because of your background rather than your actual nature. Why don't you pull a chair over to the right of my desk and sit there. Halfway between the front and back, so to speak."

I dragged one of the heavy leather chairs over to where he pointed by the side of his desk, and had just sat down when the office door opened. Angel escorted Barnaby in, then handed Herne a copy of the form that he had filled out. She left, shutting the door behind her.

"Please take a chair," Herne said, motioning to one of the chairs opposite his desk. While Barnaby settled in, his feet dangling over the edge a good eight inches from the floor, Herne glanced over the form and then set it down to the side. "So what can I do for you?"

Barnaby glanced over at me, looking wary. "She's..."

"A half-breed. I know." I stared at him, feeling defensive.

"Ember is a new employee, and she'll be working with me on a number of cases including yours. So, tell me what wrong." Herne stared at the clurichaun, and I read the unstated warning. *Either work with both of us, or get out of the office.*

Barnaby cleared his throat and let out a slight huff, but apparently he decided to cave.

"As you know, I'm Light Fae. I live in the country, away from the main court. I'm having problems with a neighbor. He's stealing my wine, and so far I've refrained from putting a *haxit* on him but so help me, if he doesn't quit looting my cellar, I won't be responsible for the outcome. I petitioned Névé but she suggested that I bring my problems to a private investigator. She suggested the Wild Hunt."

Herne nodded, his face serious. He had to be good at his job, because I was fighting the temptation to giggle. Somehow, looting wine cellars didn't seem quite too serious.

"Your neighbor, is he human? Fae?"

"He's one of them damned wolf shifters." Barnaby spat out the words *shifters* like he might have spat out the word *shit*. I had the feeling that the clurichaun didn't care very much for the shifter community.

"Ah. And what is your neighbor's name?"

"Trent. Elson Trent. He's got a little farm next to my vineyard. I wouldn't complain if he would come over and ask for a bottle now and then, but I'm running a business and I don't cotton to thieves much." Barnaby seemed to be spare on his words, but the emotion behind them was very real. He was a growly, gruff curmudgeon and I expected that he wasn't an easy neighbor to have. But he was right, stealing was not exactly the most neighborly thing to do.

"All right. What do you want me to do? What do you expect to gain from hiring me? I need to ask that, so that there aren't any feelings that I haven't done my job if you decide to engage my services."

I had to hand it to Herne. He was covering all bases.

Barnaby squinted, thinking. A moment later he said, "I'd like you to prove whether Elson is actually pilfering my *vino*. If he is, then I need proof to take him to court." He frowned. "You realize, I don't actually *like* taking people to court. I just want him to stop stealing from me."

Herne nodded, glancing over at the form Barnaby had filled out. "Well, I can look into this next week. I'm on a case right now that has priority, but next week, I can do some snooping around. See what I can find out on Elson. Will that work for you?"

The clurichaun thought it over, then nodded. "That's fine. I changed the lock three times on my storeroom. Somehow he keeps getting in. How much of a retainer do you want?"

"Why don't we start off with two hundred? I'll write out a slip and you can pay Angel at the front desk. It will be applied to the work I do as soon as I start. It's a nonrefundable deposit, providing I'm able to take on the job once I look into it. If I find that I can't take on the job, the fee will be returned to you."

"All right. Why don't you write me out what I'll need." Barnaby slid off of his chair, and waited by the desk as Herne wrote out a retainer invoice. He handed the paper to the clurichaun and walked him out to the front desk. When he returned, shutting the door behind him, I burst out into a soft laughter.

"Of all the cases that I would expect to come through your door, that wasn't one," I said, keeping my voice low. "You're seriously going to snoop around to see if Barnaby's neighbor is swiping his booze?"

Herne snorted. "You have no idea how seriously clurichauns take their alcohol, do you? If he's like the rest of his kind, he'd have an easier time if his wife were cheating on him than with somebody stealing his wine."

I wiped my eyes, shaking my head. "You know, I realize how little I know about my own people. I've had little to do with them, and my parents didn't talk much about them. They chose to live like humans because of the way they were treated. I was brought up that way. My mother taught me to respect and honor Morgana, and she taught me magic of a sort, but whenever I'd ask about my parentage—you know, grandparents, the like—I ran up against a stone wall.

"It's almost as though I have no family at all, other than Angel. Sometimes, I actually feel quite alone in the universe." I may have started laughing, but I ended on a serious note, realizing that what I had just said resonated true to the bone. I truly did feel alone in the world, belonging to no one, with no culture, no heritage.

Herne was sitting beside me, silently listening. After a moment, he let out a soft sigh and opened the bottom drawer to his desk. He pulled out a bottle of spiced rum and two shot glasses. He filled the glasses and pushed one over to me. We slammed back the drinks, and he refilled them, then put the bottle away.

"Everybody has a right to know their background. While I understand why your parents did what they did, they left you at a distinct disadvantage. Maybe we can fill in the blanks, somehow." He lifted his glass and I touched my own to his, not sure what we were toasting.

"I'm not sure if I want to. Part of me does, but

I think I'm afraid of what I might find. It's hard when you know the people you come from don't want anything to do with you. Even harder to know that they killed your parents. My parents really did love each other. I could see it on their faces every day. I could hear it in their voices with every word they said. If I could ever find a love even half that strong, I think I'd be blessed. I don't know if I would have had the courage to do what they did—to defy tradition to the point of putting my life on the line for it."

Herne said nothing, just let me ramble on. When I finished, I looked over at him, suddenly realizing just how much I was revealing. I blushed, feeling like I had said too much.

"I do understand, even though I'm not in the same position. We'll pick up this conversation later, but right now we need to touch base with Yutani and Talia." He stood up, escorting me to the door.

As we headed for the break room, I felt slightly giddy from the booze, but also from the sudden realization that I felt better after talking to Herne. He had a way of making me feel comfortable in my own skin. Until now, Angel was the only one in the world who had ever given me the space to be truly who I was.

Chapter 12

YUTANI AND TALIA were waiting for us in the break room. Viktor and Angel came right in after us as we took our places at the table. I glanced up at the clock, startled to realize it was almost seven. The day had passed so fast that I hadn't realized it.

Talia went first. "While Yutani analyzed the video, I did some digging. I have some information on this Kuveo creature. He's not actually a demon, but he is a monster of sorts. And he can be summoned with the promise of blood and life force."

"Okay," Herne said. "What is he and why would someone summon him?"

"He's a fox shifter. Kuveo is a carnivorous creature who feeds off of life energy and fear and pain. He's also known as an interdimensional assassin and he delights in torture. Which means our victims were probably alive when he ripped them to shreds. He may eat chunks of his victims, a bite here and there, but mostly he's looking for their fear and pain while he's attacking them."

Angel grimaced. "Does he normally belong in our world?"

"Good question," Talia said. "No, but he's not from the physical realm. At least not *our* physical realm. He lives out in the Dreamtime, but he can be summoned here to perform an assassination of some great magnitude. He won't go after just anybody, though. And he requires a total of thirteen sacrifices before he will turn on the target. So, if you want to summon him to destroy somebody, you must provide him with thirteen victims first."

"And Kevin was our thirteenth. Crap, that means that Kuveo is ready to go after the actual target." Herne stiffened in his chair. "Is there anything that you came across that says how long it takes after the sacrifices before he'll attack the actual target?"

Talia shook her head. "I looked, sugar. But I didn't find anything. However, when Kuveo goes after the actual victim, he'll track them until they are dead. You get your money's worth with him."

"So the Dark Fae summoned him to perform an assassination. The victims were simply payment?"

"It looks that way," Yutani said. "I did a close inspection of the video Kevin took of the summoning. And I swear that it had to be held in Under-Lake. While Castle Hall is abandoned and falling apart, there's enough of it left to house a number of ghosts. When I examined the frames one by one, it looked as though the summoning spell was done in an underground chamber. Since all of the victims were connected with UnderLake in one way or another, my guess is that they were killed there, and then dumped in other places."

"What about Kuveo? Once he performs his task, i.e., the assassination, what happens to him?" Herne leaned forward, resting his chin on his hands.

Talia shook her head. "Then he's free to go do what he wants. And he's in this realm. That's another thing I found out. Kuveo can't enter this realm without being summoned. Once he's here, he's free to wreak havoc after he's fulfilled his part of the deal."

"That means more victims after he's assassinated his target. Which means we have to take him out as soon as possible," Viktor said. "Did you find anything about his weaknesses? Does he have any vulnerabilities that you could discover?"

Talia consulted her notes. "Yes, I did. He's hard to kill. However, if someone can manage to cut off four of his nine tails, he'll be sent back to his own realm. He'll regrow them, but he won't be over here. And he doesn't have a heart like we do—literally speaking. He lives on energy. He only takes bites out of each of his victims as a ceremonial rite." She rolled her eyes, looking disgusted.

"Is there a way to kill him?" Somehow, the idea of fighting a creature that couldn't be killed didn't appeal to me.

The harpy nodded, her eyes beady. Talia had a harshness about her that both scared me and yet made me appreciate her. "Cut off *all* of his tails while he's in this realm. That will do it. Nobody has ever managed to do so, though."

Herne was playing with a paper clip. He tossed it on the table. "Wonderful. So have we figured out who his main target is? Was that in Kevin's files?"

"Yes," Yutani said, "The answer isn't good."

"Lay it on us," Herne said.

"The Dark Fae conjured him up to assassinate Névé. Apparently, Light took a potshot at Saílle recently, and this is retaliation. Kevin had his nose in everything and he made copious notes just in case something happened. Which, unfortunately, it did."

Herne groaned and rubbed his head. "We missed a previous assassination plot? Thank heavens that wasn't realized, but that means that we have to take care of this and pronto."

"So the Dark Fae are striking back." I sat back, thinking for a moment. "Is there a way we can just tell the Dark Fae to back off? I mean, if Cernunnos and Morgana have set us on this case, can we just tell them to knock it off?"

"No. We can only intercede and stop things. They can't argue our actions, but we can't stop them from trying. It's a complicated matter and this has been going on for thousands of years. But things weren't nearly so dicey until the last couple hundred years, when the cities grew and technology became so rampant. Now there's so much chance for collateral damage that we have to intervene. However, at least we know who we're fighting and how to stop him."

Talia cleared her throat. "You have to kill him, completely. You can't just send him back to his realm. Once Kuveo has been set on track and the sacrifices have been made, there's no pulling him back. Not even the Dark Fae could stop him, not even if they begged, although they were the ones who started this matter in the first place. It's like setting off a bomb that you can't disarm."

"Lovely," Herne said. "All right, the question is, how do we find him?"

"Should we warn Névé about the attack?" I still didn't fully understand how these matters worked.

"We can't. That would be intervening directly. We can stop the attack, but we can't bring it to light. The Fae courts have been warring since time began. But it's an underground war. It's understood on both sides that attacks will be made, but if we were to overtly warn Névé that her life is in danger, then she would have no choice but to declare open war on the Dark Court. That would start a catastrophic cycle of destruction."

"How so?"

"If the Fae were to openly declare war, they'd involve the entire world instead of just a few sacrifices. There would be no hiding from the destruction."

I groaned. "The politics are more complicated than just about any nation on earth."

"Actually, I've seen worse," Talia said, slipping a piece of gum in her mouth.

"Then what do we do next?"

"Did you find out anything else?" Herne asked.

Yutani shook his head. "If you could give me a couple hours, I can probably pinpoint the area in which we need to look. I was getting close but not quite there yet."

Herne slapped the table. "Then we're all on the clock tonight. We'll meet back here at 9 P.M. Angel, you don't have to come in if you don't want to. You won't be going out in the field."

She gave me a long look, then turned back to Herne. "No, I'll stay here. There's still enough here to do that I'll just stay and organize more files." She motioned to Viktor, Talia, and Yutani. "Anybody want pizza?"

While they decided on what toppings they wanted, Herne and I walked out to the main waiting room.

"I suggest we put off our cheeseburgers till later," I said. "Pizza sounds fine to me."

Herne glanced back at the break room door, which was closed. He smiled, then drew me toward him and leaned down to press his lips against mine.

It took everything I had to not pull away, even as the fear of what might happen was ricocheting through my body. But so was his kiss, and I leaned into it, the warmth of his lips warming mine, the warmth of his body flaming my own desires as he pressed himself to me. He was gentle, yet his arms held me firmly. I felt like I was swimming in a woodland pond, under a lazy, sunlit afternoon. The room was sparkling, and so were his eyes, as I gazed into his face.

"I need to tell you what you're getting into," I said.

He shook his head. "Shhh. Maybe I shouldn't have done that, and I won't again if you don't want me to. But I had to kiss you, Ember. I couldn't *not* kiss you. Was it so wrong of me?"

As the break room door opened, I quickly pulled away. But I glanced at him with a shy smile.

"No. No, it wasn't wrong at all. My heart's racing." I paused. "Ever since we met, there's been something..." I paused as the others emerged from the break room. "We'll talk later."

As we chimed in with our suggestions for pizza, my body was still resonating from the strength of his kiss. But all I did was ask for sausage, extra cheese, and mushrooms, when what I wanted to do was to drag him into his office and rip off his clothes.

WHILE WE WERE waiting for Yutani to finish his analysis of the video, Viktor and Herne went over their weapons, making sure everything was ready. They were in the armory, polishing blades and making sure that arrow tips were sharp. Talia was helping Yutani, and I returned to the waiting room with Angel to help her sort out some of the file folders.

"I'm sorry you can't go on your date," she said, eyeing me closely.

The kiss had disconcerted me as much as it had aroused me, but right now I wanted to focus on the matter at hand.

"Well, I'm sorry you can't go car shopping tonight."

"Touché." She handed me a stack of file folders.

"Here, can you put one of these colored dots on each of these files? If you put it on the top right of the folder. There," she said, pointing to where she wanted it. "I'm color coding things to make them easier to find. Blue for closed cases, green for open, red for problem cases, and yellow for cold cases."

"What color are you using for cases like the one we're on now, for the ones that Cernunnos and Morgana send us on?" I started sticking the brightly colored dots on the file folders.

"Those get orange. My least favorite color." She grinned at me. "If someone had told me a week ago that I would end up the secretary for a divine PI, I would have laughed in their face. But you know, I may have a knack for this. I worked an office at my last job, but they really didn't respect me at all and I felt underutilized. Here, I feel like I can actually participate in what's happening instead of just be directed around. Although," she looked up at me soberly, "I really wish it hadn't come down to having DJ sent away. But Herne talked to me today, and he said he'll set up a video conference with DJ this weekend. So I get to talk to him for an hour then." The smile on her face told me all that I needed to know.

"He's a good sort, Herne is. They all are, actually." I realize that I really did like Viktor and Yutani, and even Talia, even though she still made me uncomfortable.

"Yeah, that I can agree with." She paused, then handed me another stack of files. "These all get blue dots. You know, I was having a talk with Talia earlier today while you were out with Viktor and

Herne. She's had a rough life. She told me that Herne took her in when nobody else would touch her. Apparently she is not popular among her own sort anymore, especially since she lost her powers. She said it was okay to tell you."

"I guess we're all just a bunch of misfits, aren't we?" I snickered as I stuck more dots on more file folders. "Well, at least we get to hang out more together now. Speaking of which, this weekend let's go house hunting."

She nodded. "If you're sure about it? I could find my own place, but honestly, I'd rather live with you." She rolled her eyes. "Gas leak, my ass."

"As you and I always suspected, the cops are on the take. I just didn't realize it would be from the Fae. If anybody was paying them off I would have expected it to be the vampires."

"Really? The vampires don't have to pay off anybody, do they? They're so damned powerful. In fact, I'm surprised they aren't vying with the Fae for control."

I laughed and handed her back the stack of file folders, accepting another in its place.

"Think about it. The vampires are more interested in monetary power and financial empires. I have a feeling that they are buying their way into power in a different way. The Fae are probably too disorganized to see it. I doubt anything good can come from it, either way, but I have a feeling that by the time the Fae realize just how much control the vampires have, it's going to be too late."

Angel frowned, thinking for a moment before she said, "Maybe, but if the Fae are as chaotic as

Herne says, will they really care? Though I still
see the potential for an interspecies war looming
large."

"If that happens, I think I'm going to give up the
city and move out to the country and start a pig
farm and find Mr. Rumblebutt a buddy." I stopped
as the door opened and the pizza delivery man
entered. He was carrying a stack of five pizzas,
and Angel opened her desk, pulling out an enve-
lope. She paid him out of it, and asked him to take
the pizzas into the break room. After he left, she
locked the front door, and motioned for me to go
let the others know that food was in the building.

I glanced into the room used as an armory.

"Come on, guys, food's on."

Sticking my head into Yutani and Talia's office,
I told them as well, then went on back to the break
room, my stomach rumbling. Angel had opened all
the pizza boxes and brought six plates over from
the cupboard. I rummaged through the refrigerator and found two large bottles of sparkling water,
carrying them to the table.

"Somehow, getting coffee for the guys doesn't
seem like such a big deal here like in my last job,"
Angel said with a grin. "At least they don't take me
for granted."

"Nor will we ever," Herne said as he entered
the room. "Pardon me for eavesdropping, but I
couldn't help hear your comment. I value every
single employee of this agency. We all have our
duties and we all add into making it a success. And
that success is integral to keeping peace. So thank
you both for doing your best to fit in." He paused

at the table and rubbed his hands together. "Ooo, pepperoni." He looked up, a gleeful expression on his face. At that moment, his gaze landed on me, and once again, I felt a ripple through my body as his gleeful look turned to desire, and he blew me a silent kiss.

"I saw that," Angel said. She glanced at me, then at Herne. "Just be careful, you two. I can see the connection between you two. I could from the beginning. Just do me a favor and if you have a fight, leave me out of it."

Chastised, both Herne and I stared at the food, making no comment. The next moment, Yutani and Talia entered the room and we all set to eating, Yutani still tapping away on his laptop.

"So, do we know any more than we did before?" Herne began passing around plates. Given there were six of us and five pizzas, I piled my plate high. I liked to eat, and there were very few things that I wasn't willing to try.

Yutani hit enter, and set his laptop down, letting whatever program he was working on compile while he got himself some food. After a moment, a map popped up on the screen. Leaning forward, he studied it as he bit into a slice of pepperoni and sausage pizza.

Talia accepted a cup of tea from Angel. "I've found out something else about Kuveo. If you can get a silver collar on him, it's like bottling the genie. He has to obey, regardless of his prior commitments. Trouble is, getting close enough to fasten a collar around his neck isn't easy. And it *has* to be silver"

"If somebody can hold him down, then we should cut off his tails and destroy him for good," I said.

"Agreed." Viktor flexed his bicep. "I have muscles."

"I have the feeling Kuveo is pretty strong, too," Talia said with a smirk.

"I agree with Ember. This is one creature we don't want to leave alive. He's only bent for destruction, and as soon as he got free of that collar, he'd return to the hunt." Herne shook his head. "Sometimes total destruction is best. You can't give a second chance to something that won't respect it."

"Given that he's made a deal, and he has to follow through, we wouldn't dare send him back to his realm. He would just return to target Névé again." I took a bite of my pizza, my stomach rumbling. The molten cheese and the tang of the pineapple and the savory flavor of the sausage all went into making me close my eyes and focus solely on the food. Sometimes you had to pay homage to a good meal. When I opened my eyes again, after swallowing, everybody was watching me. I realized I had let out a groan of delight while eating. Maybe a mumbled groan, but a groan, nonetheless.

"Enjoying that pizza, are we?" Viktor said with a laugh. "Don't be embarrassed. I'm that way about sloppy joes. Give me a good sloppy joe and I'm in heaven."

Angel piped up. "Give Ember anything from a fast food joint and she's in heaven. I'm actually glad we're living together because that's the only way she'll get a decent meal."

"Hey, if I learned to cook then you'd stop cooking and that would be a damn shame. Besides, I live on fast food, and it hasn't hurt me yet."

"That's because you're *Fae*. If you were human, you'd be piling on the pounds and greasing up that cholesterol." She twitched her nose at me, smiling. "You know I'm kidding. Except not so much. I still think you're better off with me cooking, even though I do love pizza."

"Everybody's better off with you cooking. I never understood why you didn't go into the diner business with Mama J. You cook just as well as she did."

"Heresy, she's probably rolling over in her grave at that. But yeah, I learned from the best. I just never had the calling for it. I love to cook for friends, but if I had to do it for a living, I wouldn't love that anymore."

I glanced around. The others were watching us.

There was almost a wistful smile on Herne's face, but he said nothing, just returned to his food. I gave him a sideways glance, wondering how many friends Herne actually had. It couldn't be easy, being the son of a god. Deciding to get back to the matter at hand, I turned to Yutani.

"What's the map on your laptop?"

He blinked. "Oh, it's done? So, I think I figured out the exact location of where they summoned Kuveo. Luckily, there were enough markers in the video that Kevin shot that I was able to get a bead on it. It appears there's an underground chamber about twenty yards from the Castle Hall ruins. My guess is that we'll find an entrance in the basement. And I also suspect that it ties in with the underground tunnels that riddle the area."

"It's a long series of tunnels if it runs all the way down the Eastside." It was hard for me to imagine.

"Well, as we discussed before, there were a lot of miners around here, so there are tunnels all over the place. There were mines all the way from Renton up to Bellevue, even over to North Bend. It wouldn't take much to connect them together into a system like the catacombs."

Yutani turned the laptop so we could all see it. "Here's the UnderLake District and UnderLake Park, and here's the Castle Hall residence. And about twenty yards south is where I pinpoint the underground chamber. It's possible I'm off by a few yards either way, but this is my best estimate."

"How do we know that Kuveo is going to be there? Isn't it likely that they moved him?"

"Well, he's not going to be found aboveground, at least not between the attacks. There's no way that creature could walk around in public and not be noticed. And since they think they killed the only person who knew about their chamber, it seems likely that belowground would be the most logical place to stash him."

"Only, since his sacrifices have been made, he'll start on the attack for Névé." Talia polished off her food and pushed back her plate.

"Then we better over there as soon as we finish eating. Ember, what about your ability to talk with the water elementals? How far does that extend?" Herne asked. "For instance, if we find a puddle, could you sense anything from it?"

"That depends first on whether there are any elementals in the area. And second, if they've seen anything. Unfortunately, it may be far enough away from the water that I won't be able to pick up anything. But very strong emotions can be imprinted in the water as well as into buildings and the air, so there's always a chance." I finished off the five slices of pizza on my plate and looked around. There were still at least two pizzas left. "Anybody mind if I have some more?"

"Knock yourself out," Viktor said. "I'm still hungry too."

"Just don't weigh yourself down too much." Talia chuckled. "I do like a girl with an appetite. Salad just isn't meant for human consumption."

"I don't mind vegetables on the side, but give me a good piece of meat and bread any day. And cheese. And sauce." I took another two pieces, while Viktor loaded up his plate. "So what's our plan?"

"After we finish eating, we head over to Under-Lake. We'll search for the secret entrance to the underground chamber, and see what we find. I think we should forget the collar idea, because we need to kill him and subduing him isn't going to be any easier. I'm going to pull together my gear." Herne pushed back his chair. "Viktor, why don't you get a few extra supplies from the armory. Yutani, you're with us tonight. Ember too. Angel and Talia, hold down the fort."

As Herne headed for his office, Viktor shoved the last of his pizza in his mouth and took off for the armory. I washed my hands and helped Angel put the rest of the pizza in the fridge.

"Are you afraid?" Angel asked.

I glanced over at Yutani, who was transferring data to his phone from the laptop.

"I can't lie—yes. I've gone up against goblins and their ilk, but never anything like this. My life's been in danger, but this is big, Angel. This creature thrives on pain and torture. But we've got to do something because it's not going to stop. It's already killed thirteen people."

"I'll say this for the Fae," Talia said. "When they do something, they go all the way."

I turned to her. "How long have you worked with Herne? How long has he had this agency?"

"He's been running the Wild Hunt Agency for several hundred years. But we just came over to the US about one hundred and twenty years ago. When technology started to take off, Morgana and Cernunnos foresaw where things were headed and decided to relocate us, even as some of the Fae were relocating back over the Great Sea. But the lesser queens and kings were scattered around the world and chose to stay where they were."

"The Great Sea?" Angel asked.

This was something I *did* know about my people.

"The Great Sea—there's another name for it, but it is difficult to pronounce in English—runs between the worlds. Originally, both sides of the Fae were from the Lands of Fire and Ice, and they lived in the great cities of TirNaNog and Navane, and others like them."

"TirNaNog and Navane? Like the districts here?"

Angel asked.

"Yes, only they were spelled differently. That's where the Fae in the two districts took their names from. Thousands of years ago, some of the Fae crossed over to live in this world. They spread around the globe, which is why so many cultures have their own names for the various Fae." I turned back to Talia. "So, you came over from the UK?"

She nodded. "We met Viktor here. Yutani," she nodded to the coyote shifter, "came on about what, forty years ago?"

Yutani nodded. "I worked with Microsoft in the early days, and then moved to a startup that folded during the dotcom crash, right about the time that I met Herne. He pulled me into the agency. He had the foresight to see that everything was moving into the digital age, and he wanted to make sure that the Wild Hunt was up-to-date and on track."

"That's good," I said, staring at the laptop. "So if there are other agencies around the world, what are they called?"

"Variations on the theme," Talia said. She popped a breath mint and held out the container. "Mint?"

I took one, and so did Angel.

"In Norway, their agency's called Odin's Chase. And there's one in Finland called Mielikki's Arrow. In Italy I think it's Diana's Hounds, and so on. Cernunnos and Morgana have connected with a variety of deities around the world to form a worldwide action coalition."

That sobered me. All around the world, that

meant there were groups of people trying to keep the war from breaking out among the Fae.

"The Fae seem to need babysitters everywhere, don't they? And I know these are *my* own people. I just don't like to admit it. It's embarrassing." I shook my head, blushing. "We're no better than a pack of sputtering cats."

Yutani and Talia laughed. Talia clapped me on the back.

"Honey, if we can't laugh at ourselves, who can we laugh at? But trust me, your people can be incredibly helpful and talented, and you're magic incarnate, truly. I think someday, you'll need to make peace with your heritage. I've been around for centuries. I've seen people run away from themselves, and run away from who they are. You always end up running smack back into the person you left behind until you find a way to integrate that part of yourself into your life. And that's all I'll say, because really, it's none of my business."

I had the feeling Talia was trying to help me in her own way. I didn't want to hear it, she was right about that, but one day, I knew I'd have to take her advice. But I wasn't ready right now, and I wasn't sure when I would be.

Herne and Viktor returned, laden with weaponry and various other items.

"Let's get moving. We've got a monster to track down and kill." He nodded toward the door. "Let's just hope we can get all nine of his tails."

Chapter 13

BY THE TIME we were heading over the 520 floating bridge—like the I-90, it linked Seattle to the Eastside—night had fallen. The lights of the bridge reflected onto the water, giving off an eerie glow beneath the cover of clouds. I leaned back in the seat next to Viktor, closing my eyes. So much had changed over the past few days that I was almost dizzy with the shifts. Up front, Yutani was poring over the information he had gathered as Herne manned the wheel. I turned to stare out the window into the silent night, breathing softly as I thought about where we were headed and what we were going to do.

Yutani cleared his throat. "Whoever summoned Kuveo has to be well-versed in the magical arts."

"That may be, but we can't touch him unless he interferes with what we're doing. We're licensed to take out the threat, not to take down the person who summoned it."

And there it was again, that precarious balance beam we walked. I wondered how many times Herne and his team had gone out hunting. How many times had they stopped one military action or another? If they had been around for hundreds of years, then it stood to reason they had seen a lot of action. At least, he, Viktor, and Talia.

"Have the cops ever interfered with one of your jobs? Have they ever tried to stop you?"

In the driver's seat, Herne snorted. "They've tried, but we're still here, and the world is still relatively intact, so count on the fact that they have never really succeeded. We—and others like us—have forestalled most of the major conflicts, except for a few blunders."

"Like?" I was curious as to just what happened when they failed.

"Like the first world war. A mission gone horribly wrong. The Fae were behind that, and a dozen smaller wars, as well."

I blinked. "Really? What about World War II?"

"World War II was mostly on Hitler. Pretentious prick couldn't keep his hatred to himself," Viktor muttered.

Yutani glanced in the rearview mirror. "Some of Viktor's family members died in the war." The look on his face told me that it was better if I didn't inquire any further. Over the years, I had learned that when someone didn't feel like talking, it generally wasn't a good idea to push them. In fact, I had been on that side of the fence more than once.

The 520 bridge led us into Kirkland and onto

I-405, where we turned north on the freeway. We took the exit for Eighty-fifth Street, following it down to Market, where once again we headed north. Eventually, we ended up on Juanita Drive and from there, we wound through the Kirkland peninsula until we reached the UnderLake District. As we neared Angel's old neck of the woods, I asked if we could swing by her burned-out place.

"I just want to look, to see for myself."

"Are you sure?" Herne asked.

"Yeah," I said. "I know it sounds perverse, but if I see it and tell her, it will make it real for her. It's like when somebody dies and you aren't able to go to the funeral. Unless you're actually there, it's hard to fully accept it. If I see her house, I can help her put it in the past."

"All right, but it's not a pretty sight." Herne swung through her neighborhood. The heavy scent of soot still lingered in the air and as he slowed down in front of what remained of the house, I grimaced. He stopped the car and I quietly got out and walked up to the charred ruins.

Herne was right, it wasn't pretty. There wasn't much left—of anything. I couldn't see clearly in the dark, but Herne was suddenly standing beside me, carrying a large flashlight. The light illuminated the ruins. Even though the fire had been out for some time, the scent of soot and ash hung heavy in the air.

I slowly walked up to what had been the front of the house and stared at the pile of rubble and ashes. Blackened timbers had collapsed on themselves, glass shards were everywhere, and the entire house had collapsed. The garage, too. The skeleton of Angel's car peeked out from under the rubble. I caught my breath, staring at the destruction.

That someone had actually deliberately done this, that they had targeted Angel, made everything very real, too frightening to think about. I shivered, folding my arms as a gust of wind blew by, scattering ashes around me. At least the rain was holding off, but everywhere were pools of soot-laden water. After a moment, I turned to Herne, who had a grave expression on his face.

"This is so much worse than I imagined." It was all I could think of to say.

"Yeah. See why I didn't want Angel to come over? While it might make it real for her, it would make it *too* real. Sometimes it's better to leave things to the imagination. Sometimes the imagination *isn't* worse than the reality." He waited for another moment, then asked, "Ready?"

I nodded. There was nothing I could do. Whatever had survived, Herne and Viktor had already found it.

"Yeah, let's go." I followed him back to the SUV, where he opened my door for me and took my elbow, helping me in. I didn't need the help but it felt comforting, and so I just thanked him quietly.

Viktor looked at me. "Once Herne and I saw the mess, we wanted to spare Angel the heartache."

"Thank you." I shook my head, trying to figure out what kind of people would do such a thing when they thought a child was involved. Talia may have thought that I had to come to terms with my heritage, and she was probably right, but when I saw destruction like this, it made me want to run farther away.

"I just want to focus on stopping Kuveo. I'm used to having to kill some of the sub-Fae like goblins and the like, but the kind of brutality that we've seen the past couple of days makes my stomach churn. Do you ever get used to it?" I looked up at the ogre, hoping—and yet fearing—that he would say yes.

"No. You'd think it wouldn't bother me so much, given I'm half-ogre. But I think anybody who has any sort of empathy will find this job challenging at times. That's *why* we do it. If we didn't care, why bother? Why try to make a difference? It's always going to be difficult for those who really care. But we are the ones who can make a difference, who can put wrongs to right. Or at least, most of the time. Herne hasn't told you something, but you deserve to know."

"What are you talking about?" Herne asked.

"I know what he's talking about. Sometimes, we have to be agents of chaos," Yutani said, his voice low as he stared at his tablet.

"What does he mean?" I glanced at Viktor, who had a dark look on his face.

"Sometimes we're called on to right the balance when light overshadows darkness. There's a balance between good and evil, and it must be maintained."

"I know that," I started to say, but caught sight of Herne, who was giving Viktor a long look through the rearview mirror. He shook his head ever so slightly.

"Never mind. I'm sure things will sort themselves out." The ogre went back to looking out the window, and feeling confused, I did the same.

We entered UnderLake Park and were nearly at the turnoff to Castle Hall when Yutani asked Herne to slow down.

"Going about as slow as I can—fifteen miles an hour," Herne said.

"There should be a turnoff near the ruins. Take that and park. It's going to be difficult to see in the darkness, but you should be able to find it if you're going slow enough." Yutani consulted his tablet, then said, "On the right side."

Less than sixty seconds later Herne eased into a parking spot. I could barely see the sign indicating that turnoff, but apparently Herne's eyesight was better than mine.

"All right, everybody out and grab your bags. Try to move as quietly as you can, although I realize that's asking a lot." Herne gave us all a look that told me that this had been an issue in the past. By Viktor's response, I knew I was right.

"Dude, are you going to bring that up *every* time we head out in the field?" the ogre whined.

Herne snorted. "I wouldn't have to if you'd watch where you put your big feet."

Their sparring sounded good-natured, and one look at Yutani told me that. As much as they might poke and prod each other, they really did care.

"We need to get into the basement level. From there, we search for an entrance to the underground labyrinth," Yutani said. He paused. "You all should know that I saw a coyote on my way to work."

Herne let out a slow breath. "Just what we need. All right, thank you for warning us." He glanced at me. "You'd better tell her. She still doesn't know."

Yutani slid his tablet into his bag and switched to his phone. "Every time a coyote crosses my path, it means trouble's ahead. Sometimes it's danger, other times just chaos."

He shrugged into a denim jacket and pulled his hair back in a sleek ponytail. He slid on a black Deadman Tophat with a blue feather in the band, and suddenly he went from gangly geek to gorgeous hunk. It was amazing what the right look could do, I thought, then tried to shake off my libido, which had been on overdrive since I met Herne.

"Well, I guess I'm forewarned." There wasn't much else I could say. I showed Herne my dagger.

"That's a good blade. Looks sturdy. Nice sharp edge. You have a secondary weapon?"

I blinked. "Not on me. But I can shoot crossbow with dead accuracy. And I can fight double-handed. Two blades at once."

He motioned to Viktor, who handed me one of the small crossbows I had seen in the armory. "Have you shot this kind before?"

I glanced over it. The pistol crossbow was handmade, that much I could tell, but not dissimilar to the ones I had learned on. But there was enough variation that I wasn't sure how quickly I'd ramp up with it.

"I'd better put in a little practice with it before

I take it into a hostile situation. If you have any nunchaku, those I can use." I handed him back the crossbow reluctantly. I enjoyed target practice, and they came in handy when you didn't want to get too close to an opponent.

"I can provide a pair," he said, putting away the crossbow and handing me a pair of nunchaku.

I tested the weight and found them to be almost identical to the ones I owned, and hooked them onto my belt. The weight of the extra weapon calmed me down, and I realized just how nervous I was.

"These are good. I'm ready." I grounded myself as we crossed the lawn to the remains of Castle Hall.

The ruins were in bad shape, though—unlike Angel's house—they were still standing. Weathering and neglect had taken their toll, along with the inevitable march of time. Some of the walls were still standing, while others had caved in and crumbled. The roof was still in place, which both surprised me and made me nervous, given we were going inside. Nothing about Castle Hall looked stable, but I figured since the city owned the park, if they thought the house was going to fall down and kill somebody, surely they would have cordoned it off.

The mansion had been huge, three stories high, and it looked like most of the impacted walls were on the upper levels. A corner wall on the third story had crumbled, and on the second story a number of windows had been broken out, and the half-walls beneath them were broken through.

Up close, especially under the cover of night, the great house loomed like some massive, threatening shadow.

"And we're going in there," I murmured.

"Yeah, that's about the size of it," Viktor said, letting out a slow breath.

I glanced over at Yutani, wondering how his fighting skills were. He had his phone in one hand, and in his other, he carried what looked like a barbed dagger. I raised my eyebrows.

"That looks wicked." I pointed to the blade.

In the light of our flashlights, the smile he gave me looked feral, and his eyes flashed with a topaz light. He patted the blade against his jeans.

"Oh, she is. The blade has a silver alloy coating, and beneath it, iron. Whether I go up against vampire or Fae, it will do the trick. The Wulfine don't care for it either, but I've seldom had altercations with them, although they don't like us coyote shifters much."

That surprised me. "I would think you get along. You're both...canine." That came out wrong and I grimaced, but Yutani just laughed.

"But not all dogs pack together. The Wulfine see us as dirty mongrels, not noble like they claim to be. While the coyote shifters are street smart and cunning. Sometimes the Wulfine have too many rules for their own good. We know how to fight dirty and are willing to do so when necessary." And with that, he shrugged and motioned for me to be quiet. "We're close enough to be heard."

I wanted to point out that we had our flashlights on. Even if they didn't hear us, they could probably see us if they happened to be looking out a window. But I figured the guys had done this before, so I kept my mouth shut.

We crossed to the front door. At first I thought we should go through the back, but it occurred to me that since nobody was supposed to be living here, and all of the dirty work had been belowground. If anybody but the ghosties were hiding out inside, they were probably down in the subterranean hideout.

Herne went first, with Yutani second. I came third and Viktor took the rear, keeping an eye on our backs so that we weren't surprised from behind. I liked the idea of having an ogre covering my ass. It made me feel secure, though I had no doubt that both Herne and Yutani could hold their own in a fight.

But Herne didn't go directly to the front door. He skirted the outside of the building around to the left, and then, when we were by the side, he crept to one of the windows. I frowned, but then I caught a glimpse of Yutani's phone—the blue light was even more visible than our flashlights—and saw that he had some sort of GPS going. It didn't look like a regular map, so I guessed he had plotted out the projected route we needed to take.

Herne ran his fingers along the windowsill. Then he took out a small crowbar and pried the window open. At first, it didn't want to budge, but then it let out a creak as the wooden frame jogged free from the sill. Once it was open a couple inches, he put the crowbar away and put some muscle into it, heaving up the frame to expose enough space for us to crawl through. Leaning in, he flashed his light on the floor, then slipped through the opening.

Yutani followed him, and then it was my turn. Viktor started to offer me a leg up, but I was already half through, swinging my legs over the sill and finding my footing beside Herne. Viktor heaved himself through, and we were in.

I glanced around. The lights of our flashlight offered enough visibility for me to see that we were in what must have been a parlor of sorts. It smelled like mold and dust, and I shivered as an unexpected blast of cold air swept past.

"Ghost," Yutani said softly, keeping his voice low.

"They gather here," Herne said. "You said the trap door is in here?"

Yutani nodded. "It should be over by that bookshelf somewhere." He nodded toward a built-in that was filled with decaying books. I grimaced as we moved toward the shelves.

"What a waste, to let all of the books go to ruin." I loved to read and it pissed me off to see so many books destroyed.

Yutani began to search along the floor as Herne took one side of the bookshelf and Viktor the other. We had been looking for some sort of trigger button for about five minutes when I realized that something on the shelves looked out of place. I stood back, eyeing the bookcase, squinting as I tried to figure out what was off. And then I realized what it was. One book looked almost new amidst the sodden mass of pulp and paper. I crossed over

to it, shining my flashlight on it. The title read
ALADDIN'S LAMP.

I motioned to the men. "Found it, I think." I
pointed to the book. "It looks almost new, so it's
probably not a real book. Can we say 'Open sesa-
me'?"

Yutani's eyes gleamed as he gave me an appre-
ciatory nod. Herne let out a grunt that was almost
a laugh. He clapped me on the shoulder.

"Good work. I knew you'd be an advantage on
the team." He motioned for us to stand back as
Yutani checked around the book.

"What are you looking for?" I kept my voice low,
still worried we were being observed.

"Any visible traps." Yutani poked and prodded
the decaying books to both sides, then shrugged.
"Looks clear to me. Most people don't seem to
read much, so I assume they figured nobody would
notice."

"Here goes nothing." Herne pulled the book and
it tipped forward with a click. To the right side,
part of the built-in opened—a door in the unit. We
were staring into a small dark room with a spiral
staircase leading down.

"Okay, then. Here we are." Yutani consulted his
phone. "Down the staircase should put us near the
place that the summoning ritual was held. Let me
take the lead. I can see in the dark easier. From
here on, we'll have to rely on the light from the
dimlim."

"The what?" I had never heard the word before.

"Dimlim—slang for one of our gadgets. It's a
low-light illumination device, which basically gives

us just enough light to see by, and won't attract much attention. It's not like a beacon, unless it's pitch dark, and even then it can be mistaken for several things. Think low-level green light." He flipped the switch on a gadget that was attached to his belt and turned off his phone. "Flashlights off."

Sure enough, at that point, the darkness encroached and I could see in front of me, but not by much. Just enough to see directly in front of me. Yutani swung onto the spiral staircase and we followed him down.

The staircase was steel, and there was no way to hide the sound of our footsteps. I noticed that Herne's steps could barely be heard, while the rest of us made what sounded to me like a racket, even though we did our best to move quietly.

We moved quickly, clinging to the rail as we circled around and around, descending into the tunnel below. The dimlim illuminated our feet, but did not pierce the darkness below us. I wondered how far down we were going, as we kept spiraling, step after step. I thought back to the Market. But here, the shaft around us was roughly hewn, first out of compacted dirt and then turning into rock. I wondered how many years of rock and soil buildup we were passing through.

It felt like we had been on the staircase for hours, although I knew it was only probably ten or fifteen minutes, but eventually Yutani stepped off of the bottom stair and made way for the rest of us. I looked up, unable to see the opening above. It was all murky blackness.

The dimlim's light illuminated the area directly

around us, and I saw that there were two shafts, one leading straight ahead, the one behind us. Both were narrow passages, roughly hewn into an oval shape. The floor was rough, although it moved forward at an even grade. The walkway was wide enough for us to travel one at a time, and it occurred to me that if we met anybody coming our way, we were in for a standoff.

I took a deep breath, trying to categorize the scents that I could smell. Dampness, and the pungent scent of mold from freshly turned soil during the spring. We weren't that far from the lake, but I couldn't sense the movement of water. These tunnels probably ran straight through the earth down to where they crossed over to Mercer Island, and then across the lake.

"Anything?" Herne asked me, his voice soft and low.

I shook my head, adjusting my voice so that it would not carry. "No, just mold and soil and the dampness that's already in the air. I don't smell anything out of place."

He turned to Yutani. "Hear anything?"

Yutani shook his head as well. "If anybody's down here, they aren't in the immediate vicinity. Which is both good and bad. I'd like to get this over with, but at least there's a chance they won't have heard us coming."

"Which tunnel?" Viktor asked.

Herne looked to Yutani for an answer. Yutani closed his eyes as though he were trying to remember something, then pointed to the tunnel directly in front of us.

"This way. Straight ahead will lead us to the area where Kevin took the video. I just needed a moment to get my bearings."

I knew what he meant. The spiral staircase had turned us around so many times that I wasn't sure which way we were facing. Herne took the lead, taking the dimlim from Yutani. He pulled out his dagger, and motioned for the rest of us to arm ourselves.

As we crept along, I held my dagger firmly, but made sure I wasn't clutching it too tightly. In a fight, it was best to keep as relaxed as possible, so that your movements wouldn't be jerky. That way, if somebody caught you off guard, you wouldn't be dragged forward if the blade got jammed into something. Or someone.

We moved more swiftly now that we were on relatively level ground. Herne suddenly stopped and, in front of me, Yutani froze. Herne pointed toward the wall to his right and held up the dimlim. Yutani took a step to the left so that Viktor and I could see what Herne was pointing to.

On the wall, spreading out like some amorphous blob, was a mass of sparkling gel. It clung to the wall, and I could see the faintest of movements as it slowly spread out, stretching thinner as it did so. Or maybe, it was actually *growing*. I had no clue what it was, but Herne seemed wary and so did Yutani. I glanced up at Viktor, who was standing closest to me, and he shook his head.

"Don't touch it," he said, whispering in my ear. "That's a phosphorescent slime. Not only will it give you a severe acid burn, it will then infect you with some pretty horrible diseases. It's riddled with bacteria. They breed like amoebas, splintering off from each other, which is probably what it's doing now. Give it a wide berth, and now that we know one's down here, be on the lookout for more."

I shuddered. It was beautiful in an eerie way, like a sparkling iridescent gel. But knowing it could kill me seemed to drain away some of the fascination. Yutani had heard Viktor and now he nodded in confirmation. We all pulled to the left after making sure there weren't any others on the left side of the tunnel, and skirted around it as best as possible. Herne began checking the floor as we went, and I realized that the slimes were probably not confined to the walls. We'd have to be careful with every move we made. It made me wonder just how many other creatures there were that I didn't know about, and how many we might find down here.

We had gone probably two hundred yards down the tunnel when Herne stopped again, holding up his hand. He pointed forward, and pulled aside so we could see. Ahead, there seemed to be a faint light coming from the left, and I realized there was a branch in the tunnel.

Herne glanced at Yutani, a question in his eyes.

A moment later, Yutani pointed toward the turn-off.

Herne gave him a nod, and once again began to move forward, preparing to turn the corner. I felt my breath quicken, and tried to calm myself. One thing was for sure: this wasn't a profession for anyone with high blood pressure.

For a moment, I wondered what Angel and Talia were up to, briefly envying their jobs. But this was what I was cut out for. I was born for this sort of work, even if it was a pain in the ass at times. I steadied myself, straightening as Herne neared the turnoff. From here, it was obvious that the tunnel we were entering was wider than the one we had been in, and Herne motioned for Yutani to scoot next to him. We'd swing around going two abreast.

As we rounded the corner, we abruptly found ourselves not in another tunnel, but in a large cavernous chamber. It must have been fifty yards wide, and probably that much and more long, with two exits on the other side, one opposite to us, and one to the right.

A series of sparkling lights circled the ceiling, from what looked like a sea of delicate floating witch balls, all illuminated from within. They were beautiful, and seemed to move on their own, floating softly in what appeared to be a random pattern. I knew they weren't will-o'-the-wisps, but I wasn't sure what they were. They seemed alive, and I wondered what kind of magic had created them. They provided enough light for us to see the edges of the cavern.

As I was staring at the lights, Yutani poked my side and nodded to the center of the chamber. On the floor was a large symbol carved into the rock, about three feet in diameter, and painted with what looked like a ruddy brown paint. For a moment, I wondered why they had painted it such an ugly color before I realized that wasn't paint. It was probably blood.

Herne held his finger up to his lips as we crept further into the chamber. I couldn't see anybody around. On one hand, I was relieved. On the other, the tension was growing the farther we went.

Yutani stared at the symbol for a moment, then pulled out his phone. He consulted his pictures, and showed them to us. There, from a still taken from Kevin's video, we saw a group of Fae standing around the same symbol.

"This is where they summoned Kuveo." He glanced around the chamber, suddenly stiffening. "We're not alone."

As he spoke, there was a rustle from the walls as three figures moved forward off of the rock, carrying large swords made of shadow. And they were headed right for us.

Chapter 14

"WHAT THE HELL are those?" I wasn't worried about being heard now. The jig was up and we were in for a fight.

"I'm not sure," Herne said, pulling out a second dagger in his other hand. "But I think we're going to find out."

Yutani whipped his pistol grip crossbow off his shoulder, where it had been hanging on a sling. Within seconds, he had aimed at one of the shadows and fired. He was fast, faster than I had expected him to be. The arrow drove through the shadow, disrupting for a moment, but the inky darkness reformed immediately as the arrow tip bounced off the wall, falling to the floor.

"Crap, arrows won't work." He immediately slung the bow back over his shoulder and pulled out a blade. "Let's hope silver does the trick. Or iron."

The shadows advanced, moving quicker now, and we spread out so that we could all manage an attack. My breath was tight in my chest and I forced myself to exhale, then breathe in again slowly. I had faced unknown enemies before, opponents where I hadn't a clue how to attack them, but they had all been corporeal, flesh and blood.

The next moment, I dismissed thought from my mind because the shadows were close enough to attack. I moved in with Yutani on one as Herne and Viktor took the others.

The fact that the shadows were carrying swords made it more difficult, even though I had a feeling their blades were actually just extensions of themselves. But they had a long reach, and I wasn't sure at all what the damage would be.

"Distract him," Yutani said.

I darted to the side, yelling at the shadow. As it turned to follow me, Yutani came sweeping in from behind, driving his blade through the smoky form. The creature let out a yowl, sounding like a wounded animal, but kept coming my way. It looked a bit thinner, however, its form less dense.

As it swung at me, I leapt into the air, dodging the blade as it rounded beneath my feet. As I landed, my feet touching the floor again, I plunged forward, driving my dagger toward the shadow. My blade bit deep, and as soon as the silver touched the shadow, the creature shrieked again and once more thinned out, the remaining shadow stretching out to fill the gaps.

Yutani attacked from the back at that moment, and the shadow swung around, striking him with the blade before he could move out of the way. The coyote shifter let out a choked cry, and fell to his knees.

I rushed in toward the back of the shadow, driving my blade into the thick again. This time I stayed put instead of darting away, holding the blade firm inside of the shadow. The shadow struggled to get away from me, its shriek reverberating through the chamber, and then, as it tried to turn on me, it vanished in a puff of smoke.

A quick glance at Herne and Viktor told me they were well on their way to defeating their opponents, so I knelt beside Yutani.

"Are you all right?" I couldn't see any blood where the shadow's blade had pierced him, but he was obviously wounded and in pain.

He grunted, nodding. "I think so. Help me up."

He wrapped his arm around my shoulder as I helped him struggle to his feet. He was shaky, and he felt jarred, as though his energy had been disrupted. At that moment Herne and Viktor ran over, the other two shadows gone.

"What happened?" Herne patted Yutani down, pulling his hand away quickly as a crackle and spark jolted both of them.

"It disrupted his energy field." I wasn't sure how the shadow had done it, but I knew what was happening. Yutani had been wounded on an energetic level, and the question was, would he continue to lose energy or would the gash heal over enough for him to go on?

"I feel strange." Yutani wavered. "I feel like I'm going to faint, and I never faint." He glanced around, looking panicked. "I don't know what to do."

Herne stared at him for a moment, then said, "I know what you need. Change into your coyote self. That should help you heal faster."

"But what about—"

"Just do it, man. Otherwise, I think you're in danger of dying." Herne began grabbing Yutani's things off of him. He pulled away his bow and grabbed the blade from his hand.

Yutani struggled to get out of his jacket, so I took hold of the collar, yanking it off of him. His phone dropped to the floor and Viktor snatched it up, making certain that it was still all right. As Yutani struggled out of his jeans, sitting on the floor, Viktor helped him take off his boots.

It was obvious that Yutani was having trouble doing much of anything, but he was finally naked, and as he rolled over on his side and whimpered, he began to shift shape.

I gathered up his clothes as Viktor kept an eye out for anybody else who might enter the chamber. A moment later, Yutani lay there in coyote form, a gorgeous, lean specimen of an animal, with haunting topaz eyes and a thick bushy tail. He whimpered again, but had stopped panting, and now he rested his chin on his front paws.

"How long will it take him to heal enough to change back?" I knew very little about shifters, although I knew they healed better in their natural shape. And their natural shape was that of the animal whose nature they shared.

"I don't know," Herne said. "Hopefully not too

long. I hope it's before Kuveo decides to come meandering along."

I stacked Yutani's clothes by his side, and knelt, slowly stroking his forehead. He whimpered and looked up at me, and I wanted nothing more than to give him a hug, to reassure him that he'd be okay. I sought for any water elementals that might be in the area—sometimes they could bring a healing force with them—but there were none, and I let out a sigh of exasperation.

Viktor pulled out a small bottle from his backpack. "Aren't you glad I remembered to bring this?" He held it up so Herne could see it.

"Man, I could so kiss you for that. Get it down his throat *now*." Herne was keeping watch on all three of the exits from the chamber.

I joined him, blade at the ready. "What is it?"

"There are certain restorative potions that can heal life force lost. They're expensive to buy, and they take a long time to make, but whenever we're going into what's likely to be a highly dangerous situation, I try to make certain that we have some at hand. I forgot this time, but thank heavens Viktor remembered."

I glanced over at Viktor, who was holding the bottle for Yutani as he poured it into the coyote's mouth. "How fast will it work?"

"If it does work against this sort of attack, it should be almost instantaneous. If Yutani was unconscious, that might be a different matter. Or if he had lost a great deal of blood. Potions like this can't replace blood lost from the body, and they can't take care of amputated limbs or anything of that nature, obviously. But they can go a long way to helping somebody get back on their feet." Viktor stood back, waiting. A moment later, Yutani struggled to his feet, shaking his head. He really was a beautiful creature.

"I hear something," Herne said, as Yutani began to shift back. I wanted to watch him—I had seldom seen anybody change shape and it was a fascinating process—but Herne needed me as backup. Yutani was struggling into his clothes, protected on one side by Herne and me and on the other by Viktor, as a loud noise sounded from the tunnel ahead.

"I don't think that's a person," I said. The growling and snarling couldn't be human *or* Fae.

As we prepared to meet the oncoming opposition, Yutani finished dressing and cocked his pistol crossbow. He gave us a grateful nod. "Thanks, guys."

"Are you up to this?" Herne asked.

"I'd better be. Yes, I'm ready," Yutani said. "Let's do this."

As he finished speaking, a figure appeared at the edge of the tunnel, rushing into the room. Over seven feet tall and bipedal, the monstrous fox form with nine tails entered. Here was the creature we had come to slay. *Kuveo.*

OVER THE YEARS I had fought some interesting creatures, but never one quite so terrifying.

His muzzle was narrow, with sharp teeth protruding from the edges of his mouth, and the light in his eyes was cunning and deadly. He was bulky, as wide as two men, and his arms were long and thick, with sharp claws instead of nails. He was naked, and I really didn't need to see the massive penis that was standing at attention. Apparently, facing enemies gave him a hard-on.

"Crap," I muttered, back up a step. "We've got trouble."

Yutani immediately fired an arrow toward Kuveo's heart. It bit deep but the creature barely seemed to notice it, yanking out the quarrel and tossing it aside. He let out a low growl and his tongue lolled out the side of his mouth, slobber dripping down.

"Fuck that. He's hungry." Visions of his victims flashed through my mind, their bodies ripped to shreds. I didn't have any plans on joining their company. I edged to the side, holding my dagger ready. I needed a distance weapon, I thought. Tomorrow, I'd be out in the field, practicing with the company bows, provided we survived this.

Herne pulled out a blowgun and several darts. The darts looked small and useless against such a large creature, but that didn't seem to faze him as he began shooting.

Viktor unsheathed his short sword and began to edge around the side of Kuveo. He was going to try for the tails, but he would need a distraction. I glanced down at the floor and saw several loose rocks lying around. I swept up several and began pelting Kuveo with them, hitting him square between the eyes. While the rocks bounced off, I managed to get his attention and he turned toward me, offering Viktor better access.

Herne managed to land two of the darts. He dropped the blowgun and pulled out his dagger. "We need to buy several minutes, but that should slow him down."

"They were coated?" I asked, dancing out of the way as the creature charged toward me. He was fast, faster than I had expected, and I barely missed being eviscerated. It was easy to see how he mutilated his victims now, and I forgot all about my question as I started to run, with Kuveo right after me.

The heavy thumping of his feet behind me left no doubt as to how close he was. I could feel his breath on my neck in the damp, cool air. I dodged to the left, around a stalagmite on the outer edge of the chamber, and then circled in a figure-eight pattern around yet another one.

Kuveo tripped on a boulder, sprawling forward as he skidded along the rough floor, but before I could swing around to try slicing off one of his tails, he was on his feet again, charging after me. The moment's respite gave me just enough time to figure out where I was and I took off again. Viktor and Herne were just catching up—apparently I could run faster than they could. At least when I had a raging maniac monster behind me.

I saw a corner up ahead behind a pile of rocks that looked long and narrow enough for me to hide in and be out of his reach. At least, I thought Kuveo was too large to follow me in there. As I slid into the v-shaped niche and struggled to push myself back as far as I could, Kuveo lashed out, his long arms coming perilously close to ripping into me, but there was about twelve inches to spare. I sucked in my gut, just to make sure. The question was, would he be able to rip out the rocks in order to get to me before the others could take him down?

"Keep his interest!" Herne's voice echoed from behind Kuveo.

"I don't think I can do much else!" I yelled back, jabbing at his long, furry paws with my dagger. Kuveo let out a shriek of frustration and began to thrash against the rocks.

I snorted, but then he grabbed hold of my blade, cutting his paw as he wrapped his fist around it and yanking it toward him. Luckily, I was still taking my own advice and hadn't been holding it tightly. I let go before he could drag me forward.

Then Kuveo froze before raising his head. He let out a shriek that echoed through the chamber, almost deafening me.

He dropped my dagger and spun around, and I saw that three of his nine tails were gone. He was bleeding profusely and for a brief moment—but only briefly—I felt sorry for him.

I grabbed my dagger as Kuveo charged toward the others. I saw the tails on the ground, and Herne's blade was dripping with blood. We needed to knock him down to cut off the rest, because if we only took out one more, he would vanish back to his realm with his mission still intact.

I estimated whether I could body slam him from

here. I probably could, but I doubted if my weight would knock him off his feet. The next moment, my theorizing became moot as Kuveo charged toward the others, breaking through them as he headed for the tunnel from which he had come. He moved like the wind, so fast that it seemed to defy how big of a creature he was. As he vanished into the tunnel, leaving a trail of blood behind him, I stumbled out of the nook.

"Should we go after him?" I didn't relish chasing him through the tunnels.

"No," Herne said. "That space is too enclosed. We'd be at a distinct disadvantage." He let out a sigh. "He's going to find someplace to heal. But there may have another way to track him." He knelt by the tails and the puddle of blood. "Yutani, have a body bag?"

I blinked. "You carry body bags?"

"Figure of speech," Yutani said, handing what looked like a large plastic bag to Herne. "We carry bags that seal reliably for cases like this."

Herne gingerly picked up the three tails and dropped them into the bag. "Come on. We need to get a move on before Kuveo heals up enough to go after Névé. I wish I could warn her, but we can't. Let's go." He turned, motioning for us to follow him back through the tunnel to the spiral staircase. I fell into line, wandering what he had in mind next.

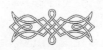

AS WE SHUFFLED back to the car, I hoped that we were done for the night.

While the three of us scrambled into our seats, Herne stayed outside, leaning against his door as he put in a call to someone. I leaned against the backseat, exhausted. I was pretty sure my body would be a kaleidoscope of colorful bruises by morning. Viktor looked just as ragged, and Yutani still looked green around the gills. I had the feeling he was going to have one hell of an energy hangover by morning. I yawned, just wanting to close my eyes and rest.

"Here," Viktor said, stretching out his arm. "Rest. Ogres make great pillows."

I was so tired I didn't even question him. I just leaned my head against his chest. Damned if he didn't make a good pillow, all right. And he didn't smell anything like I would expect an ogre to smell like. In fact, he smelled a little like Calvin Klein or some other designer fragrance.

"You're not used to this. At least, not with our group. I imagine you've pulled a few doozies on your own." He sounded so friendly that I couldn't take offense. In fact, it felt good to sprawl out on the car seat.

I snuggled closer, drifting. It had to be past midnight, or at least it felt like it to me.

"Call me in the morning," I said, closing my eyes.

"Not so fast." Herne slid back into the driver's seat, frowning when he saw me curled up on Viktor's arm. He buckled in. "Sit up and fasten your seatbelts. We're making a stop in Medina."

"Is that where you think Kuveo is headed?" I felt all sorts of grumpy. I didn't *want* to go to Medina. I *wanted* to go home.

"No, but that's where my source lives who can tell us where he might be." He sounded a little bit reticent, and Yutani gave him a long look.

"Oh *please*, don't tell me we're going to go visit *her*. The last time we did that, you warned Viktor and me to stop you the next time you got the bright idea to bring her in on a case. Newsflash, dude: *it's the next time*." Yutani sounded so disgusted that I forgot about being tired and straightened up, buckling my seatbelt as I watched the interplay.

"I know what you're thinking. I really do. And normally, I'd agree. But we can't give up. And you know that she can help." Herne seemed dead set on whatever it was he was planning.

Viktor let out a little huff. "Fucking hell. You know he's right."

"Who's right?" Herne asked. "Yutani or me?"

"Oh, for fuck's sake. *Both* of you. I feel the same way Yutani does and I'm not going to hide it. If I never lay eyes on that woman again, it will still be too soon. I'd die a happy man if we could pretend she's dead and gone. Happy ogre. *Whatever*."

"Then you think we shouldn't go see her?" Herne glanced over his shoulder at Viktor, looking ready to argue.

"Crap, I don't know. She can probably help, especially given we have three of Kuveo's tails in the bag, so it's your call. You're the boss."

I couldn't stay quiet any longer. "Who the hell are you talking about?"

Viktor snorted while Yutani muttered something under his breath.

"They're talking about a certain witch I know." Herne shrugged as he turned on the ignition and backed out of the parking spot. "She rubs them the wrong way. It's always been a hate-hate fest between the three of them."

"You can't tell me *you* feel any different than we do, especially after what she did to you." Yutani tapped away on his phone, bringing up a picture that he handed to me.

The woman in the picture was gorgeous, that was for sure. Tall, statuesque, really, with long blond hair, and boobs that exceeded my own in size. But she was thin and leggy, and looked like a porn star. I swallowed. Hard.

"She's...well... Wow."

"Wow is right. Her name is Reilly. She's a witch and a priestess of Aphrodite. And she used to be Herne's snuggle bunny until he found out she was snuggling with everything that walked on two feet and had money and a cock." Viktor shook his head.

"*Enough*," Herne said from the front seat.

At that, Viktor and Yutani shut their mouths and stared out the window. A moment later, Herne sighed as he turned swung onto the road that would take us to the freeway.

"Okay, here's the deal. The guys are right. Reilly can be bad news. But she can also be helpful. As to my past with her, it would have been one thing if she had told me about the others, but I had to find out the hard way. And I found out that not only was she screwing around on me, but she was scam-

ming the other guys for whatever she could get
from them."

I tried to take in what he had just told me. "And
you still keep in contact?"

"We parted amicably enough. I told her we were
done. She burned down my garage and threatened
to shrivel up my dick. I reminded her I'm the son
of a god—and goddess—and she said we were even.
We don't stay in touch much, but I still hire out
her services when absolutely necessary. She's good
at what she does."

I blinked. "That's a lot of information to take
in." Then, before I could help myself, I added, "So
what's she so good at?"

Herne glared at me through the rearview mirror,
but then laughed softly. "I should have expected
that. To get it out of the way, yes, she's great at
casting lust spells. But she's also a talented medi-
um and she's very good at divining the locations of
missing people. And *monsters*. It helps if you have
something that belongs to the missing person, and
since we have Kuveo's tails, I think Reilly should
be able to get a good bead on him."

Reilly. Sexy witch. Lovely.

"Will she do it?"

"I called her. She's home and still up. She said
for us to drop by. It will cost me two-fifty—that's
two *hundred* and fifty—but it's worth it."

"She won't scam you?"

He shook his head. "That's one thing about
Reilly. When she gives her word on a business
deal, she keeps it. She's lousy at relationships, but
she's an astute and savvy businesswoman."

I pressed my lips together, staring at the back of the front seat. Astute and savvy businesswoman, my ass. She was sex on legs. The thought of her and Herne together needled at me, and I realized I was jealous, even though I had no right to feel that way. Or, perhaps, *threatened* was a better word. They had a history. Herne and I had shared a kiss. That was it.

I felt something poke me in the side and glanced up to see Viktor giving me a knowing look. He couldn't have seen Herne kiss me, only Angel had been there, but then again, I wasn't sure who knew what anymore.

"Ember? Ember?"

Herne's voice jolted me out of my thoughts.

"What?" The word came out more sharply than I had intended, but I cleared my throat and added, "Sorry, I was off in my thoughts. What did you ask?"

"I asked if you're okay? Did Kuveo hurt you?"

I snuck a glance at his face in the rearview mirror. He looked concerned and I had to force myself from kicking the back of the front seat. I was frustrated and tired, and aching from the bruises that were starting to come on full force.

"Yeah...I mean no. I'm bruised up a bit, but I can take it. Nothing I haven't dealt with before." I leaned back, glancing at Viktor. "Mind if I rest on the way to the witch's place?"

He shook his head and held out his arm again. I ignored Herne's glances in the rearview mirror as I leaned against the ogre's chest and closed my eyes, listening as the wheels of the car ate up the asphalt, spinning the road out behind us.

REILLY LIVED NEAR Medina, one of the prici-
est areas near Bellevue. Outside the window, the
houses passed by, growing more lavish and expensive as we went. I had seen my fair share of expensive homes, but these were sprawling behemoths
that promised a life of glitz, glamour, and massive
property taxes.

I wondered what it would be like to live here in
one of these grand houses.

I had never been wealthy. Even my parents had
lived modestly, given they had been cut off from
their families when they were kicked out of Tir-
NaNog and Navane. They had left with what little
they possessed. All told, it afforded them a tidy
little house in Seattle, but when they died, I had
asked the lawyers to sell the house, with almost everything in it, and I invested what was left as best
as I could.

I had lost a little of the money on poor specula-
tions, so I didn't touch the bulk of it until I was
eighteen and moved out of Mama J.'s house. She'd
invited me to stay, pointing out that Angel wasn't
leaving yet, but I really didn't want to take advantage of her any more than I already had. Mama J.
had a huge heart, and if she could have, she would
have gathered up every stray dog, cat, and kid that
came her way. There were others who needed her
help more than me, so I got a job and moved out

to make room for them. Two years later, Angel and I roomed together at junior college, and two years after that, Mama J. gave birth to DJ.

"What are you thinking about?" Herne asked. "You look a million miles away."

I was surprised he had noticed. "My past. Where I came from, and where I'm headed. All sorts of things." My mood had turned from snarky to introspective and I decided to tone it down. It really wasn't my place to be jealous. One kiss didn't mean much, nor did two.

We were on Twenty-fourth Street and had just passed the Overlake Golf and Country Club when Herne took a left onto Seventy-ninth. As we wove through a new development of McMansions, I shook off my thoughts, especially the one that needled me with wondering how I looked. I was better off if I just ignored that particular train of thought. There was absolutely no way to compete with a sex goddess when you were covered in bruises and blood.

Halfway down the block, Herne eased into the driveway of a house that looked modest compared to the others, but fancy compared to what I was used to. It had the typical pillars in the front, common to current design, and was a two-story house on a narrow lot. I glanced at Viktor, who raised his eyebrows and shook his head. His lips were set in a thin line.

We got out of the car, and followed Herne up to the door.

I glanced at my phone. It was almost two in the morning. "I'm surprised she's still up."

"I'm not," Yutani quipped. Herne flashed him a dirty look and the coyote shifter simply shrugged and shook his head.

"Play nice or she might not help us." Herne's sigh told me he wasn't so blasé as he sounded.

He rang the bell.

A moment later I heard the yipping of a tiny dog, and the door opened to reveal one extremely statuesque woman dressed in old-fashioned pajama pants. Her top was open down to her navel, barely concealing a pair of extremely large, firm, and upright breasts. Given mine were about the same size but in no way able to defy gravity like that, I wondered how much she had paid for them.

"Herne, darling, come in." She glanced at the rest of us. "I see you brought your *friends*. How nice." She sounded anything but pleased, but ushered us into the house, passing through the living room and leading us to the dining room, where she had placed a crystal ball on the table. She motioned for us to take our seats and she wedged herself next to Herne.

I sat across from him, with Viktor on my left and Yutani on my right.

Reilly ignored them but stared at me for a moment. Finally, she thrust out her hand in a smooth, well-practiced gesture. "I'm Reilly. I don't believe we've met."

I reluctantly took it, surprised by how firm her grip was. "Ember. I'm working with Wild Hunt now."

She nodded, graciously, but there was a searching look in her eyes. "Fae?"

I blinked. It wasn't all that polite to ask on first meeting what somebody was, but I decided that must be part of her dubious charms.

"Yes." I wasn't about to tell her I was mixed blood.

Reilly waited for a beat, but when I didn't say anything else, she cleared her throat and turned back to Herne, the smile returning to her face. "So, you mentioned a job?"

He nodded, all business. "We need to locate someone and the sooner the better." He paused, then added, "It's an emergency."

Reilly started at his tone. "Bad?"

"Yeah. Bad enough for me to come to you in the middle of the night."

I wondered how she felt about what he said. But if she took offense, she didn't show it.

"Then no delays. Let's get busy." She glanced at the table. "Am I going to want the tablecloth on the table, or off, when you bring out whatever it is you've got as an anchor?"

I laughed. She had obviously done this before. She glanced at me, breaking into a wide grin.

"Trust me, I've learned the hard way. This is but one of many reasons we're not together anymore, regardless of what he's told you." She rolled her eyes, and pushed back her chair. "Help me clear the table. Nobody touch the crystal ball."

We scurried to help her as she lifted up the ball. While the men took the other knickknacks off the table, I pulled off the tablecloth and folded it nicely, draping it over the back of one of the unused chairs. Reilly set the crystal ball back down, pulling it toward her. She disappeared into another room and returned with what looked like a small plastic tarp the size of a very large cutting board. She spread it out on the table.

"You really *are* used to this," I said. I had to hand it to her, she didn't seem like the bimbo I thought she'd be. Oh, I believed what Herne said about her cheating on him and her calculating nature, but that just reinforced the intelligence that I now sensed was back there.

"I'm far more used to this than I'd like to be." She resumed her seat, placing her hands on the sides of the crystal ball. "All right, let's see it."

Yutani silently lifted up the bag, spreading the three fox tails out on the tarp. He was careful not to splatter blood on the white carpeting, and I found myself glad that he at least observed some niceties, regardless of what he thought of her.

Reilly stared at the tails for a moment, then let out a sigh. "I can't even… All right, let's get this show on the road. I'm not going to ask, and I don't want to know. I will tell you what I see, and you will pay me, and then you will leave so I can get on with the rest of my evening. Do we understand each other?"

He nodded. "Clear as a bell. Let's get a move on."

As she placed her right hand on the crystal ball and her left on one of the tails, I saw her shudder. She seemed to fall into a trance, and I kept my mouth shut along with the others as we waited for her to pick up whatever it was she could find.

By now, I realized that Herne was still a lot more miffed over their relationship than she was. She had hurt him far more deeply than he had hurt her.

Forcing my mind away from speculation, I looked around the room where we were waiting.

The walls were pale gray with stark white trim. One accent wall was black, with silver and crystal sconces attached to the wall. In the center of the accent wall, a fireplace with a white mantel and a gray marble hearthstone was the focal point. It truly drew the eye.

I had to admit, she had excellent decorating taste. The house felt gracious, inviting, and quietly elegant. It seemed a stark contrast to Reilly herself, but she fit in somehow, in a way I could never see Herne managing. I wondered if she had owned the house before they met. That led to wondering how long they had been together. Finally, once again I dragged my thoughts away from where they were headed.

After a few moments, Reilly opened her eyes. She looked like she was reeling from something, and she shook her head, looking slightly confused.

"Whatever the hell this is, it's bad. It's big and it's hungry and it's on the rampage. I don't know what you've gotten yourself into this time, but if you mean to go up against it, you'd better take extra muscle with you. Either that or plan a sure-fire way to take it down for good." She shoved the tails away from her, grimacing. Her left hand was covered with globs of congealed blood.

"Can you tell me where it is?" Herne asked.

She closed her eyes again, placing both hands on the crystal ball, pressing bloody fingerprints against the side of the orb. A moment later, she let go of the sphere.

"Would somebody please get me a wet paper towel and some soap from the kitchen?" She glanced over at Yutani, who silently rose and exited through the swinging doors leading out of the dining room. When he returned she washed her hands, drying them on the dry paper towel he had also brought.

"I can give you a general location. Bring up a map on your phone."

Yutani pulled out his tablet and brought up a map of the area. He shoved the tablet over to her, and she took it, expanding the picture by pinching two fingers together and spreading them over the map. She scanned the picture, staring intently at it until suddenly she expanded it and pointed to an area near Seward Park.

"I can tell you this. He's confused. When you cut off three of his tails—I have a feeling there are more—it not only hurt him, but sent a shockwave through his system. He hasn't regained full composure yet. I have a sense that there's something he supposed to do? But right now he can't remember what it is. He's trying to find a place to heal as far away from where he was hurt as possible."

"That makes sense. If he can't remember that he supposed to assa—" Herne stopped, rolling his eyes. "If he can't remember what his mission is right now, then we have a leg up on him. Do you know if he's on the move?"

Reilly scanned his face closely, but said nothing about his slip. "No, he's hunkered down, hiding in an area near the lake. I think you have a few hours before he's regained enough strength to be clear-headed. That's the best I can tell you."

"That's more than I expected to find out. Thank you." He pulled out his wallet and tossed three one-hundred-dollar bills on the table. "A tip as well, for being willing to see us this late. For being willing to take the job on at all."

"As I said, I don't want to know what you doing. I have no interest in it, so in this matter, my part is done. Now, if you will wrap up your tails—you can take the tarp with you—and go, I'll get around to the rest of my evening." She pocketed the bills, and stood up.

Yutani wrapped up the tails and slid them back into the bag.

I turned to Reilly. "Do you want help putting your tablecloth back on?"

"No, thank you. I need to disinfect the table first. Or rather, I need to have the maid disinfect it. I have business to attend to tonight and it can wait. Unless you think that thing is diseased?" She glanced at me, rather than Herne.

I didn't know what to say, so I glanced over at Viktor. He shook his head.

"I have no clue. If I were you, I'd probably disinfect it now. It won't take much. A little bleach, or antibacterial soap." The burly man picked up the bag, taking it from Yutani. "Come on, let's go wait in the car."

Yutani followed him, and they looked at me, waiting. I wanted to stay, to see how Herne and Reilly said their good-byes, but it was obvious that

Viktor and Yutani thought I should go with them. I waved, then followed the two men out to the car.

A few moments later, Herne jogged back to the car and slid into the driver's seat. As he turned on the ignition, buckling his seatbelt, I waited for him to say something. Part of me wanted to hear him say he was glad that was over, or at least now we could get on our way, but he remained silent as he eased out of the driveway and set a path for Seattle and Seward Park.

Chapter 15

WE REACHED SEWARD Park within less than twenty minutes. This time of night there was barely any traffic. My mind churned with a myriad of thoughts to the point of where it was exhausting me.

"How often do you have nights like this?" I asked.

Herne let out a laugh from the front seat. "Not very often. I guarantee this isn't a daily event. Most of the cases we work on aren't nearly as deadly or time-sensitive. Well, you saw Barnaby today. That's going to take us all of a couple days, and all we will have to do is have a talk with the neighbor and warn him that Barnaby is going to throttle him if he continues to steal the wine. He probably has no idea of how unpleasant clurichauns can be when they feel they're being crossed."

That brought another thought to mind. "What's

the percentage of cases? Outside cases as opposed to stopping mayhem between the Fae?"

"Oh, I'd say probably sixty to seventy percent are outside cases. Some are pretty edgy, but others, not so much. Out of the cases concerning the Fae, the majority usually do have a high degree of danger in them, but they don't often involve summoned creatures. I hope this isn't the start of a trend."

"Could be just an anomaly," Yutani said.

"That's nice to hope for, but I have a feeling that something has escalated the tension between the two courts. It's always been bad, but lately it seems like there are more assassination plots. The past three cases we've had dealt with assassination attempts. This one just happens to already have collateral damage." Herne shrugged. "Whatever the case, that's what we're here for."

He slid into a parking spot outside of the gates of Seward Park. "Were going to have to go on foot from here. The park closes at dusk."

"Why can't we just open the gates?" I asked. "Those things aren't difficult to hack."

"You would think, but the last time I tried that, I managed to set off a sensor. Of course, it was a private golf course and not a public park, so maybe that had to do with it." Herne paused, then shrugged. "You can try if you want, but if we get interrupted, it's just going to prolong our search for Kuveo."

"Oh, let's not prolong this night any more than we have to." I shoved open my car door, slipping out into the chill of the night.

Once again, the clouds had eased up, and it was a relief to feel the chill of the night without the driving rain to go along with it. The cold air braced me up and I blinked, feeling alert again.

When we were ready, with all of our gear, Herne led us around the gates that were blocking the road. They were low enough to step over, and we headed down the winding road toward the water.

"Is there a chance you can use your water witching and find out exactly where he is? Reilly said he was near the water."

We were close enough, so I figured that might be possible. I motioned for them to stand back as I reached out through the moisture in the air. I could feel the lake whipping in the wind, the waves driving and crashing against the shore. It wasn't long before I caught hold of an elemental's attention and opened myself to communication.

I forced my words into emotions, doing my best to query the elemental so it would understand. *Friend, I'm looking for something. Something dark and evil has crossed the lake, and it's hiding near the shore. Is there a chance that you can sense it?*

There was a pause, as the elemental considered my thoughts and feelings. It was wary, but then a rush of compassion washed over me and I realized it was bound to the positive. Sometimes water elementals found themselves caught in a certain energy. Whether they were bound by a witch or not, I did not know, but this one wanted to help. And anything evil would be anathema to it.

A picture began to crystallize in my mind. I saw

the shoreline, near the parking lot. And there, I could see a small cave, partially submerged, and in it, I felt Kuveo lurking. The confusion that he was feeling passed through the elemental and into me, and I let out a whimper as I reeled back.

Herne was standing next to me, and he caught me before I tripped.

"Are you all right?"

I nodded. "Yeah, I just touched the creature. A water elemental showed me where Kuveo is. I sensed his energy. He's still confused, but we have to be very careful because like any wild animal, confusion and pain lead to danger. We need to head down this road."

As we wound through the trees, the sound of the lake became louder. The waves were choppy, driven by the wind, and even in the dark of the night, as the road curved toward the water, we could see them crashing against the shore in a frothy mix of foam and sputum.

The road curved until it intersected another road that ran parallel to the shore. We crossed over the pavement to the shoreline. I led the others past the pilings that marked off the parking spaces, onto the rocky embankment leading down into the water.

"The cave isn't far from here. The entrance is partly underwater, but I think the cave itself slopes up into the side of the hill so we should be fine once we find the entrance."

"That's a handy talent you have," Viktor said.

"Thank my mother," I said. "I have an odd feeling that I'm going to have a talk with Morgana soon. My mother was pledged to her and it feels like I'm walking down that same route."

"I think you're right," Herne said. "My mother calls those to her whom she chooses. And both she and my father were insistent that you be brought into the agency."

I nodded, gauging our next move as we stood on the shore. I didn't want to make any unnecessary mistakes.

"Is there a ledge that leads to the entrance, or are we going to have to swim for it? Either way, I'm not looking forward to this." Viktor sounded grouchy. "I can't swim, by the way."

"I think there's enough of an outcropping to allow us to walk through the water. If what I saw is correct, it should only be about knee-deep, if that." I wanted to use my flashlight, but I was afraid of alerting Kuveo. "Yutani, do you have your dimlim? I think Kuveo is in enough pain that he won't notice a light that faint."

Yutani handed it to me, showing me how to strap it to my wrist. Turning it on, I breathed a sigh of relief. It made the going much easier.

I took over the lead, since I was the one who had had the vision, and eased my way along the embankment until I reached the edge of the water. Cautiously, I reached out with my toe, feeling for a foothold. Sure enough, about shin deep I came to a ledge about a foot wide. It would be enough to walk on. With my right hand I braced myself against the side of the embankment, leaning against it as I slowly worked my way forward, testing each step as I went. The others followed my lead.

I could see the entrance to the cave from where I was, but I refused to hurry. Haste made for easy accidents. Sure enough, on the next step as I tested my footing, the ledge beneath me gave way. If I had been in a rush, I would have fallen into the water. As it was, I paused to regain my equilibrium, then took a longer step over the gap, testing to make sure the next step would hold. I glanced over my shoulder.

"There's a gap in the ledge," I said softly. "Test each step as you go."

Two more yards and I was at the opening. I wasn't sure how far back Kuveo was in the cave, so I paused to listen, straining to hear anything. Yutani, who was behind me, noticed what I was doing and he leaned in beside me, listening as well.

A moment later he shook his head and whispered, "I think it's okay."

Trusting that his hearing was better than mine, I swung myself into the cave, crouching as quietly as I could. I was still ankle-deep in water, but two more yards and I stood on dry ground.

I paused as my eyes adjusted. I was hiding the dimlim, pressing it against my jacket so that it barely gave off a glow. If Kuveo was nearby, I didn't want him seeing us before we were ready.

Herne and Viktor joined us, and we all caught our breath. A moment later, I glanced at the others, and Herne motioned to me. He leaned in, his mouth close to my ear.

"Would you like me to take over from here? We should arm up here."

I realized that we were close to the creature. I gave him a nod, and slipped behind Yutani, giving him the dimlim back. We drew our weapons, and Herne took over the lead, motioning for Viktor to join him. We started off again, heading into the cave.

The cave might have started out sloping up into the embankment, but it quickly leveled off.

It was also shallow, and I wondered where Kuveo was hiding. There was only one chamber, but it was filled with massive boulders, so he was probably behind a pile of rock and rubble. The fact that he hadn't come after us yet meant he was likely still in a lot of pain.

The next moment, my musing was interrupted as Kuveo leapt out from behind a nearby rock. Yutani shot the dimlim on him so that we could see while Herne and Viktor immediately went on the attack. The thought occurred to me that we could further disorient him if we had a bright light.

I poked Yutani. "Flashlight! The bright light will disorient him."

He nodded and I took that as a go-ahead, yanking my flashlight off my belt.

"Close your eyes!" I yelled as I switched it on, aiming it directly at Kuveo's face.

The creature let out a howl, waving his hands in front of his face as he stumbled back. I was right, he was more disoriented than ever. Herne took the opportunity to dash around behind him, and the next moment he slammed himself against Kuveo's back and knocked the creature forward.

"I need help to keep him down!"

Viktor raced over and straddled Kuveo's back, helping Herne hold him face first on the floor. "Somebody cut off his tails! Hurry, because he's too strong to hold for long!"

Yutani's hands were full, so I tossed my flashlight on the ground and skidded to a halt beside them. Yutani flashed the dimlim my way, giving me enough light to see by.

Kuveo's tails were a bloody mess, the stumps of the three we had already cut off still oozing blood, and for a moment I felt horribly sorry for the creature. He couldn't help his nature. But he had destroyed thirteen lives and was set on destroying another. And he would kill us if he had the chance.

Resolved, I grabbed hold of the stump that conjoined all of his tails to his body and, taking a deep breath, brought my dagger down. My blade was sharp—I kept it razor-sharp—and it sliced smoothly through the thick trunk, cleaving it from the creature's body. Kuveo let out a loud shriek, and I stumbled backward, scrambling away from his flailing feet.

Herne and Viktor were thrown to the side as Kuveo thrashed. I tossed the tails to Yutani, not sure if Kuveo could make use of them to heal himself in any way. But the next moment, there was a loud humming noise, and another shriek, and as we watched, Kuveo's flesh disappeared in a cloud of black dust, and all that was left was his skeleton. The tails that Yutani was holding vanished as well.

I dropped to the floor, staring at the bones. "Cripes on a shingle."

"Yeah," Victor said, groaning as he picked himself off the floor. "You got them all? I don't want a rematch."

"Yeah. I cut all the rest off." I felt queasy, but forced myself to breathe slow and steadily.

"We should take the bones with us," Yutani said. "I'd like to study them."

"Morbid much?" I asked.

"The more you know about your enemy, the better. Even if he was the only one of his kind—and we don't know that—there's always something to learn." He prodded the bones and began to pull them apart in order to take them with us.

I sat there, unsure of what to do next. "What now? Do we talk to the Fae? Or does this just end here? What will they do when they realize that we've destroyed him?"

Herne let out a slow breath, sitting down on the boulder next to me. He looked about as tired as I felt.

"Now we go home, clean up, and sleep. Tomorrow I let Cernunnos and Morgana know that we've closed out the case. The Fae can't do anything about it, since they're bound to the agreement I told you about."

"And that's it?"

"That's the thing about this job," Herne said. "There's no fanfare. Unless it's a private case, there's seldom anything to mark that we finished. We're the only ones who really know what we're up to. The Fae will realize we killed Kuveo but they can't do anything about it, nor will they acknowledge it in any way, given their actions started the whole mess. Private cases? Sometimes our clients take us out to celebrate. But we don't do this for any glory."

"It's all in a day's work?" I asked.

He nodded. "Pretty much."

There wasn't much I could say. I wasn't sure what I had expected, but what he said made sense. We worked behind the scenes. We might have just saved war from breaking out, and we had potentially stopped a number of other deaths, but nobody would know. Nobody except the gods and the Fae, and the latter wouldn't be throwing us any congratulations party.

"I'm ready for some sleep," Yutani said. "I still feel shaken up from earlier. It's going to take me a while to regain my equilibrium."

Wearily, I stood and stretched. "I'm ready for a shower. I feel covered with gunk and dirt."

"Welcome to our world, Ember. We're a grimy little bunch." With a laugh, Herne wrapped his arm around my shoulders. "Come on, let's get back to the office and put this one to bed."

And with that, we headed out of the cave, dragging along Kuveo's skeleton for Yutani. I glanced back at the water as we headed up the road toward the car.

From the depths of the lake, I could hear a call. Yes, I needed to have a talk with Morgana. I could feel her calling, although what she was saying I couldn't quite understand. But I had a feeling it wouldn't be long before I'd be standing in front of her and she would be very very clear about what she wanted out of me.

Chapter 16

THE NEXT DAY I slept until three. When Angel woke me up, she was still in her pajamas. Herne given us the day off, considering we had just finished the case.

I was still reeling with emotions over what had happened over the past few days, but at least I'd slept deep without nightmares. Mr. Rumblebutt purred as I picked him up and gave him a big smooch on the forehead. He squirmed out of my arms and ran into the kitchen, chirping for breakfast.

"Doofus, I already fed you." Angel turned to me, yawning. "So, what do *you* want for breakfast, Supergirl?" She and Talia had been awake and waiting for us when we got back. Angel had driven us home, because I was so punchy that I didn't trust myself behind the wheel.

"If I'm Supergirl, then I fear for the state of the

world. Look at me." I slipped out from beneath the covers. I slept naked most of the time, and I wasn't embarrassed. Angel had seen me plenty of times without my clothes, given we traded backrubs now and then. Not to mention we had lived in the same room together for three years as kids and had been roomies in college.

I stared down at my body. I was covered with bruises, most of them bright purple although a few were already turning yellow, which meant they were starting to heal. I also had a nice assortment of cuts and scrapes, and I suspected a bruised rib, though it didn't hurt enough for me to go to the doctor.

"You sure got rough and tumbled. I suggest you buy a gallon of Icy Balm. Meanwhile, why don't you take a hot shower and I'll rustle up some waffles." She paused. "By the way, Ray Fontaine called again on the landline. He left you a rather long message, and I have to say I don't like the tone of it."

I sighed. I kept a landline for clients to reach me on before I accepted their cases. Most often, I didn't give them my cell number. It kept my private life, private.

"Yeah, he's a problem I'm going to have to deal with pretty soon. I should never have gone to see him the other day. It seems to have rekindled his undying devotion to me. Either that, or an unhealthy obsession."

As she headed back into the kitchen, I climbed into the shower and turned it on full blast, as hot as I could handle it. I had taken a shower when I had come home the night before, but my muscles were protesting their stiffness, and the only thing I could think of was to soak the ache out of them. I washed my hair while I was at it, and finally, reluctantly stepped out of the water. Toweling off, I padded into my bedroom.

Just then I heard Angel let out a shriek and, before I realized what I was doing, I raced out to see if she was okay, buck naked. I skidded to a halt, my hair still slicked back against my head, dripping down my back, only to realize I was staring at Herne, who was definitely staring back at me. Angel was picking up a pan from the floor and staring at a dozen eggs that were splattered all over the linoleum. She gave me a speculative look.

"Yes?"

"I heard you shout. Are you okay?" I didn't bother covering myself, since it would only draw more attention to the fact that I was standing there nude.

"I dropped a dozen eggs and the pan when I saw a spider on the counter. Um, Herne's here, if you haven't noticed." She turned away, and I swear she was suppressing a laugh.

"Yeah, I noticed. I'll just go get dressed and be right back." Feeling incredibly exposed, I started to turn, though the smirk on his face made me want to smack him.

He waved me off. "Don't bother on my account, but if you feel like it, knock yourself out."

I stomped back to my room, where I yanked on a pair of jeans. I fastened my bra, then slid a V-neck tank top over my head. As I threaded my leather belt through the belt loops, I couldn't decide whether I was more angry with him or myself. Actually, I couldn't decide whether I was really angry or just embarrassed.

By the time I returned to the living room, Herne had taken a seat at the table, and Angel was setting out plates filled with waffles, eggs, and bacon. My stomach rumbled as I slipped into a chair.

"Any chance you—"

"Latte coming up. I taught myself how to use the machine. Quint shot, just the way you like it. What flavors you want?"

"Chocolate peppermint."

As she slid the iced drink in front of me, Herne bit into his waffle.

"These are so good," he said, his mouth full. A moment later, he added, "You two fit right in. I can't tell you how happy we all are to have you. Viktor, Talia, and Yutani all think you're great." He glanced at me. "How are you feeling this morning?"

"A little roughed up, but nothing that time won't heal." I paused long enough to take another bite of my waffle. As the maple syrup drained down my throat, tickling my taste buds, I let out a contented sigh. "We really need to look for a better house with a full kitchen. I want you to make everything you ever wanted to bake."

Angel snorted. "You just like the fact that I cook."

"True that. But I also like that we can drive into work together. Plus, there's the fact that there's nobody I'd rather have for a roommate than you."

I meant every word. Then, looking at Herne, I said, "So what brings you over today? Besides to see me naked?"

"Oh, that wasn't my intent, although I must say, I consider it a bonus." A twinkle sparkled in his eye. But then he sobered. "Actually, two things brought me over. According to your contracts, now that you're both settled in, you're required to get the company tattoo."

"Both of us?" Angel said. "I thought just Ember."

"No, this marks you in the field as protected. And it shows that Cernunnos and the Wild Hunt claim you as one of his bounty hunters. Since that's what we do. We may be peacekeepers in one sense, but in reality we're hunters."

"So when do we do this?"

"When we finish eating. Talia is a licensed tattooist. We'll go down to the shop and she'll take care of you."

I let out a long breath. "If I've got the mark of the silver stag on my ass, I should have a tattoo for the Wild Hunt on my arm. It seems like this was destined for me from the beginning, even though I hate the concept of destiny. I don't like anybody controlling my actions."

"You'd better get used to it. You're living in my world now." Herne held my gaze. "My mother and father are lenient to a degree, and so am I, but the moment you signed that contract... No, the moment you were *born*, Ember, and you too, Angel, you belonged to the gods. Trust me, they aren't interested in controlling *all* of your actions. But you will answer to Cernunnos and Morgana, and you will answer to me."

"What about the receptionist before me, the one who left?" Angel asked.

"She asked permission to leave and start a family. We relocated her and her fiancé to a safe place. Because of the work she did, though, she'll always be in danger. Once you leave the Wild Hunt, we can't protect you. If you leave, the tattoo will vanish and you'll be open to any retaliation the Fae choose to pay out. Only when you're under our umbrella are you truly safe."

Angel and I glanced at each other. There wasn't much to say. Neither one of us had chosen for this to happen, but there was no other option than to make the best of it.

"Oh, speaking of my mother," Herne added. "She wants to see you today, Ember. After you get your tattoo."

We finished our breakfast in silence, and as we slid into our coats to go back to the agency, I felt like I was spinning. Life was changing so fast that it felt like I didn't know where my roots were, anymore.

MY ARM STUNG as I looked down at the fresh tattoo. The blade was exquisite, beautiful, and green vines wound around it. The tattoo was the same one Viktor had, and Yutani and Talia and Herne, only somehow on me it looked prettier, I thought.

Angel had gone home after she got hers. Herne told her he would bring me back after I talked to Morgana. I was surprised that Angel had acquiesced to the tattoo so quickly. It didn't seem in her nature, but as Talia inked it onto her skin, the image seemed to flow along, to become part of her as it had me.

Now, I was sitting in the break room. I had expected to be taken somewhere, maybe deep into the forest, or into some other dimension to meet the goddess. But Herne had insisted that his mother would be coming to the agency.

It suddenly occurred to me that, perhaps, I should have dressed up. Shown some respect for Morgana. But *shoulda, woulda, coulda*.

At that moment, the door opened and I yanked my head up.

A vision of blue light entered the room, and all I could see for a moment was a blinding blue flash. Then I was standing in the middle of the ocean atop a rock jutting out of the waves. The wind was bracing, blowing my hair every which way, and my brand-new tattoo stung as saltwater lashed against me, the spray washing up and across me in a long sweep.

I gasped, looking around for some anchor to hang on to, something to tell me I was still in the room, but there was nothing there. Feeling faint, I crouched on the rock, doing my best to hang on as the rolling waves around me made me dizzy. I felt like I might topple off, fall into the water and drown, drawn down below the dark surface.

Then in front of me, a ripple formed as a throne

of shining crystal rose out of the waves. Steps led up to it, crafted from mother-of-pearl.

The throne was carved with seashells, and pearls dripped down off the top, and seaweed drifted in the waves around it. A woman sat on the throne, clad in a gown as indigo as the night sky, with shimmering stars dappling the surface.

Her hair was long and black, flowing past her shoulders, draping down to coil around her waist like some ancient serpent. I realized that night had fallen as the moon rose into the sky, the silver orb mirroring the light in her eyes. She wore a diamond tiara, only the diamonds were interspersed with sparkling black crystals.

I trembled, staring up at Morgana. Herne's mother. The goddess my mother had followed.

"Approach me," Morgana said, motioning for me to climb the stairs to her.

Trembling, I obeyed. When I was at her feet, I crouched, bowing my head, afraid to look into her eyes. "My Lady."

"Ember Kearney, stand in my presence."

I stood.

"Your mother served me before you, and her mother before her. My husband marked you at birth. You belong to him, as your father before you did. Now, you will serve me as well. You carry the blood of the Water Fae."

I nodded, unsure of what to say. "My mother, she was one of the Water Fae."

Morgana's gaze seemed to pierce right through me. "Your mother refused to use her magic in her own defense. It frightened her. You, however, will learn to use my magic. You will conquer the fear that tripped her up."

I could only return her gaze—I couldn't look away.

"The magic of water, the magic of the tides, the magic of the moon. They are intricately bound together." Her voice echoed over the water, sending waves crashing against the rocks below. I could barely breathe, her presence was so overwhelming, that for a moment I was afraid I would fall and she would let me drown.

I opened myself up to her, and found myself swept into the night where the magic of the hunt ruled. The magic of the moon and water and the dripping forest surrounded the world. The scent of ferns and trees washed over me as rain pounded against the ground. Water soaked deep, coiling up through the tendrils, feeding the plants, creating the life of the world. And all of this buoyed me up, welcoming me into its realm.

"You begin to understand," she said. "Everything is connected, and everything in your life has played a part to bringing you to me, in bringing you to the Wild Hunt. Kneel now, and give yourself to me."

I took a deep breath. There was no turning back. Seeing Morgana in front of me, my heart swelled with a passion that I didn't yet understand, but it was my path—*she* was my path. I would not turn away.

"Will you be mine, in life and in death? Will you obey me?"

There was only one answer. There had only ever been one answer.

"I will. I give myself to you. I am yours, Lady. Command me." And as quick as my words came, the bargain was sealed.

She reached out and lifted me up to my feet, placing in my hand a silver necklace. The pendant sparkled, and I realized it was a crow.

"Fasten this around your neck. Forever you will wear it as a sign that you belong to me."

I lifted the chain and draped it around my neck, fastening the clasp. As I did, I realized that I had just made the biggest oath of my life.

"Listen for me in the water." A veiled smile passed over her face. "And about my son..."

I blushed, hanging my head.

"Don't fear your emotions. Don't fear passion and love. No human can ever claim you. But love may yet come. Time will tell. Remember your oath to me. Your life depends on it."

The next moment I opened my eyes and found myself back in the break room, alone. The necklace was firmly fastened around my throat, and I knew it would never again come off. I was bound for life.

HERNE AND I sat in his SUV, the silence thick between us. Finally, he cleared his throat.

"I've made arrangements for Angel to talk to DJ next weekend."

"I'm glad," I said. "She needs to." I wasn't sure what else to say. I stared up at my apartment building, thinking I should just get out of the SUV and go home, and sort everything out later.

As I reached for the door handle, Herne's hand wrapped around my wrist.

"Ember, wait."

I turned to look at him, holding my breath. We stared at each other, the air thick. I glanced down at his fingers that were wrapped around my arm. He had taken care not to grab the fresh tattoo, for which I was grateful.

"I'm not sure what this is, between us," he said. "I'm not sure what you want it to be."

"Do you know what *you* want it to be?" I waited, afraid to close my eyes.

"I never want to take advantage of my authority. I don't ever want you to feel that I'm doing something like that." He paused, the expression on his face so strained that it made me dizzy.

"I will never allow you to abuse your authority over me. I'm not that kind of person. I'm not the kind of woman who does what you want just because you say so. I've been on my own a long time, Herne. I'm not a sex goddess. I'm not very genteel. I don't forgive easily and I've seen far too much in the short time that I've been alive. Do you think you can handle that?"

His eyes lit up and he smiled.

"I'd like to give it a try," he said. "But you have to know that I'm protective. I'll do my best to keep you safe, whether you want me to or not. But I'll never stand in your way. You belong to my mother and my father now, but so do I. We answer to them. The question is, do we want to answer to each other?"

The world seemed to pause, waiting for my reply. Finally, after a long moment's struggle with myself, I nodded.

"Let's see where this takes us."

As I spoke, he gathered me into his arms, kissing me deeply. Outside, the city passed by, gritty and dirty, and in its usual hurry. Yet Seattle was my home, and it was Herne's home, and at the moment, I loved every single part of it.

If you enjoyed this book, never fear—there will be more Wild Hunt books out this year! The second will be titled OAK & THORNS, and the third, IRON BONES. And more to come after that.

Meanwhile, I invite you to visit Fury's world. In a gritty, post-apocalyptic Seattle, Fury is a minor goddess, in charge of eliminating the Abominations who come off the World Tree. The first story arc of the Fury Unbound Series is complete with: FURY RISING, FURY'S MAGIC, FURY AWAKENED, and FURY CALLING.

If you prefer a lighter-hearted paranormal romance, meet the wild and magical residents of Bedlam in my Bewitching Bedlam Series. Fun-loving witch Maddy Gallowglass, her smoking-hot vampire lover Aegis, and their crazed cjinn Bubba (part djinn, all cat) rock it out in Bedlam, a magical town on a magical island. BLOOD MUSIC,

BEWITCHING BEDLAM, MAUDLIN'S MAYHEM, SIREN'S SONG, WITCHES WILD, BLOOD VENGEANCE and TIGER TAILS are available. And more are on the way!

If you like cozies with an edge, try my Chintz 'n China paranormal mysteries. The series is complete with: GHOST OF A CHANCE, LEGEND OF THE JADE DRAGON, MURDER UNDER A MYSTIC MOON, A HARVEST OF BONES, ONE HEX OF A WEDDING, and a wrap-up novella: HOLIDAY SPIRITS.

The newest Otherworld book—MOON SHIMMERS—is available now, and the next, HARVEST SONG, will be available in May 2018.

For all of my work, both published and upcoming releases, see the Bibliography at the end of this book, or check out my website at Galenorn. com and be sure and sign up for my newsletter to receive news about all my new releases.

Playlist

I often write to music, and THE SILVER STAG was no exception. Here's the playlist I used for this book:

Arcade Fire: Abraham's Daughter
AWOLNATION: Sail
Band of Skulls: I Know What I Am
The Black Angels: You on the Run; Vikings; Don't Play With Guns; Holland; Love Me Forever; Always Maybe; Black isn't Black; Young Men Dead; Phosphene Dream
Black Mountain: Queens Will Play
Black Rebel Motorcycle Club: Fault Line; Feel It Now
Bobbie Gentry: Ode To Billie Joe
Boom! Bap! Pow!: Suit
Broken Bells: The Ghost Inside
Camouflage Nights: (It Could Be) Love
Celtic Woman: Newgrange; Scarborough Fair
Chris Isaak: Wicked Game
Cobra Verde: Play with Fire
Colin Foulke: Emergence
Corvus Corax: Filii Neidhardi; Ballade de Mercy
Damh the Bard: The Cauldron Born; Tomb of the King; Obsession; Cloak of Feathers; The Wicker Man; Spirit of Albion
David & Steve Gordon: Shaman's Drum Dance
Dizzi: Dizzi Jig; Dance of the Unicorns
Donovan: Sunshine Superman; Season of the Witch
Eastern Sun: Beautiful Being (Original Edit)
Eivør: Trøllbundin
Faun: Hymn to Pan
FC Kahuna: Hayling
The Feeling: Sewn
Foster The People: Pumped Up Kicks

Garbage: Queer; #1 Crush; Push It; I Think I'm Paranoid
Gary Numan: Ghost Nation; My Name is Ruin; When the World Comes Apart; Broken; I Am Dust; Here In The Black; Love Hurt Bleed; Petals
The Gospel Whiskey Runners: Muddy Waters
Gypsy Soul: Who
The Heathen Kings: Rolling of the Stones
Hedningarna: Tuuli; Grodan/Widergrenen; Räven; Ukkonen; Juopolle Joutunut; Gorrlaus
Huldrelokkk: Trolldans
Ian Melrose & Kerstin Blodig: Kråka
In Strict Confidence: Forbidden Fruit; Silver Bullets; Snow White; Tiefer
Jessica Bates: The Hanging Tree
Julian Cope: Charlotte Anne
The Kills: Future Starts Slow; Nail In My Coffin; DNA; You Don't Own The Road; Sour Cherry; No Wow; Dead Road 7
Lorde: Yellow Flicker Beat; Royals
Low with Tom and Andy: Half Light
Marilyn Manson: Personal Jesus; Tainted Love
Mark Lanegan: The Gravedigger's Song; Riot in My House; Phantasmagoria Blues; Wedding Dress; Methamphetamine Blues
Matt Corby: Breathe
Motherdrum: Big Stomp
Orgy: Social Enemies; Blue Monday
A Pale Horse Named Death: Meet the Wolf
Pearl Jam: Even Flow; Jeremy
S. J. Tucker: Hymn to Herne; Witch's Rune
Scorpions: The Zoo
Sharon Knight: Bardic Voices; Mother of the World; Bewitched; 13 Knots; Crimson Masquerade; Star of the Sea; Siren Moon; Song of the Sea
Shriekback: The Shining Path; Underwaterboys; This Big Hush; Now These Days Are Gone; The King in the Tree
Tamaryn: While You're Sleeping, I'm Dreaming; Violet's in a Pool
Tempest: The Moving-On Song; Slippery Slide; Buffalo Jump; Raggle Taggle Gypsy; Dark Lover; Queen of Argyll;

Nottamun Town; The Midnight Sun
Tom Petty: Mary Jane's Last Dance
Tuatha Dea: Irish Handfasting; Tuatha De Danaan; The Hum and the Shiver; Wisp of a Thing (Part 1); Long Black Curl
Wendy Rule: Let the Wind Blow; The Circle Song; Elemental Chant

Biography

New York Times, *Publishers Weekly*, and *USA Today* bestselling author Yasmine Galenorn writes urban fantasy and paranormal romance, and is the author of over fifty books, including the Otherworld Series, the Fury Unbound Series, the Bewitching Bedlam Series, and the upcoming Wild Hunt Series, among others. She's also written nonfiction metaphysical books. She is the 2011 Career Achievement Award Winner in Urban Fantasy, given by RT Magazine. Yasmine has been in the Craft since 1980, is a shamanic witch and High Priestess. She describes her life as a blend of teacups and tattoos. She lives in Kirkland, WA, with her husband Samwise and their cats. Yasmine can be reached via her website at Galenorn.com.

Indie Releases Currently Available:

Wild Hunt Series:
The Silver Stag

Bewitching Bedlam Series:
Bewitching Bedlam
Maudlin's Mayhem
Siren's Song
Witches Wild
Blood Music
Blood Vengeance
Tiger Tails

Fury Unbound Series:
Fury Rising
Fury's Magic
Fury Awakened
Fury Calling

Otherworld Series:
Moon Shimmers
Earthbound
Moon Swept
Knight Magic
Otherworld Tales: Volume One
Tales From Otherworld: Collection One
Men of Otherworld: Collection One
Men of Otherworld: Collection Two
For the rest of the Otherworld Series, see Website

Chintz 'n China Series:
Ghost of a Chance
Legend of the Jade Dragon
Murder Under a Mystic Moon
A Harvest of Bones
One Hex of a Wedding
Holiday Spirits

Bath and Body Series (originally under the name India Ink):
Scent to Her Grave
A Blush With Death
Glossed and Found

Misc. Short Stories/Anthologies:
Mist and Shadows: Short Tales From Dark Haunts
Once Upon a Kiss (short story: Princess Charming)
Silver Belles (short story: The Longest Night)
Once Upon a Curse (short story: Bones)
Night Shivers (an Indigo Court novella)

Magickal Nonfiction:
Embracing the Moon
Tarot Journeys

For all other series, as well as upcoming work, see Galenorn.com

Made in the USA
San Bernardino, CA
15 April 2018